Choices

Choices

Dedication

This book is dedicated to my darling son Brett, who introduced me to the concept of parallel worlds.

Choices

Barbara Knight

One World

Chapter One

Jenny pushes open the heavy door and is instantly assailed by the smells of beer and cigarettes. During her years as an art student she'd smoked, both tobacco and cannabis, but had given up when she met Don. Now she really can't stand being in the same room with someone who is smoking, but to get to the beer garden out the back she has to pass through the bar area. As she makes her way through the crowds, trying not to breathe the polluted air too deeply, a man jostles her as he steps back suddenly from the bar.

He slobbers belligerently, 'What's your hurry, sweetheart?'

She mumbles an embarrassed, 'Excuse me,' before continuing through the throng.

By the time she reaches the glass doors that lead to the outdoor area she feels flushed and dishevelled. Looking around she sees her two friends seated in their favourite spot under a big shady tree. They both look so cool and immaculate, Sonya in a forest green pants suit and cream silk shirt and Emma in black that matches her shoulder-length blue-black hair.

She wishes she'd remembered to pack a fresh blouse this morning. She had meant to but what with packing the children's lunches, making sure they all had their home readers and that Grace had something to take for show and tell, she had forgotten to put in the new silk blouse she'd planned to wear tonight.

Emma spots her standing at the doorway and calls, 'Over here,' and Jenny weaves her way among the tables to join her friends.

Sonya stands and gives her a hug and Emma pulls out a chair saying, 'What kept you? We've already had our first wine.'

As she settles herself into the chair and puts her heavy tote bag under the table she heaves a weary sigh, 'I've been trying to convince one of my girls that she should apply for a scholarship to study art next year. She's absolutely brilliant. The problem is her parents aren't very well off, and they don't want her going on to Art School. They want her to get a job.'

'I can't understand parents like that,' Sonya drawls in her deep husky voice. 'You'd think, if their kid's got talent, they'd do anything they possibly could to encourage her.'

'Of course you don't understand those sorts of parents,' Emma says abruptly and glares at Sonya. 'You grew up with a silver spoon in your mouth, and teach at a private school for the rich and privileged. The parents of most of our students are already battling. Putting someone through university or art school is something they just can't afford, even when the kid has a part time job to help out.'

Sonya answers laconically, 'There's no need to be so aggressive Em. I do understand.'

Jenny is upset by Emma's glare. She likes peace and harmony. To break the tension she says, 'Let me get us all a drink. What are you having?'

Sonya grins, 'Mine's a Shiraz and my friend here is having chardonnay.' As she says this she puts a long arm around Emma's shoulder and gives her a hug. Peace restored Jenny once more pushes through the crowd to get to the bar.

While waiting at the bar for their drinks Jenny wonders, as she has previously, what is behind Emma's occasional sudden shows of animosity towards Sonya. She knows Sonya has wealthy parents and that Emma comes from a working-class background, and just occasionally this seems to cause tensions between the two of them. Evidently they had attended the same high school but hadn't been friends until they met again during their second year at university. When Jenny met them two years later they were absolutely best friends and still are, but sometimes Emma makes the odd snide remark like the one this evening about Sonya's more privileged background. When this happens Sonya looks uncomfortable and does her best to smooth things over. Jenny doesn't like to pry but she would dearly love to know the reason behind these occasional flare-ups on Emma's part.

When she returns to their table, carrying a small tray laden with three wines and a bowl of cashews, she's pleased to see Sonya and Emma are chatting happily about what they have been reading during the past week.

As Jenny clears the tray Emma asks, 'Have you read any of Alice Munro's books Jen?'

'Gosh no,' Jenny answers almost apologetically. 'I never seem to get time to read any more. What with school, and the kids, and Don away so much I'm lucky to get time to read the Sunday newspapers.'

Emma looks horrified. 'But you must make time to read. You should try one of her books. I've been telling Sonya about her. She's wonderful. A lot of her books are short stories; you could read her when you have a spare hour or so.'

'Watch out', Sonya interjects. 'You're beginning to sound like an English teacher. You know the rules. No talking about kids, those we teach or those you two have borne, and no talking shop.'

Emma flushes at Sonya's rather bossy edict. She sips her drink then mumbles, 'I wasn't actually talking shop so you needn't be so bossy. I was merely suggesting that Jenny read an author whom I happen to love.' She knows she's overreacting, but the least criticism from Sonya can still make her feel like the nerdy scholarship girl she was when they first met.

Sonya senses she may have been a bit abrupt with Emma. She says, rather humbly for her, 'Sorry love. I guess I came on a bit strong, and you're right. Both of us should probably make more time for reading.' She sips her wine then continues. 'Actually I've been reading something lately that I wanted to discuss with you two. It was an article in a journal one of the other teachers lent me.'

'Do tell,' Jenny says, pleased to have harmony restored.

'It was about parallel worlds and when they are created. According to this writer there are only a few times in everyone's life when important decision are made, times when one's life could take a totally different path, and these are the only times a parallel world is created.'

Emma pretends an interest she doesn't really feel, 'Like in the film Sliding Doors?'

Sonya takes a sip of her wine before continuing, 'No. Actually the author mentioned that film, but as an example of a negative. I haven't seen the film, but evidently in it the woman created a parallel world simply by not catching a train when she'd been meant to. According to this writer's theory an alternative world wouldn't have been brought into being by this because the woman didn't make an important decision.'

"I'm kind of surprised that you find this sort of thing interesting,' Emma says, raising her well-shaped eyebrows. 'I've always thought of the concept of parallel worlds as something dreamt up by physicists or science fiction writers to keep themselves amused.'

'I probably would feel the same as you except for an odd experience I once had, when just for a moment I felt as though I was in another life. It was really weird but I was very unhappy and stressed out at the time and wanted out from the mess I'd made of my life. The other thing that makes me think there's something in this parallel worlds concept is that I've had some very vivid dreams; ones that were so real I felt as though they must somehow be part of another life I could be living.'

Jenny is finding the concept interesting and says eagerly, 'The thing that has sometimes made me think there could be parallel worlds is the way you can meet someone for the first time but they feel really familiar; as though you've known them somewhere before.'

Sonya adds, 'And when you go to some place for the first time, and feel as though you know exactly what it's going to look like.'

'Actually I think psychiatrists have an explanation for that feeling,' Emma says cynically. 'It's something to do with the subconscious brain registering what is being seen at a faster rate than the conscious brain.'

'Well I think the concept of parallel worlds is just as believable as that so-called explanation,' Sonya states definitely. 'And I found this writer's theory interesting, mainly because it limits the number of worlds one would create to the few times in your life when you make important decisions. It seems so much more manageable than having a new world pop up every time you make the smallest change in your life.'

As though humouring her friend Emma asks with a sigh, 'Okay, so what sorts of decisions are sufficiently important to create a parallel world?'

'Well the writer mentions things like what work we choose to do, who and when we marry and whether or not we have children. These important decisions are like junctions in a path, and at these times we open another pathway that runs parallel with the one in which we're living.'

Emma interjects, 'So at these junctions, where another world is created, there is still another you living in the already existing world. What have you gained from making this decision?'

Sonya answers, 'What you've gained by making an important decision is that you create a world of your choosing. You determine how you now want your life to be, while the first life continues on another plane.'

'Well I like the world I've got, so even if I could I wouldn't want to create another.'

'God, you sound so smug. Then again you've always seemed to know what you wanted, but I certainly haven't, and I know I made some bad choices. Mind you some of the time decisions were made for me, so I don't take responsibility for all the parallel worlds I may be in.'

Jenny perks up at this, 'How do you mean?'

'Well to create a parallel world, according to the article, you have to make a decision of your own free will. It got me thinking about what decisions I've actually made. How many times have my choices really been mine, and not what I was led to do because of influences by my parents or society in general? Quite frankly I couldn't think of all that many times when I've been free to choose; free from pressure of one sort or another. I don't think there are many other versions of me out there that I'd have willingly brought into being.'

Jenny has been listening with interest to the discussion. Now she says, 'Whether or not you felt free to choose wouldn't make any difference would it? If you made the decision you'd have created another world.'

'I guess so, but that doesn't mean I'd be happy with that world.'

Emma laughs at this. 'So you think there may be some worlds out there that you were pressured into creating because you didn't feel free to choose? I can't believe a strong-minded woman like you hasn't always done exactly what you chose to do.'

'Well I don't feel I have. I've given this quite a lot of thought. I definitely chose to become a teacher, even though my dear mother tried to talk me out of it.' When she says this her full generous lips turn down in a sneer. 'As for the rest, I don't feel I've had much say in how my life's gone.'

'What about your husbands?' Jenny interjects. 'I seem to remember you choosing them.'

'It may have seemed that way but, looking back I think my marriage to David was decided by his and my parents; although I did love the man I thought he was. I married Jeff because he was persistent, and he made me feel like a woman again after the sham of my first marriage. So you see I don't feel I made those life-changing choices freely, although I did choose to divorce both times. I guess those decisions helped me escape from the other worlds I didn't want. Anyhow all this talking has made me thirsty. I'll get the next round.'

With a graceful motion she collects the glasses and tray and walks to the bar.

Jenny turns to Emma, 'Did you notice she didn't mention her decision not to have children, and that's one of the most important decisions women make? She's so fond of her students, and so great with our kids, it's always surprised me that she hasn't ever seemed to want a child of her own.'

'It is something she never talks about.' Emma looks uncomfortable. 'Perhaps she can't have them, or it may be that she didn't feel secure enough in either marriage to complicate the relationships with children.'

She looks towards the bar and sees Sonya returning with their drinks so says hurriedly, 'Let's change the subject. Can you go to dinner tonight? Bruce got off work early to pick up the kids from school, and is going to cook them a gourmet meal of hamburgers and chips. I'm a free woman for the evening.'

'Don's out of town on business, so Mum's minding my lot. They're staying with her overnight so I can go to dinner, and have a lovely lie-in in the morning.'

As Sonya rejoins them she hears the last part of the conversation, and putting down the three glasses of wine says, 'Let's go to the new French restaurant that's opened up on the waterfront. Pierre and I went there last week. He reckoned the food was as good as anything you can get in Paris.'

'So you're still seeing our resident Frenchman? Emma says teasingly. 'I thought, from what you were saying a few weeks back, that you two were having problems.'

Sonya tosses back her thick mane of auburn hair and gives a wry laugh, 'We went through a rough patch, but things are good again. We don't see eye to eye about everything, but he makes me laugh, he's good company and he's great in the sack. What more could a girl want?'

Emma and Jenny exchange glances. They both think Pierre is a charming womaniser and fear he may not be completely trustworthy. They worry at times that Sonya may get hurt.

She catches the look that passes between the other two and says defensively, 'Look, I know neither of you trust him, but he suits me. You may not see him as husband material, but then I don't want another husband. To get back to what we were talking about before, he's my choice for now. He suits me at this time in my life, although I don't think for a minute that our relationship will be life changing. Anyhow drink up my darlings and I'll give La Cuisine a ring and book us a table.'

Chapter Two

The restaurant is only a couple of blocks from where they had met for drinks so they decide to walk. They pass brightly lit shops, still full of late night shoppers, then enter the area where many of the best restaurants in town are housed in the solid sandstone buildings that line one side of a wide cobbled road. On the other side of the road is a grassed space shadowed by gnarled plane trees, and then the waterfront with its mishmash of old and new buildings. These are built on the reclaimed spurs of land that jut out into the still dark water where fishing boats, sporting an array of nets, craypots and buoys, swing slowly at anchor.

As the young women tap in their high heels across the cobbled road in the soft, summer twilight they feel light hearted and free. It's the end of the working week, and for a few hours they are able to forget their responsibilities of work and home, of children and husbands and lovers

They push open the heavy wooden door. Jenny and Emma both give a sigh of pleasure at the sight of the room before them, and Sonya says, 'It's lovely isn't it?'

Before they can answer the maître d' appears. He is slim, dark and foreign-looking with sleek black hair and a small moustache over full red lips. Sonya gives him her name and he says in a strongly accented voice, 'Follow me madams,' and mincingly leads the way to a circular table in a corner of the room.

Jenny sighs, 'This is what I call luxury,' as she gazes admiringly around the room. It is softly illuminated by concealed wall lighting and candles that glow on each table in red cut glass shades. The tables are all covered with heavy white cloths and each one has a red rose in a specimen vase as its centrepiece.

'The décor's great but wait until you taste the food.' says Sonya, pleased her friends are so obviously taken with her choice.

'You've been here before so what would you suggest?' Emma asks as she looks down the extensive menu.

'I had the pigeon pie, which was divine, but Pierre had beef bourguignon and he raved about it, so that's what I'm having tonight.'

'Sounds good to me,' says Emma, and Jenny agrees.

They give their orders for food and wine and a short time later the waiter returns with the wine Sonya had ordered.

She waves aside his offer to taste with an imperious, 'Don't bother with that. I know we'll like it.'

After the waiter has poured each of them a glass of the rich, almost purple Burgundy Jenny takes a sip then says, 'You know what you said earlier Sonya, about not being free from undue influences when you've made important decisions?'

Sonya nods and murmurs agreement to encourage Jenny to continue.

'Well on the way here I was thinking about the important decisions in my life. I really don't think I've had much say in anything that's happened to me. Perhaps if I'd been stronger my life would've been different.'

Sonya and Emma are aware that Jenny has not been happy during the past months, but they are not prepared for the look of sadness that now distorts her pretty face. Tears appear in her round blue eyes. She brushes them away, smearing her mascara and giving herself the look of a sad clown. Both friends reach across the table simultaneously. Their hands are clasped tightly with Jenny's when the waiter arrives with the food. He looks taken aback, and Sonya thinks that perhaps he imagines they are a trio of lesbians. They release each other's hands and are silent while the delicious-smelling beef bourguignon is placed in front of them.

Jenny smiles, 'Sorry. I don't want to spoil our evening, but I guess I'm just feeling a bit bogged down at the moment. Thinking about what you said Sonya made me realise just how much of my life has been decided for me.'

Sonya and Emma are surprised for most of the time Jenny seems happy. She speaks lovingly of her children and appears to enjoy her job. At times they have sensed there may be problems between her and Don, but no more than in most marriages. Although they both think him rather autocratic and domineering, Jenny has always seemed to accept this and loved him regardless.

Sonya once more reaches for her friend's hand across the table and says, 'You look so sad. Is there something you want to talk about? Is there anything we can do?'

Jenny squeezes her hand, a silent thank you, and says, 'No, I'm okay. I've just had the blues a bit lately. It's probably hormonal. Let's get stuck into this gorgeous food. It smells divine.'

The evening passes pleasantly as the three women enjoy their main course and follow it with a light lemon tart and a second bottle of the wine. They chat about mutual friends, a film they have all seen and a concert they are planning to go to together. They are all feeling relaxed and slightly tipsy. While drinking second cups of good strong coffee and discussing the logistics of taxi sharing, Pierre appears at the door.

Sonya waves him over saying quite loudly, 'Ah! My knight in shining armour. How did you know where to find me?'

He strides across the room, acknowledges Jenny and Emma with a smile, takes Sonya's hand in his and kisses it with a gesture of exaggerated gallantry.

'I can find my princess whenever she needs me,' he says laughing. 'And also you did say you would like Emma and Jenny to try the oh so wonderful food here.'

There is a gaiety and light-heartedness between the two lovers that is appealing, and Jenny and Emma exchange almost maternal grins. While they don't quite know what to make of Pierre, they know that for the past year he has brought happiness into the life of their friend.

They finish their coffees and are calling for the bill when Pierre intervenes, 'No, no. I will take care of this.'

Before they can object he strides across to the bar area and settles the account.

Sonya smiles complacently. 'Let him do it. He can afford it and he loves making chivalrous gestures.'

The three women join Pierre at the door and he holds it for them while they walk out into the balmy summer air. He opens the passenger side door of his BMW and helps a giggling Sonya into her seat before turning to assist the other two into the back.

Emma enters the car straight away but Jenny says, 'It's very kind of you Pierre, but I'm only a few blocks from home, and I really would like to walk. It's such a lovely evening.'

Before any of them can remonstrate with her she has set off, striding purposefully along the street and round the nearest corner.

Pierre watches in dismay. 'Did I do something to offend her?' he asks. 'I don't like to think of her wandering these dark streets by herself.'

Sonya puts her head out the window. 'It's nothing you've done darling. I think she just wants to be alone and, as she said, she lives quite near to here.'

Pierre shakes his head but then gets into the car. As he starts the engine and moves smoothly from the curb, he feels Sonya's hand gently caressing his thigh and smells the perfume in her hair as she softly kisses the side of his neck. He is eager to get her home and enjoy the sensual pleasures she is silently promising. Selfishly he thinks it is a good thing they have only one passenger to off-load.

Jenny

Chapter Three

I turn the key, open the big, heavy front door and switch on the light. I feel the emptiness even before I've gone two steps into the entry. Usually I enjoy this first view of my house; the expansive foyer tiled in a diamond pattern of black and white, and the graceful sweep of the curved stairway that leads to the upper floor. Tonight I am only conscious of the way in which my heels tap noisily across the tiles. They seem to echo in the silence, but this must be my imagination. I'm not used to coming home at night to an empty house.

I open the first door on my left and go into the sitting room, my favourite part of the house. It's a long rectangular room with a generous bay window at one end and a fireplace at the other. This room never fails to please me with its golden walls, glowing timber floors and amber velvet curtains that now cover the window and match the couches and chairs placed strategically around the room.

I walk to the small drinks table that's at one side of the fireplace and pour a small whiskey before collapsing onto a couch. I know I've already had quite enough to drink, but feel the need of the warming comfort the whiskey will bring.

When I'd told Emma I would be alone tonight and tomorrow morning I'd felt a sort of freedom at the prospect; had really been looking forward to being by myself for once and able to do as I wished. Now I feel lonely in a way I haven't experienced since I was a child.

I was certainly alone much of the time in primary school; I didn't really have any close friends, but in high school I always had Nina and at the college, where we studied art, we had hung out with a bunch of fellow students. At the end of our final year Don had come into my life and although we weren't always together he was there, a presence in my life, even when he wasn't around.

Now Don is frequently away on business, either around the state or in Melbourne or Sydney, but then the children are with me, filling the house with their laughter and their needs.

As I sip my whiskey and let my tired body sink into the comfortable velvet I think back over the evening. I feel ashamed of myself for the self-pitying tears I'd shed in front of my friends. They both always seem so on top of everything, and I don't like to feel inferior. I don't want them being sorry for me either, but lately I feel as though I'm living a life of constant stress and pretence.

The big problem is the way things are between Don and me. He's either out or away so much it's almost as though we're living separate lives. Sometimes I wonder if he's having an affair, but so far I've been too cowardly to accuse him. I keep silent, shying away from what he might tell me. I'm not ready to hear what I fear put into words. If he were to confess to infidelity I know I would have to act, respond to the knowledge of his rejection of me. At present I don't feel strong enough to cope if this is so.

I finish my drink and stand, sighing wearily as I cross the foyer to the kitchen, and rinse my glass at the sink. I walk up the stairs and along the wide passage, looking into each of the children's room as I pass. I know they're not there, but do it out of habit. Seeing the empty beds only makes me feel even lonelier.

Later as I lie in bed willing sleep to come and thinking back about the evening. I really can't understand why the discussion about choices and life changing decisions upset me so. Perhaps it's because at present I don't feel quite in control of my life, but it also made me think about just how few important decisions I've actually ever made. All my life I've felt the need to please the ones I love. Perhaps this has stopped me speaking out when I should have; stopped me from standing up to Don about things that were important to me.

Chapter Four

When I got into bed I felt so tired I thought I would go to sleep instantly but it's now 1 o'clock and I'm still wide awake. My outburst about never having made any important decisions in my life is still bugging me. I guess because I know it's true. I let others make choices for me because I had a frantic need to be loved and approved of. I think this stems from the fact that I grew up knowing I wasn't important to my father. By the time I came on the scene he had his three clever athletic sons, and didn't know how to relate to the accidental daughter who was born soon after his fiftieth birthday.

In photos taken at that time he holds me diffidently, a bemused look on his face. He looks as though he doesn't quite know what to make of me. He had thought his parenting years were coming to an end; had already begun planning for his retirement. He never came to terms with being the father of a girl child, didn't seem to quite know how to treat me. As a result of this I grew up uncertain of male approval.

My relationship with Mum was completely different. After years of being a lone woman in a house of males my mother loved having a daughter, and spoiled me totally. From her I received unconditional love. Even if she didn't always understand my rather fey ways, my mother accepted that anything I felt or did was all right. But is it enough to get such love and approval from your mother when your father, the member of the opposite sex, ignores you?

From a very early age I knew I didn't see the world in the same way as my brothers and parents. For me colour was something you could feel and taste as well as see. I remember standing transfixed before a beautiful sunset, or a rainbow shimmering across the sky to an unknown place where a pot of gold was to be found. I was so entranced by the colours of flowers in my mother's garden I felt I must eat them, savour their taste upon my tongue. Nasturtiums tasted as they should, sharp and bright and orangey, but the velvety purple pansies were disappointingly bland and flavourless.

I also had very definite ideas about clothes, and my doting mother allowed me to choose what was bought for me to wear from the time I was about four. Thinking back I can see that my mother spoilt me, but at the time I'd thought it only reasonable. I understand now she gave me what choices she could for she was well aware how limited they would be.

Growing up in a male-dominated world I was very aware that my mother's and my concerns were of secondary importance. Although Mum encouraged me to express my wishes and gave me choices, these only related to small things. Big decisions were made by men.

My father and brothers ruled the house. As soon as Mum heard my father's car in the drive she would get me to pack up my artwork that was spread over the kitchen table, and then she'd bustle around the room putting finishing touches to the evening meal. Talk at the dinner table always revolved around the doings of my brothers; how one had gone at football training or of an important test another had sat that day.

My brothers filled the house with the sounds of heavy boots on the stairs and mud-splattered jerseys and shorts in the laundry. Later, when they become studious and serious uni students, I moved quietly around the house fearful of disturbing them and their important studies.

Slowly I patterned myself on my mother; became the pliant, pretty little daughter of a doting mother and a largely disinterested father.

Later I would tell myself I didn't really care about my father's lack of interest in me but for many years I tried so hard to win his love and attention. I remember when I was about seven I decided to make him a really special card for Fathers' Day. For hours I worked on the card, embellishing the blue cardboard with flowers and twining leaves. On the outside I wrote Happy Father's Day in my very best printing, and inside painted a big red heart with the words Daddy and Jenny within it. He gave me a hug and thanked me for the card, but didn't put it on the mantelpiece where Mum displayed such offerings.

I wondered what he had done with it and a week later, when everyone else was outside, I crept into my father's study hoping to see the card on his desk. It wasn't there, so feeling very nervous I searched the drawers that ran down one side of the desk. In the second drawer I found the card buried beneath some of my father's papers. Tearfully I crushed the card in my hands, and then went to my room where I tore it into the tiniest pieces before flushing them all down the toilet.

I knew then that in my father's eyes I would never be as important or interesting as my brothers. Only my fascination with colour made me different and this wasn't even understood by my father although it was encouraged by my mother.

As the years progressed Mum became convinced I had what she called, "an artist's eye," and gave me an enormous box of coloured pencil and reams of paper. Later she bought real stretched canvases, tubes of paint and numerous brushes for me. I know Mum spoiled me and I think it was her way of trying to make up for the total lack of interest my father showed me.

With all this encouragement from Mum I became a bit of a child prodigy. In art classes it was always my work that the teachers pinned first to the display board as they predicted, 'I can see you will become an artist when you grow up.'

Few children like such attention drawn to them. They know the outcome will be playground bullying, jibes of, 'Teacher's pet,' snarled behind pudgy hands and, 'Don't you think you're smart?' accompanied by a rough push in the back when the teacher isn't looking. Throughout primary school I copped all of this and more. The bullying and taunting made me even shyer than I had been. Living in a house dominated by my father and brothers and with mainly only Mum for company I didn't know how to talk to other children and I had few friends..

There was also the problem with sleepovers, which were just beginning to become popular in Australia. If you liked another girl you invited her to your house for the night and your mother cooked a special meal. There would also be treats to be taken to bed and munched on while you discussed clothes and fairies and what you wanted to be when you grew up.

I was invited for a few sleepovers during my later years in primary school, and enjoyed brief friendships. I didn't feel, however, that I could ask a friend to my house. It wasn't that there was anything wrong with it, in fact it was a large, almost luxurious home, but I didn't feel comfortable at the thought of any of my friends being there. It was too full of brothers, and a father who might look critically at another girl child around the place.

Because I didn't reciprocate with sleepover invitations my friend of the moment dropped me. Two of the girls who had been friends, and with whom I'd shared sleepovers, began saying around the school I was a snob; that no one was good enough to go to my house. This hurt me and I became even more of a loner.

My first really close friend was Nina who I met when I started high school. We sat next to each other in classes, and for both of us our favourite subject was art. I invited my new friend to stay with me for the weekend so we could paint together.

By now two of my brothers had moved out of home. Bob, my oldest brother, was doing his internship as a doctor, and Jake was working interstate as a journalist. Steve, my youngest brother, was completing his final year of a degree in Computer Science, and spent most of his time at home glued to the computer in his bedroom.

The weekend went well. Mum was thrilled that I had a friend to stay, and my father even stopped and joked with us before heading off for a day on the golf course.

Nina and I decided we would paint on the verandah overlooking the long sweeping drive and colourful flower-filled gardens that were Mum's pride and joy. We set up easels and were soon engrossed in our paintings. As we worked we chatted about what we were painting. I loved the fact that Nina saw the world as I did, felt the same rapture about the beauty and colour surrounding us. We discussed the shadows beneath the big oak tree, and both saw the blues and pinks and purples where other less aware eyes would see only grey. We both felt we had found a soul-mate.

When Mum came out later with sandwiches and cool drinks for us she admired our paintings and praised them both, but I could see Nina's painting had that special something mine lacked and I think Mum could see that too.

That weekend was the beginning of a long and close friendship. Nina and I finished high school and enrolled together to do the degree course in fine art at the local college.

During the following three years I changed. I met others who saw the world as Nina and I, and I moved away from the close but overprotective force of my mother's love. I thought of myself as mature, analytical and self-motivated, but of course I was still being influenced by preconceived ideas of how I thought artists should look and behave.

Nina and I began to dress and behave the way we thought artists would. We now wore only black; black jeans, black sweaters or tee shirts and black boots in winter. We even painted our fingernails black. We hung out with fellow students in a seamy café that sold strong black coffee and dubious organic food. The owners turned a blind eye to the thin hand-rolled strange-smelling cigarettes passing from hand to hand around the crowded table, and encouraged our patronage because we lent a touch of colour to their establishment.

My friends and I spent long hours discussing the paintings of the Great Masters, the Fauves, the Cubists, the Impressionists and Post Impressionists. We criticised the works of those who had gone before us with the arrogance of youth, but secretly wished we had a fraction of the talent of those long-dead masters.

The boys who I met during that time were so different from my conventional father and brothers and I found them fascinating. They didn't follow the footy or the cricket, or dress in business suits or smart casual gear the way the men in my family did. They wore faded jeans, black sweaters or paint-stained shirts and sported shoulder length hair. Two of them even had dirty woolly-looking dreadlocks. I liked to listen to their talk of paintings they were working on, and the ways in which they hoped to achieve certain effects by the use of techniques and colour.

During the final year I began to realise I lacked the talent to make a living as an artist. Nina and some of the other students were now producing the most amazing works, and I knew I wasn't in their league. My paintings were competent, but lacked that essential something that makes a work of art. I discussed my future with my favourite tutor and although he recognised my limitations as a painter he said I had an exceptional colour sense that should be used in another sphere. He suggested I enrol in the Interior Design course being offered by the college the following year.

Feeling rather nervous I broached my father about the possibility of him funding me for a further two years of study but he told me grumpily he wouldn't back me in another airy-fairy course. I was hurt by the arbitrary way in which he dismissed my fine arts degree as airy-fairy and by his refusal to fund me in further study. For a while I toyed with the idea of trying to get a job and financing myself through the interior design course but couldn't think of anything I would be able to do. Some of the other kids doing the fine arts course with me had worked in bottle shops or packed shelves in supermarkets during the evenings but I couldn't imagine doing menial work like that.

When I told Mum about my father's refusal she suggested I apply for a scholarship to do a Diploma of

Education so that I could teach art. She further annoyed me by saying, 'Teaching will be so convenient when you have a family.'

Suddenly I felt my adored and adoring mother had never really understood me; had never really understood the need I felt to create. I knew I had the flair and colour sense to design and create beautiful home interiors, and that this was the field in which I wanted to train.

For the first time in my life I felt cross with Mum. I'm ashamed to admit it but I remember shouting at her, 'You don't understand. I want to create something myself. I know I can't paint well enough to make it as an artist, but I feel that with training I could become extremely good as an interior designer.'

Seeing the sadness on Mum's face I lowered my voice and said more quietly, 'Please talk Dad into bankrolling me for just two more years.'

'He won't listen to me darling,' Mum said rather wistfully. 'He never has and he's not going to start now. At least think about my suggestion. If you qualify as a teacher you'd be earning your own money, and could perhaps do the interior design course sometime in the future.'

I loved my mother and hated us being at cross purposes; hated seeing her looking worried, and knowing I was the cause of her concern. In time I saw the practicality of Mum's suggestion and put in my scholarship application, although it wasn't what I wanted to do. I continued to feel resentment towards my father for he had happily paid for my brothers' educations; but then I'd always known I was not as important to him as they were.

At the end of the final semester my classmates and I organised a party to celebrate the completion of our three-year course. Only fifty of us graduated from an initial enrolment of eighty. We had watched the others disappear, some because they found the assignments too demanding, or realised they lacked sufficient talent to succeed, others left because of financial problems. We remaining fifty called ourselves "The Survivors" and were determined to finish the year with a bang.

The boys cleared the largest studio of easels and tables and we girls put up streamers and balloons to decorate the room. One of the boys brought in a sophisticated sound system from home, and we pooled our money to buy numerous wine casks and biscuits, long loaves of French bread, pates and various cheeses.

At the party I was talking and drinking with a small group of friends when I looked towards the door and saw a couple of strangers, who were peering around the semi-darkened room looking rather lost. The woman was tall, darkly good-looking and wore a severe blue-grey suit, but it was the man with her who caught my eye. He too wore a business suit, and was one of the handsomest men I had ever seen. He had big dark eyes, a strong chin below a wide curving mouth and tanned skin that glowed against his immaculate white shirt. They looked totally out of place amongst this group of students dressed in their habitual blacks or more colourful hand-painted gear. I drew the attention of the group to their presence.

To everyone's surprise Justin, one of the dreadlocked boys said, 'Gee that's my sister Joyce. I kind of invited her, but I didn't think she'd come.'

He moved quickly across the room and soon returned with them in tow.

When he introduced Joyce and her friend Don, the sister said in a cool precise voice, 'What a beautiful top. Where did you get it?'

I know I blushed at being complimented by this elegant woman and sort of stammered, 'We learnt screen printing last year and this was one of my experiments.'

'Well it's really lovely,' Joyce said, before turning to her boyfriend. 'Isn't it Don?'

He said the one word, 'Beautiful,' but the look on his face showed that he meant more than just the top, and I was glad I'd taken a bit of trouble dressing up for the party. I was wearing the colourful screen-printed silk top over black tights that fitted snugly inside my long black boots, and had pulled my blonde hair up into a high pony tail to show off the gold dangling earrings I'd found recently in a shop selling second-hand jewellery.

Soon Justin led Joyce and Don away to get drinks for them and introduce them to more of his friends. I found it touching that he was so obviously pleased his sister had come. Even though they looked almost as if they came from different planets there was evidently a strong bond of familial affection between the brother and sister. I thought how embarrassed I'd have been if one of my brothers had turned up to this college do; not that I'd have ever thought of inviting any of them, not even Steve.

During the summer I loafed around the house, sometimes with Nina, but often alone. I found myself daydreaming about Don; imagining he would follow up the obvious look of interest with a phone call. I told myself I was being ridiculous; he wouldn't even know my number. It had also been obvious he and Joyce were close, and they certainly looked good together. Evidently he was attracted to tall elegant women, not short slightly scruffy blondes.

Despite telling myself these things I still couldn't resist quizzing Justin about his sister and Don when a group of us met for coffee. I began by saying how great it had been that his sister had come to their party.

Justin answered with a grin, 'Yes, she's a good sort, even if she doesn't always approve of what I am doing or the way I dress. She's the square one in the family and I'm the rebel, but by doing the right thing and qualifying to be a lawyer she's taken the heat off me with Mum and Dad.'

'And what about her boyfriend?' I asked in what I hoped was a casual voice. 'Is he a lawyer too?'

Justin shook his head. 'No he's in business. Actually I'm not sure he's still around. Last time I was home Mum said something about them breaking up. I was pretty surprised about it because they've been going together for a couple of years. I think Mum was already planning the wedding.'

At this news my heart gave a little lurch. Suddenly I felt surprisingly happy, but knew I was being foolish if I thought that now he might get in touch with me. After all, as far as I knew, he didn't even know my surname.

A couple of days after this conversation with Justin I was sitting on the verandah trying to sketch my cat that was sleeping in the shade of a pot plant. He seemed to be still, but every time I took my eyes off him he moved ever so slightly and that made my drawing completely wrong.

I heard the phone ring inside the house, heard my mother answering it and then she appeared at the door looking slightly flustered, 'There's someone on the phone for you. He didn't seem to quite know whether he had the right number. I hope it's not a nuisance caller or a stalker.'

I giggled at Mum's look of concern, 'It's probably someone wanting me to buy something or give to a charity.'

I walked inside and picked up the phone.

As soon as I said hello, his deep voice came on the line, 'This is Don Fielding here. You may not remember me, but we met at a party a month ago. I was with Justin's sister Joyce,'

My heart thudded in my chest making me feel breathless. I wanted to say, 'Yes, yes, of course I remember you. I've been thinking about you ever since.'

Instead I took a deep breath before answering as casually as I could, 'Yes, I do remember being introduced to you. How did you get my number?'

Sounding a bit embarrassed he answered, 'I rang Justin on his mobile, and asked him about the beautiful blonde with the dangling earrings. I've broken up with Joyce, and she and her parents are a bit dark with me at the moment, but Justin was okay. He just said these things happen and gave me your number, without putting me through the third degree.'

With an effort I kept the delight from my voice when I asked flirtatiously, 'And what can I do for you kind sir?'

'I was hoping you would let me take you out to dinner. There's a very good Italian restaurant not far from where you live. That is if you like Italian food, but if you don't we can go somewhere else.'

With my heart beating wildly I said I'd love to come and that my favourite food was pasta.

Before the date, I searched frantically through my wardrobe trying to find something suitable to wear. For the previous three years I had happily worn clothes bought from the op shops, or cheap jeans and sweaters. In dismay I saw I had nothing smart and fashionable to wear, nothing suitable for a date with a man like Don.

There was a little money in my bank account, saved from the meagre student's allowance I had received during the past year. I splurged most of it on an elegant dark green dress and new black very high-heeled shoes. Over this I planned to wear a silk shawl I had designed and printed in second year. It was covered in a swirling pattern of gold, black and a green that matched my dress exactly.

When the evening of our date arrived I was ready early, and rushed to open the door as soon as I heard the bell. I had thought that perhaps during the intervening weeks since we'd met my mind had exaggerated how handsome he was, but now I saw he was just as gorgeous as I remembered.

He put a warm hand on my arm and said, 'I've so wanted to see you again.'

Throwing caution to the wind I laughed and said, 'And I've wanted to see you too.'

Chapter Five

As I lie alone in my bed unable to get to sleep, I think back to that perfect night, remembering how enchanted Don and I were with each other then. Did we both fall in love with an illusion, or is our changed relationship to be expected after fourteen years of marriage and three children?

I know I have changed from the girl I was back then. Even for a twenty-year old I had been very naïve and unworldly. I was also extremely inexperienced as far as the opposite sex went. Perhaps it was the result growing up in such a male dominated household, but until I mixed with the boys at college I'd felt rather intimidated around males.

Nina and I had gone on double dates to the occasional movie with boys from school, but my only serious boyfriend had been Saul, who was in my English class at Matriculation College. He took me to the Leavers' Dinner and we'd hung out together during the following summer. He was a nice boy, gentle and intelligent, and I felt comfortable with him. One summer day we found a secluded old boatshed and in the following weeks often went there after a swim at the nearby beach. Here we kissed and petted on an old dusty sail we'd found rolled up in a corner and when Saul became insistent that we go all the way I gave in but didn't enjoy it much. I felt pressured into something I wasn't ready for yet but wanted to please Saul. When the summer holiday ended he left to study math and physics at the university in Canberra. We kissed goodbye beneath the trees in my parent's garden with both of us tearfully promising to keep in touch.

For a while we phoned each other every week and talked about how we missed being together. We planned endlessly what we'd do during the mid-year vacation. Gradually our calls tapered off as we became involved in our very different courses and made new friends. By June, when Saul came home for two weeks, we had become almost strangers to each other. We hung out together but anything that had been between us had gone and I was actually glad when he went back to Canberra.

Amongst the boys at college I had lots of friends, but I didn't feel attracted to any of them in a romantic way. We went out in groups, Nina and I and some of the boys, to movies and cheap restaurants, exhibitions and plays. It was always fun and of course we all paid for ourselves.

Don was the first man I had ever dated and soon I was deeply in love with him. Compared with the boys I had known before, Don seemed so mature and sophisticated. At twenty-eight he was self-assured, successful and worldly-wise, or at least that's how he seemed to me. I was to learn he had his share of faults but at the time was too young and in love to see them or to question his behaviour.

Strangely the only time I felt critical of him in those early months was to do with Joyce. I knew from what Justin told me that Don had broken up with Joyce shortly before he began dating me. I hadn't thought much about this past love until one day when I went to town to buy a new dress for a party one of Don's friends was giving.

As I crossed the mall I saw Don and Joyce together. They were drinking coffee, and seemed to be engrossed in an intimate conversation. Feeling a surge of jealousy I turned around and retraced my steps. All that afternoon I agonised about why they would be meeting. Did it mean he had tired of me and wanted to get back with Joyce? Had he realised he'd made a terrible mistake?

That evening, as he was helping me into his car I said, as casually as I could manage, 'I saw you with Joyce today in the mall. I didn't know you still kept in touch.'

He looked a bit shamefaced but answered abruptly, 'We don't. I hadn't seen her since I started dating you, but she rang me and said she wanted to have a talk so we met for coffee.'

He shut my door and went around to the driver's seat, but before he could start the car I asked, 'Did she know you were interested in me when you broke up?' This was something I had wondered about and now seemed the perfect chance to ask.

He shrugged, 'Look, I didn't tell her at the time. I just told her I didn't see any future for us, that our feelings weren't strong enough for a lifetime commitment. She was upset but seemed to accept it. Now she's found out about you and she's furious with me for what she calls my deceit. That's why she wanted to see me today. She gave me the third degree about whether I'd been seeing you before we split up. She was pretty upset.'

Feeling sorry for being the cause of another woman's pain I said, 'Poor Joyce.'

'She'll get over it,' Don answered rather curtly. 'It's her pride that's hurt more than anything.'

As we drove to the party I couldn't help but think Don's attitude towards this woman, who he once loved, was very cold and unsympathetic. I felt a shiver of dismay that he could be so dismissive about Joyce. A small voice in my head said he might not be as perfect as he seemed, but to think this seemed disloyal so I pushed it from my mind.

During our first year together I met many of his friends at dinners and parties, and he seemed to enjoy introducing me as his artist girlfriend, ignoring the fact that I was by then training to become a teacher. Sometimes this led to embarrassing situations when people asked me what I was working on at present. I told them about the diploma course but implied that this year of study was simply a form of insurance, a stopgap until I could get back to my real work. When I said this I always felt a bit hypocritical but I wanted Don to be proud of me so went along with the image he wanted me to project.

When we went out with his friends he encouraged me to wear some of the more outlandish clothes I had made for myself during my college years. I knew I looked very different from the other girlfriends and wives who wore smartly elegant clothes, but figured I was dressing to please Don and he obviously wanted me to appear arty and a little bit bohemian. If this was the image he wanted me to project I was happy to go along with it because for the first time in my life when Don looked at me with approval I felt beautiful.

Common sense told me I had an attractive collection of features, large blue eyes, a neat nose, curving mouth and pretty, blonde hair. Mum had always made much of me and told me how pretty I looked, but girl children get their view of themselves from their fathers. Although he was never deliberately cruel my elderly father had never made me feel beautiful or loved.

In contrast, Nina's father, who was also elderly, treated his precious only child as a princess. He was always buying her surprise gifts, and telling her how lovely she looked as he hugged her when he returned from work. Seeing this show of fatherly love and approval had made me feel somehow less worthy than my friend, and certainly less attractive.

Now Don made me feel I was special, not only lovely to look at but interesting and exciting as well. When he proposed at the end of our first year together as a couple I accepted eagerly.

I had completed my Diploma of Education and been assigned to a local high school. Don suggested that we marry in April, and became quite angry when I said we would have to wait until the end of the first semester in June.

He had never shown much interest in my work; treated it as something I was doing to fill in time until we married. I hated him being angry with me but there was no way I could just up and leave my classes in the middle of term. To get him out of his mood I used what feminine wiles I could muster.

I was a bit of a novice in this department but insisted I'd need at least two months to find the right dress and that Mum would need probably longer to organise everything.'

When I said this I'd thought I was just placating Don, but it proved to be true. By then my three brothers were all married, but this would be the first time Mum could be actively involved in the wedding plans. As mother of the bride she had the pleasure of arranging the church and reception venue and we spent happy times together having endless discussions about "the dress" and the flowers.

Once the wedding date was set I arranged to meet Nina for coffee to tell her I was engaged and to ask her to be my chief bridesmaid.

Instead of squealing her congratulations, as I'd expected, Nina said quietly, 'Are you sure he's the right one for you?'

Nina had first met Don at my twenty-first birthday celebration. Although our social life revolved mainly around Don's friends and acquaintances, we had gone out to dinner with Nina and a friend on a couple of occasions. I'd thought the evenings had gone well, but now Nina's question and lack of enthusiasm about my news upset me.

I remember being sort of hurt by her response and saying, 'God, that's not what I expected you to say. I thought you'd be thrilled for me. You know how much I love him and, yes, of course I'm sure he's the right one for me.'

Seeing how much her remark had bothered me Nina said apologetically, 'I didn't mean to upset you Jen, but it's just that since you met Don you've changed. You let him dominate you completely. He tells you what to wear, chooses for you at restaurants, and even tells you what books you should read. Soon he'll be telling you what to think.'

Feeling hurt and distressed I stood up from the table, said, 'I don't think I want to continue this conversation,' and left Nina sitting alone, open-mouthed and dismayed.

I spent a miserable afternoon. I was terribly upset by Nina's remarks, partly because I knew there was some truth in what she had said. At times I did feel Don was too domineering, but generally I accepted this was the way men behaved. After all this was what my father was like with my mother.

That evening Nina rang and apologised for what she'd said and we sobbed together over the phone.

Neither of us would allow this little disagreement to ruin our long friendship, and years later I was to wish I'd taken more heed of Nina's warning.

My other two best friends, Emma and Sonya, who I had met at university the previous year, were to be my other bridesmaids. During the next few months the four of us met often to discuss the dresses and later for fittings. Afterwards we'd go for drinks and dinner, and my hurt feelings about Nina's criticism of my relationship with Don were forgotten.

I can't really remember those months very clearly. They seemed to pass in a blur. What with getting used to my new job, planning the wedding and still having precious time to spend with Don, I often felt thoroughly exhausted. At times Don complained about me always being tired, and I would be cross about his lack of empathy, but I tried not to show it. Soon we would be married and be able to spend lots of relaxing, loving time together.

Chapter Six

We began married life in Don's rather luxurious flat in the bay area. I loved the flat with its compact, modern kitchen, large bathroom equipped with spa bath and stereo and the spacious lounge room with its views across the river. I had thought we would live there for the first few years of our marriage, but this was not to be.

Soon after our return from a honeymoon in Fiji Don suggested we begin looking for a place that would be more suitable as a family home. He began talking about starting a family, and his sense of urgency about this surprised me. After all I was only twenty-two and not yet ready to take on the responsibilities of motherhood. As far as I was concerned there was plenty of time before we changed our lives in this way.

Absurdly, we had never discussed the issue of when we would want to start a family. We both agreed we wanted to have children, but had not actually talked about the timing of this event. Now, when I said I wanted to wait for at least a couple of years, Don looked quite baffled.

He asked, 'Why should we wait? I'm going to be thirty this year, and I don't want to be an old man with my kids or to die before they've made their way in the world.'

Don had also been the child of older parents and we had commiserated with each other about this; felt it was another bond between us. In his case, though, both parents had died in a car accident when he was only eighteen. Belatedly I realised this was also something we had not discussed, but should have. I should have tried to find out how being orphaned at such an early age affected him. Perhaps not having any parents accounted for the importance he now placed on starting a family of his own.

Unwillingly, I stopped taking the pill. I'd heard that once you had been on it for a while your body could take some time to readjust, causing a delay in becoming pregnant. I hoped this would be the case for me for I really wanted more time with us just being a couple.

Within a month I missed a period and began to feel slightly nauseous in the mornings. I told myself it couldn't happen so quickly. I wasn't ready yet to be a mother or for all that motherhood entailed. After my second period was a week late Don insisted we must find out, and bought a pregnancy kit from the chemist. When the test confirmed my fears he was jubilant. He thought my tears were tears of joy but that couldn't have been further from the truth. I didn't tell him how I was really feeling but my mind was shrieking, 'I'm not ready for this.'

Now we were going to have a baby we began house hunting in earnest. We found a house I loved. It was very modern with a beautiful kitchen and three good-sized bedrooms. There was a large flat back yard. I could see it would make a perfect playground for the child I was carrying inside me and any subsequent siblings.

Don said the house was much too small, and refused to even consider it. I felt very disappointed but accepted his decision without argument. We were buying the house with money left to him by his parents so my sense of fairness made me feel he should have the final say about the purchase.

He found the house we were to buy almost by accident. He was driving along Bay Road and pulled up when he saw a "For Sale" sign fixed to a high stone wall. The house was hidden from view by this wall, but when Don pushed open the tall metal gates he could see a long driveway leading up the steep incline to a magnificent sandstone mansion. Within an hour he contacted the real estate agent listed on the sign and arranged a viewing.

That evening when he arrived home excited about his find I felt put out that he had looked at the house without me, but his enthusiasm made me feel I was being petty. He talked so happily about the enormous rooms, the wide verandah that surrounded the house on three sides and the private back yard full of old trees, apple and quince and even a walnut.

From Don's description I really hadn't known what to expect, but when I saw inside the house my heart sank. It was old, built for a wealthy merchant in the 1850s, and would have been very beautiful in its heyday. Now it was dilapidated, wearing the years of neglect like an ancient dowager in a faded ball gown.

For the past fifteen years it had been rented as student accommodation. The kitchen was a shambles, and some of the larger bedrooms upstairs had been roughly partitioned to provide added sleeping spaces. I looked around the house in dismay. I couldn't see anywhere in that great barn of a place where my baby could be warm and comfortable. Tears filled my eyes, and as I unconsciously rubbed my bump the baby kicked as if, he too, objected to what would be his new home.

Seeing how upset I was Don assured me he knew it needed a lot of work, and that we wouldn't move in until at least some of the rooms had been restored.

The next time I saw the house the kitchen had been gutted and all the old mouldy floor coverings and temporary partitions had been removed. Don showed me the changes he had organised and said to me proudly, 'Now you have a clean canvas to work on.'

I must have looked as woebegone as I was feeling because Don put his arms around the bulge where my waist used to be and said apologetically, 'I know I've railroaded you into this, but I want you to love this house too. You'll have a free hand with the decorating. You have such an eye for colour I know you will make it beautiful and a great home for our children.'

He looked so earnest and concerned I felt a rush of love. I had been feeling manipulated; first into a pregnancy too soon, and then into a house I didn't like. Now he seemed only concerned about providing a lovely home for me and our children and I felt guilty for thinking him self-centred. Talk about being manipulated.

Chapter Seven

I look at the clock on my bedside table. Two o'clock and still wide awake even though I feel exhausted. My thoughts about choices and decision-making have led me on a mental journey to the past, and what I remember reinforces what I told my friends. I haven't had much say in the way my life has gone.

Lying alone in the large, king-size bed I feel lonely and bereft. I wonder if Don is feeling the same, or if he has someone warm and willing to share his night. As a tear rolls down my cheek I tell myself to stop imagining things. I have no proof he is being unfaithful to me. He is away tonight on legitimate business, has given me his itinerary and phone numbers where he can be reached at all times. Nevertheless I still harbour doubts, for all is not right between us. During the last few years we have drifted apart, and it seems we are only held together by the shared love we have for the children.

I know I'm not going to be able to sleep without something to help so put on a warm dressing gown and walk past the empty bedrooms, down the staircase and into the kitchen.

This was the first room to be rebuilt and decorated to my design. During the last three months of my pregnancy, when I'd felt too large and lumpish to do anything more active than clean the flat and cook the evening meal, I had spent my days pouring over catalogues and colour charts. I wanted to create a kitchen that was an attractive and convenient room in which to work, but one that would fit into an old house. I knew I needed to retain the charms of yesteryear without losing the efficiencies of a modern kitchen.

In my final plan I had sleek, varnished Blackwood cupboards with greenish-grey granite tops and a matching slate floor. The large black German stove I'd selected had the efficiency required by the modern cook but would sit inconspicuously among the dark timber cupboards. The fridge/freezer was to be hidden in the pantry cupboard and the dishwasher behind one of the cupboard doors. Instead of a breakfast bar, a feature very popular at that time, I chose to have a small circular Blackwood table at one end of the room. For the large window over the sink I selected a blind the same colour as the green in the bench tops but a shade lighter.

Don organised the work on the kitchen, and it was completed two weeks after I returned home from the hospital with our beautiful son Josh. He took me to see how it looked, and when I held my baby in my arms and looked around the lovely room I had designed I'd felt an overwhelming sense of achievement.

As I enter the kitchen now I still feel pleased with this room. It has such an ageless charm about it, and looks as attractive as it did thirteen years ago.

I take a small pot and fill it with milk. To this I add a good dollop of honey before placing it on the front hotplate on the stove. While it is heating I get the bottle of whiskey from the drinks table in the lounge room and add a nip to the warmed milk before pouring the lot into a mug.

I sit at the little circular table thinking back to that first year of motherhood.

Although initially I had been a slightly unwilling mother I absolutely adored my baby boy on sight, and he proved to be an amazingly good first child. From the beginning he fed from my breasts without any problems. I saw other mothers having difficulties and felt a sense of achievement that my son and I could do this so easily. From the time we came home from the hospital he slept contentedly between feeds and within a couple of months went through the night without waking.

When Don told me what a natural mother I was I gloried in his praise.

By the time Josh was three months old one of the bathrooms had been refitted and redecorated to my design and the painting of the master bedroom had been completed. Don decided we should move in and complete the renovations while living there.

I wasn't happy about this but he argued logically by pointing out how much we would save by not renting the expensive apartment and that this money could be put into the restoration and refurbishing of our own home.

When I continued to argue against the move he appealed to my creativity by saying, 'Once we're living there you'll get the feel of the house. It will give you a better idea of what you want to do with it, what changes you want to make.'

I would have preferred to stay in the comfort of the flat, at least until Josh was a bit older, but I agreed, albeit unwillingly, to the move. Although I felt I was once more being manipulated I gave in just the same. This had already become the pattern of our marriage.

Despite it not being my decision to move I soon adjusted to the change. Living in our ramshackle old house helped me realise how beautiful it could be once all the rooms had been renovated to the same standard as the kitchen and master bedroom.

For the next few months I spent many happy hours cleaning and painting the walls of the long lounge room. Josh either slept peacefully upstairs or played happily on a rug in a corner while I worked. Once the painting was completed I sanded down the wide skirting boards before organising to have the floor sanded and varnished and velvet curtains made for the wide bay window.

I furnished the room with such care, selecting rugs and settees that blended with the soft gold walls and the amber curtains. I didn't allow Don into the room while work was in progress but when he saw the finished product he was thrilled.

He held me close and said fondly, 'What a clever little thing you are. This room is a work of art. We must have a party to show it off.'

At the party I enjoyed the compliments from their guests, but most of all I gloried in Don's obvious approval.

This is what I miss now. I feel nothing I do really pleases him. Mind you, if I'm honest with myself, I must admit I no longer try as hard to be the perfect wife as I did in the early happy years of our marriage.

Sometimes I wonder if I was as happy as I remember. Perhaps I have glossed over the bad times.

Chapter Eight

I still remember vividly the way I felt when I was first pregnant with Sam. When Josh was nine months old I started to wean him and was looking forward to not sharing my body. Although I had been fit during my pregnancy, and enjoyed breast-feeding my precious little boy, it would be nice to have my body to myself again. I looked forward to once more being an independent entity.

The problem was Don had already begun talking about us having a second baby.

He said things like, 'Everyone should have a brother or a sister,' and, 'You don't want him to be lonely the way you and I were as children.'

I said I would like to put off having another baby until Josh was older but Don thought it important that siblings be close in age. Despite feeling I was being rushed into things I gave in, acceded to his wishes and stopped birth controlling. Although this was not what I wanted I had become used to accepting what he decided.

While I was breast-feeding my doctor advised me against taking the pill and had fitted me with a diaphragm. When used in conjunction with spermicidal jelly it was an effective safe form of birth control, but one I had found both tedious and messy. It was a relief not to be using it any more. Optimistically I thought it would probably take a while to get pregnant again, but this wasn't the case. Within a month I was sure I had conceived and a few weeks later the test proved to be positive.

I moaned to Don about not wanting another baby so soon.

When he tried to soothe me I remember shouting at him, 'It's all right for you. You don't have to put up with a body that is out of shape, or milk leaking all over the place if you so much as eat an ice-cream.'

He would hold me close and say things like 'I think you're beautiful when you're pregnant,' and 'How great it will be for Josh to have a sibling so close to him in age.'

Don managed to make me feel I was behaving like an immature brat instead of the nurturing, caring woman he envisioned me to be. Eventually I became reconciled to the fact that inside my womb another little life was forming. As the months passed and I began to feel the baby kicking I was ashamed with myself for not having wanted it. I'd rub my stomach and talk softly to the little person inside me assuring it of my love.

During the next few months Don and I worked together painting and decorating the room next to our bedroom. We went shopping and chose a single bed with a matching chest of drawers and wardrobe. By the time the room was finished Josh was fifteen months old, an active and delightful little boy. He knew he was going to get a new baby brother and often put his little hand on my stomach and said delightedly, 'Baby come soon.'

We moved him into his room two months before the baby was due, hoping he wouldn't feel that the newcomer was displacing him.

I looked down wistfully on him in his new bed and worried that he was too young for this change. Until then he had been sleeping in a cot next to our bed. Josh and his cuddly toys had filled the cot, but now he looked tiny in the bed, a small bump at the top of an enormous doona. I doubled it over and made a game of shaping it into a cave for him. Soon he was asleep, one chubby arm clutching his favourite doggy and his head resting on a soft bear.

For the next week Don and I lay in our big bed listening for sounds of distress from the next-door room, but there were none. Josh adjusted straight away to the change and loved his big boy's bed. He'd come into our room in the mornings, favourite doggy clutched in his arms. Don would lift him up so that he could snuggle between us for a while each morning, but at night he went happily to sleep in his own room.

I felt awash with love for my husband and our child and the baby who would soon complete our family. I wondered why I had been so distraught just a few months before and think Don knew what was best for us as a family.

When Sam, our second son, was born I was delighted for he proved to be as good as Josh had been as a baby. After an initial bout of jealousy Josh adored his baby brother.

By the time Sam was four months old and could sit propped up the two boys played together. I'd put them in the playpen with a soft rug underneath and all the toys that were safe for the baby. There they happily amused each other while I spent many productive hours sanding down the staircase.

It is a magnificent structure, but looked a mess because it was scratched and stained after years of neglect. When I completed the sanding I coated it with a special finish supplied to me by an antique dealer who made the mixture himself. After several coats the timber in the staircase had the patina of golden satin, and contrasted strikingly with the black and white tiles I had chosen for the floor of the foyer.

Gradually I redecorated all the rooms, and by the time all the work was completed I loved the house. I found it hard to remember why I had been so upset about Don insisting on buying it at the beginning. I conceded that once more he had made the right decision.

During that time I often saw Emma, who also had two boys a little younger than my own. We visited each other's homes, or took the children for picnics in the park or to some of the playgrounds around the city.

We rarely managed to catch up with Sonya. When she married David, the son of friends of her parents, it had been a very glamorous and social event. I had still been breast-feeding and Emma was pregnant at the time, and we both felt dowdy and matronly amongst the other elegant guests.

Sonya continued to teach at the private school where she began her teaching career. There she achieved rapid promotion, becoming the Principal in her early thirties.

During the school holidays, she sometimes joined Emma and me and our sons for a day out at a park or the beach. The boys all loved her because she never failed to bring them treats and played energetic and boisterous game with them. She talked fondly of her students, and obviously had a rapport with kids, but seemed to have no desire to have a child of her own.

My other great friend, Nina, had virtually disappeared from my life. After completing her Masters in Fine Art she went travelling with a fellow student, backed financially by her doting parents. I only knew where she was by the sporadic arrival of hastily written postcards and the occasional letter.

I had a small room at the back of the house. Originally I'd called it my studio, had set up an easel in one corner and paints and brushes on a long purpose-built shelf. Although I knew I would never become a great artist I had still felt the need to create. Don encouraged me in this and happily minded Josh while I sketched or painted.

As my second pregnancy progressed I felt less inclined to paint. At times I felt that all my creativity was being directed towards producing the child who was growing in my womb, and at other times blamed my lack of inspiration on what was being called "baby brain". Once Sam was born I had little time to pursue what had really become just a hobby, and told myself the house was my work of art.

In time this room became a repository of miscellaneous objects, but also the place where I thought about Nina. In there I had a pegboard to which I pinned Nina's postcards, from the Tate in London, the Louvre and Musee D'Orsay in Paris and the Prado in Spain, as well as photos of her and her travelling companion Simon, taken in out of the way places all over Europe. In her letters Nina sounded supremely happy, said they are painting wherever they went and planned to have a big joint exhibition when they finally returned to Australia.

Sometimes I'd shut myself away in my little room and imagine the exciting life my friend was living. I'd feel slightly jealous of Nina's free and creative life but basically I told myself I was happy with my lot. Don was a loving husband and father, our sons were growing up healthy and happy and I was proud of the beautiful house I had created.

During this time my relationship with my father even improved or, more to the point, I began to develop a relationship with him. He adored his grandsons and this shared bond brought us closer. For the first time in my life I felt as if my father actually approved of me.

This peaceful time was shattered when my father died suddenly from a massive heart attack. Later I was to feel glad that at least we'd had that time when we had enjoyed each other's company and that my sons had known and loved their grandfather. At the time though, all I felt was the loss and regret for the wasted years when we had been so distanced from each other.

With his death, Mum became a ditherer, seemingly unable to make the most basic decisions. When I visited her I'd find her wandering aimlessly around the house like a lost child. All her married life she had worked at being the woman her husband wished her to be, the devoted wife, loving mother and efficient homemaker. It seemed that without him there with his expectations of what she should do and how she should do it she had ceased to function properly.

I spent worrying months, visiting her every day, taking her shopping and encouraging her to start living again.

Now that Mum was alone the house was much too big for her and too far from town. To add to the problem, public transport was almost non-existent and my mother had never learnt to drive. Eventually I convinced her she would be better off in a smaller house closer to town. I took her house hunting and together we found a little cottage, not far from our house. Once Mum moved into the cottage she improved, but it was the birth of Grace that really restored her interest in living.

Chapter Nine

Thinking about Grace makes me smile as I walk to the sink and rinse out my cup. Once more my mind returns to my outburst to Sonya and Emma about not having a say in the way my life had gone. To a large extent I do feel I'm living a life not of my choosing; that too often through the years I have let Don make all the major decisions. Despite these feelings I never regret the existence of my children, even though I had little say in the timing of their conception.

Don decided when we should try to conceive Josh and Sam but fate determined the conception of Grace. Although each time I conceived my initial reaction was not one of joy I soon adjusted to impending motherhood. Now our three children are such a source of pleasure in their different ways.

Josh is dark and serious and already very ambitious to be the best in class and on the soccer field. Sam is blonde like me and has the sweetest nature, but can be quite mischievous at times, and Grace is a lively, loving child who moves like a ballet dancer through her imaginary world of princesses and fairies.

As I stare out the kitchen window at the dark night sky I think of how it was chance and not a thought out decision that brought our beautiful little daughter into the world.

I conceived Grace while Don and I were on a holiday in Tahiti. At the time Josh was six and a half and Sam five and both were at school. I had decided to at last follow my dream and enrol in the Interior Design Course at the art school.

Don was very encouraging; pleased I was going to develop what he saw as my creative talent. During the early days of our courtship he had proudly introduced me as his artist girlfriend, and in later years, praised my accomplishments as an interior designer whenever we had guests to the house. At the time I enjoyed the rather boyish pride he took in presenting me as artistic and creative. By enrolling in the design course I was once more living up to his vision of me, but this was also something I wanted to do.

Don had planned our Tahitian holiday as a treat for me before I started the course. It was to be our first time away together, just as a couple, since our honeymoon. Mum had agreed to move into the house to mind the boys. She had been so much better since she began living in her little cottage, and I felt confident she would have a happy time caring for Josh and Sam.

The holiday began really well.

Don had booked us into a lovely resort where we stayed in a lavish bure, built over the crystal clear waters of a bay. We ate in the five star restaurants or had gourmet meals delivered to our bure. During the warm, sunny days we swam, snorkelled and walked the white beaches, and at night made love in the wide, comfortable bed with the peaceful sounds of slow waves swishing beneath us.

One day we caught the bus into Papeete and wandered the busy streets, buying gifts for the boys and my mother, as well as sarongs for me and a beautiful silk shirt for Don. We held hands as we walked along the streets and ate at the open-air food stalls. We felt young and carefree and I felt closer to Don than I had for a long time. He worked such long days, and the boys took up so much of my time and attention that sometimes I felt Don and I were drifting apart. Now I found the pleasure we were experiencing during this time together reassuring.

That night after our day in Papeete I woke with the most excruciating pain in my stomach, and barely made it to the toilet before vomiting into the enormous shell vanity basin. I spent the next day alternating between lying curled up on the bed and racing to the bathroom to be sick. Don tried to comfort me through the night, and in the morning sought medical aid. The resort doctor diagnosed food poisoning and gave me some tablets to ease the pain. They took a long time to work. It wasn't until the end of the next day that the vomiting had stopped and by that time I felt and looked wan and exhausted.

The following day we were due to return home, and I felt guilty about spoiling the last part of what had been, until I got sick, a lovely holiday.

When I said how sorry I was Don answered, 'Oh darling, it's not your fault. I probably shouldn't have suggested that we eat at those stalls.' He laughed. 'It could just as easily have happened to me, and I'd have been a much worse patient.'

On the plane trip home we drank champagne and toasted each other, to my success in the course I was soon to begin and to seeing the boys again. By the time the plane landed we were both slightly drunk. I shed sentimental tears while I cuddled the strong little bodies of my sons and nestled my face into their warm smooth necks.

Soon after we returned I commenced my course.

It was strange, being in a classroom situation after so many years. Everyone seemed so young.

During the first week we were introduced to our different lecturers, who then gave a summary of the course work they would be teaching. I spent most of the time in a daze as I moved with the other students from one room to another. At lunch times I sat alone in the canteen, watching the young ones chatting and laughing together. Although I was only twenty-eight I felt old amongst this group, and experienced again the loneliness I had often felt in the schoolyard as a child.

To further complicate my unhappiness I had begun to feel quite ill each morning and sometimes even vomited. Initially I attributed this to the bout of food poisoning I'd experienced in Tahiti. I thought perhaps my body might still be harbouring the bacteria that had caused me so much pain.

When my period failed to materialise the following week I became worried; I was always so regular. After I missed a second period I told Don of my fears and made an appointment to see my doctor.

When he told me I was pregnant I couldn't quite believe him because I was on the pill and had been since I'd weaned Sam.

When I pointed this out to the doctor he said, 'Yes I know that.' He smiled benignly. 'What you young women don't seem to realise is that the new lower dose pills are riskier than the older high dose ones. That bout of food poisoning you told me about would have been enough to leave you unprotected.'

Later, as I sat drinking a coffee in the café beneath the doctor's surgery, I forced myself to come to terms with the fact that once more I had an unplanned baby growing inside me. I thought back and remembered how I had felt guilty for initially not wanting Sam. To be honest I hadn't been all that pleased when I had conceived Josh so quickly. Now they were so important to me I couldn't imagine life without them. I was determined to welcome this tiny creature right from the start, rubbed my still flat stomach and whispered, 'Perhaps this time you'll be a little girl.'

I was surprised by Don's reaction to my news. He had been overjoyed when we conceived Josh, and talked me out of my distress when I had become pregnant so quickly with Sam.

Now when I told him quite happily that we were going to have another child he looked baffled, 'But how? You've been on the pill. I thought that was foolproof.'

I didn't like the way he said, 'foolproof,' with a slight sneer in his voice but damped down the sudden rush of anger I felt towards him and explained that the low dose pill had probably ceased to be effective because of the violent stomach upset I'd had.

He sighed deeply, 'Well you seem to be taking it in your stride this time. I must say I'm surprised. I'd sort of thought we had our family, and with the boys at school you'd be able to get into doing something creative again. Does this mean you'll have to give up your course?'

'There's not much point in going on with it is there? I answered rather ruefully. 'I wouldn't be able to finish.'

I felt regret at having to give up the course for I was beginning to enjoy many of the lectures, especially the ones given by a well-known architect Byron Solange. Initially I had felt out of place amongst the young students, but some of them had begun chatting to me before classes or would join me for a coffee in the canteen and my feelings of being the odd one out had gone.

With mixed emotions I put aside my new textbooks and began planning for the arrival of another baby.

During the pregnancy I moved Sam from the room next door to our master bedroom to one along the passage and redecorated the nursery. From the ultrasound I knew I was going to have a little girl, so painted the walls soft shell-pink and hung white diaphanous curtains at the windows with heavier rose pink drapes ruched across the top and down the sides. I spent many happy times with Mum for she was as thrilled as I at the thought of me having a baby girl. We'd meet for coffee, and then go shopping, spending lavishly on little pink frocks and nightdresses and flower-trimmed jackets.

Grace arrived and I was delighted with our little girl, but Don wasn't quite as attentive or hands on as he had been with the boys.

When I quipped him about this he'd say, 'I guess I'm just not as comfortable around a girl child.'

At times I thought I should insist on him being more involved with Grace but I didn't. I was rather shocked to realise how similar his attitude to Grace was to that of my father's to the birth of a daughter. I realised that in many ways I was replicating my parents' marriage.

Don continued to be a good father to the boys, spending what little free time he had from work playing with them and later helping them with their homework. I usually felt it would be churlish of me to insist on him paying more attention to our daughter. In darker moments I wondered if his lack of interest in Grace was because, unlike with the boys, her conception had not been his decision, for he always seemed to need to be the decision-maker.

Once Grace began toddling around the house, looking rather like a drunken midget, we sometimes laughed together at her antics. Occasionally Don picked her up and she giggled excitedly as he threw her into the air and caught her in his strong Daddy arms, but these times were rare.

Initially Josh and Sam were fascinated by their new baby sister and sat, round-eyed, watching her feed from my body. When she lay gurgling on her play mat they would hand her toys and jiggle the mobile for her amusement, but the novelty soon wore off and they returned to their own games.

By the time Grace was three they virtually ignored her. Josh was ten and Sam eight and a half and they didn't want an annoying little sister tagging along. They had always played well together, and were now forever kicking a ball around the big back yard or having secret meetings in the little house Don had built for them in the old spreading walnut tree.

Seeing Grace standing sadly at the window watching her brothers play, or sitting in the garden having a pretend tea party with her dolls reminded me of my own lonely childhood. I certainly didn't want this for my daughter, and enrolled her at a nearby childcare centre for three days a week so she could have the companionship of other children her age.

Grace loved going to the centre and chatted happily about her new friends and the games they played. With Grace away three days I was now the one who felt lonely. I had worried about my daughter's lack of companionship, but hadn't realised how much I had come to depend on her company.

Although Don and I entertained quite often, and attended parties and dinners regularly, the people I met at these events were generally work associates of Don's. I became quite friendly with a couple of the wives, but Emma and Sonya still remained my best friends.

I didn't see them often, but during school holidays we'd catch up. Emma had returned to teaching at the local high school once her younger son started school, and Sonya was now vice-principal at the private girls' school where she began her teaching career.

Sometimes when I listened to these two discussing their work I'd feel left out of things, and remember how I had quite enjoyed my one year of teaching. I hadn't ever thought of going back because I knew Don wouldn't like the idea of me working again and I no longer felt confident about my capability to educate and inspire the young.

Shortly after Grace started at the childcare centre I ran into Emma in the street, and we went into a nearby café for a coffee and chat.

As soon as we were seated Emma said excitedly, 'I was going to ring you so it's a bit of luck running into you like this. One of the art teachers has pissed off. He's gone to Vanuatu or Tahiti or somewhere to find himself. He was always a bit strange. Anyhow there doesn't seem to be anyone available to take his place. At staff meeting today the principal asked us if we knew of anyone who could come in until a permanent replacement can be found, and I thought of you. You were saying you don't know what to do with yourself now Grace is in childcare three days a week. What do you think?'

I spluttered, 'Oh, I don't think I could do it. It's been so long I think I've probably forgotten all I ever knew about painting. Anyhow, I only have three free days. They'd want someone who could work full time.'

Emma interrupted my excuses, 'You'd soon get into the swing of things again, and I reckon the timetable could be adjusted so you only had to work three days. If that can't be done I'm sure your Mum would love to mind Grace the other two days.'

When we parted I told Emma I would think about it and let her know the next day. As I drove home I felt quite excited about the prospect of returning to work, but also nervous about telling Don about it.

I waited until the children were in bed before mentioning it. Although I hadn't expected him to be particularly pleased I was annoyed by his reaction.

At first he simply said quite calmly, 'If you want something more to do why not go and do that course you started before you had Grace, or take up painting again.'

I told him it was too late in the year to re-enrol in the design course and that I knew I didn't have enough talent to ever be more than just a hobby painter. I pointed out to him that teaching was something I knew I could do, even though at this stage I wasn't actually feeling all that confident. I also pointed out that teaching would fit in with the boys' school times.'

I've never forgotten his answer. With a sneer on his face he'd replied, 'Well it's up to you. I must say I'm surprised. I always thought once the children were off your hands a bit you'd do something more creative. There's an old saying, "Those that can do, those that can't teach." I'm disappointed that you'd want to do anything so pedestrian.'

With that he turned and left the room leaving me fuming silently.

All our married life I had fitted my life around him and his wishes, had tried to be the person he imagined me to be. Perhaps he would have been happier if I had finally followed my dream and become an interior designer, but I felt I has lost the drive and ambition needed to complete the course and then start in a whole new profession. Don made it perfectly clear he didn't think much of me returning to teaching, but I was tired of constantly trying to please him. I felt I had spent our whole married life doing what he had wanted and now when I was going against his wishes he had responded by sneering and putting me down. Well too bad. I needed to do something, and teaching again might be just what I needed to stimulate my mind and fill the empty days. I decided that the next day I would tell Emma I would take the job and arrange an interview with the principal.

Chapter Ten

I have now been teaching again for three years and quite enjoy my job.

The first few months were difficult as I adjusted to a new life as a working mother. I seemed to be forever rushing from one task to another and was always tired, but slowly I developed routines that worked.

The other two art teachers helped me when I first returned to the classroom, and now the three of us work closely to ensure our students have a stimulating and exciting place in which to develop their talents.

I enjoy being with the students. They are at that stage in their lives when they are not yet adults, but have left childhood behind.

Some of them see art as an easy option, a pleasant way to gain a pass in a matriculation subject, but each year there are always some with real artistic talent. These students take themselves and their art seriously, and soak up new information and ideas with sponge- like tenacity. They love to experiment. After a lesson on Seurat, interesting pointillist works adorned the walls, and a film about Jackson Pollock results in a rash of drip paintings in glorious colours.

I enjoy seeing how they will take a suggestion or idea and develop it to create a work that is uniquely theirs. These talented young people remind me of Nina and some of our other fellow students from our art school days.

When I'm feeling down, however, seeing what they produce reinforces in me the sense of failure Don's attitude to my teaching evokes. I feel frustrated at not actually creating something beautiful myself.

Don has continued to be derogatory about my work, and never helps with the household chores. I know Emma's husband often cooks the meals, vacuums the floors or does a load of washing. Sometimes I feel hard done by because of Don's lack of support, but then the habits of a lifetime kick in and I make excuses for him. His job is very demanding and he does have to travel a lot.

At times I regret that I didn't go back and complete the Interior Design Course. I know I would have found a career as an interior decorator more satisfying than teaching, but I like my students and am free to spend the school holidays with the children, something I wouldn't have been able to do in another job.

I have returned to bed but the honeyed milk and whiskey drink has not done its usual trick. Although the digital clock says 3.30 I am still awake, staring into the dark and thinking. Why do I feel so dissatisfied with my life and often even downright depressed? I have three gorgeous children who I adore, and Don is basically a good father.

Although they don't see much of him during the week, he takes the boys fishing and camping at weekends during the summer and coaches their soccer team in winter. Grace gets little attention, but he does give her the occasional cuddle or reads her a bedtime story. This is at least more attention than I ever got from my father.

The big problem, of course, is my relationship with Don. Once I returned to teaching he changed, became less affectionate and more critical. He makes me feel I have somehow fallen short of his expectations of me. My decision to return to teaching was the first time in our marriage when I had gone against his wishes. I realise now how malleable I had always been. I really had let him make all the major decisions and weakly let him convince me to go along with his every suggestion. Because this had been the pattern in my parents' marriage I had been so accepting of his right to be the decision-maker but it hasn't brought me happiness.

My thoughts return once more to the conversation I'd had with Sonya and Emma about decision-making and parallel worlds. I had become stupidly upset because so much in my life and the person I have become has been determined for me, first by my father and then by Don. Was there another world where I hadn't relied on my father to fund me but had found part-time work in order to finance myself to do the Interior Design Course? Perhaps in that world I didn't meet Don, or if we had met I'd been confident enough to withstand his domineering ways. Alternatively I might have heeded Nina's warning about how controlling he was and dumped him for someone who allowed me the freedom to be who I really wanted to be. While mulling this over I think about my children for I know I would always have wanted to be a mother. I would have different children if I had married another man and they would be different ages if I had chosen when I would conceive. This would mean that in another world I wouldn't have Josh and Sam and Grace. Just the thought of that makes me feel bereft and tearful. I can't even begin to imagine a life without them.

Tomorrow Don's flight arrives at eleven o'clock, so I will have to pick up the children from Mum's by ten if we are to be at the airport on time. If I don't get to sleep soon I won't have the energy to do what I know I must. All this introspection has forced me to recognise how little control I have had concerning how my life has gone. The conversation tonight with Sonya and Emma has made me recognise how few choices I've ever actually made concerning the important aspects of my life. Now I am determined to put an end to the constant nagging suspicion that Don is being unfaithful. Tomorrow night, once the children are in bed, I'm going to have it out with him. Instead of continuing to be accepting and malleable I will act decisively and find an answer to my doubts, one way or the other.

As I close my eyes I think once more of the evening with my friends and the discussion about parallel worlds. Will my decision to force the issue of Don's probable infidelity create a different world for me while another feebler me meanders on unhappily in my old life?

Emma

Chapter Eleven

I tell Pierre how to get to my house, and then relax into the soft leather upholstery feeling pleasantly drunk. I must have dropped off to sleep because the next thing I feel is a cold rush of air as the door is opened. I hear Pierre saying in his deep, accented voice, 'Time to wake up Sleeping Beauty,' and Sonya giggling quietly from the front seat. He helps me from the car and insists on escorting me to the front door. As I fumble with the key I hear the BMW roar off into the night.

The light is on in the hallway, but all is quiet except for a soft murmur coming from the lounge room. I open the door to see Bruce sound asleep in front of the television set. His hair is awry and his glasses have slipped to come to rest on the end of his nose. I tiptoe across the room and gently stroke his hair into place.

He wakes abruptly, pushes back his glasses, and says sleepily, 'Hello darling. I must have dozed off. Did you have a nice evening?'

I sit next to him on the couch and take off my shoes. I really love them, but they have been hurting my feet for the past hour. They have high, stiletto heels and I can only wear them for a while with any sort of comfort, but I couldn't resist them when I saw them in the shop window. They are the sort of shoes Sonya wears all the time and they reek of class and glamour. I had changed into them from my more practical work shoes before leaving school and now, after five hours, my feet are hurting.

I point to the discarded shoes, 'Well, except for the fact that those things have been killing me for the past hour, I had a lovely time. We went to this really gorgeous place, La Cuisine. Had a top meal and of course I always enjoy catching up with Sonya, and talking to Jenny away from the workhouse. How did you and the boys get on?'

Bruce grins. 'I don't reckon our meal was quite as good as yours, but we made hamburgers and chips and they weren't half bad.'

'What time did the kids go to bed?'

He answers rather sheepishly. 'I let them stay up to watch "Police File" but they were off by half past eight. I figured that was okay for a Friday night.'

''Course it was. Oh darling, you're such a good Dad.' I give him an affectionate and half-drunken hug. 'I do love you very much and I'm so glad we're together.'

Bruce hugs me back and says with a grin, 'I'm not sure what's brought that on, but I'll make the most of it. Let's have a nightcap, and then go to bed.'

Although I know I don't need anything more to drink I pour two small glasses of Glayva and hand one to Bruce before curling up close to him on the couch.

I sip slowly then say, 'Sonya was all hopped up tonight about an article she'd read. It was about parallel worlds, and how you create one when you make an important decision. Quite frankly I thought it was a load of old rubbish.'

Bruce gives me a quizzical look and says, 'I wouldn't have thought that was the sort of thing Sonya would be interested in. She's always struck me as such a practical woman, interested in the here and now.'

'Yes I know, and that's why I was surprised by how seriously she talked about it.' I sip my drink before continuing. 'Oh! And the other thing; later on Jenny started getting so upset she almost cried.'

Bruce is fond of Jenny and asks affectionately, 'What did she get upset about?'

'I'm not really sure. It was to do with the article Sonya had been talking about. Jenny said she hadn't made any of the important decisions in her life. I think her exact words were, "I really don't think I've had much say in anything that's happened to me." Then she almost cried.'

'I'm not surprised that's how she feels.' Bruce gives an impatient sigh, for he doesn't really like Don. 'The few times I've seen her and Don together he's seemed to be nit-picking about something she's said or done. I don't know why she puts up with it.'

'He's always been like that, but until tonight I thought she'd pretty much accepted him being that way. I think there may be trouble looming there.'

Bruce curls his arm tighter around my shoulder in a comforting gesture. 'So it hasn't all been just a fun night out?'

I turn my face to his. 'Oh it's been fun, even though it had some serious moments. But, you know, all the talk about parallel worlds made me think about how happy I am with you and our boys. I wouldn't even want to imagine a world where I'm not with you.'

Bruce finishes off his drink and pulls me to my feet. 'And with that beautiful and sentimental statement I'm taking you to bed woman.'

Chapter Twelve

Much later I lie contentedly in bed with Bruce's warm body spooning into my back and one of his hard, muscular arms curled around my waist. Usually after making love I slip easily into sleep, but tonight I feel wide awake. I keep remembering the forlorn look on Jenny's face, and wonder what it must be like to feel so disempowered.

While I was growing up I saw many women who had little say in the way in which they lived their miserable lives, but they were poor and uneducated. I really can't understand why a woman like Jenny, who is well-educated, talented and capable, lets her husband dictate to her as he does.

As I snuggle happily in the arms of my sleeping husband I think back to my childhood years.

I lived in one of the most wretched suburbs in the city. It was a place of basic weatherboard houses, built by the government to provide accommodation for those unable to afford the rent on better properties or to save the deposit to buy a house. Most of the gardens were neglected and weed-filled, but in a few of them the women had planted flowers or decorated parched lawns with cheery gnomes and swans. More generally the front yards were home to rusting car bodies, discarded household appliances and other items that had overflowed from the pokey, crowded houses.

In the midst of this desert of neglect and hopelessness our home and gardens were an oasis. Inside Mum kept the house immaculate and orderly and outside flowers bloomed around a neat green front lawn, while the back yard was a haven for children. Here my mother had installed a homemade seesaw and a rope swing attached to a strong branch of one of the few old trees that had been left when the land had been subdivided. She also had a thriving garden where she grew vegetables and berry fruits, which she shared with her less provident neighbours.

My mother, Madge, also provided sympathy, advice and sometimes even a safe haven for neighbouring women who came to her beaten and battered by abusive husbands. From a very early age I saw the results of domestic violence, women with bruises and blackened eyes. I often wondered why these women didn't stand up to their husbands the way my mother did when Dad came home drunk and abusive. I also wondered why they didn't just leave.

I remember asking Mum this and her answer has stayed with me because for the first time I realised just how vulnerable many women were. She said 'The poor things haven't nowhere else to go, and so they just go back to them brutes of husbands. What we need are shelters, where they can be safe 'til they can be found somewhere else to live. And we need more lawyers, ones who'll look out for the rights of women like Suzy Jones and Doreen Brown.'

Although both of these women had been hospitalised by abusive husbands they hadn't had any option but to return home, their bones mended but their spirits broken.

I said to Mum, 'When I grow up I'm going to do that. I'm going to be one of those lawyers who look after women who can't stand up for themselves.'

Mum hugged me and said, 'You're such a clever little girl. I bet there isn't anything you couldn't do. I reckon you'd make a real good lawyer.'

That year I was in grade five and shortly after this conversation with Mum our teacher asked us all to write on a piece of paper what we wanted to be when we grew up and I knew exactly what I planned to do.

When called upon to share what I had written I read out, "When I grow up I am going to be a lawyer, and stand up for all the women who get treated badly by their husbands and who can't speak out for themselves."

The girls in the class tittered at this and I sat down, blushing furiously.

Miss Jones rapped her table and said ominously, 'There's nothing funny about Emma's ambition. It shows that she thinks about others, and I'm sure she would make a very good lawyer. It's certainly more laudable than wanting to be a film star or model, which is what most of you other girls seem to be setting your sights on.'

The other kids were suitably silenced and I glowed from my teacher's approval.

If you're lucky you get a special teacher once in your life, one who will change the way you think about yourself and the world in which you live. For me, Miss Jones was that one.

Around the school she had a name for being tough. At the end of final term, when the pupils were allocated to their classes for the following year, all the talk was about who would be going into Miss Jones's class.

The tougher boys bragged, 'She won't know what's hit her when she gets me.'

The quieter, well-behaved pupils, like me, sighed with relief and looked forward to the following year.

Miss Jones was a stickler for good behaviour, good work and good grammar. Boys who thought they would run riot in the classroom, as they had with lesser teachers, soon cowered beneath her scornful glare and became model students. She expected only the best behaviour from her pupils and even the naughtiest boys buckled beneath her relentless expectations. By the end of the year her well-behaved class achieved the best results in the school and most of them spoke, as she put it, "Like little ladies and gentlemen," at least in her hearing.

During the fifteen years she had been teaching at Hillsborough Primary School she had taught hundreds of children. She did her best for them during their year under her care, but knew many of them would slip back, and very few would go any further than year ten. Most of them came from poor homes and had parents who placed little importance on education.

Occasionally she got a pupil in her class who she thought showed exceptional ability, and she tried to help them achieve their potential. I was one of the lucky ones who she felt should be given the opportunity to get the best possible education.

On the day I had written about wanting to become a lawyer Miss Jones called me aside after school, and asked if my mother could come to the school to discuss something with her.

When Mum heard that Miss Jones wanted to see her she asked fearfully, 'You haven't done nothing wrong have you love? You're always such a good girl.'

I reassured her that I didn't think I was in trouble, but still I felt nervous all the next day, wondering why Miss Jones wanted to see my mother.

After classes finished I waited anxiously at the school gates for Mum to appear. Miss Jones had asked me to bring my mother to the classroom so that they could have a talk. When I saw Mum hobbling along the footpath in unfamiliar high heels and the black and white tweed suit she only wore for funerals my heart thudded. She looked so serious and had obviously made an effort to look her best for the meeting. I ran to greet her, and held her hand tightly as we crossed the quadrangle and entered the classroom.

Miss Jones gave Mum the loveliest smile and said, 'I'm so pleased you could come Mrs. Williams. Won't you take a seat? And you sit next to your mother Emma. I've been thinking a lot about Emma of late, and I'm concerned about her progress in this school.'

Mum looked upset and said in a flustered voice, 'But she isn't having no problems with her schoolwork is she? Her report cards are always good.'

I wasn't sure what was going on or why this meeting was taking place but was glad Miss Jones had asked to see Mum and not my father. Not that he would have come anyway, but he always said "aint" instead of "isn't." He also said "bloody" a lot, a word that got the boys into really big trouble if a teacher heard them say it. Mum made some mistakes but she didn't say "aint" or use swearwords.

Miss Jones smiled at Mum's look of concern, 'Yes, her report cards are always good, and she's a very attentive and willing pupil. The thing is, you have a very bright little daughter, and I don't think she'll get the education she deserves at this school.'

My mother looked confused, 'I don't understand what you're sayin' Miss Jones. She has to go to this school 'cause it's the one for the area.'

In a voice that I thought sounded condescending Miss Jones said, 'That's what I wanted to discuss with you. The feeder school for here is Waymere High, and very few students from there finish year twelve, let alone achieve sufficient grades to go on to university. Your daughter should be given the opportunity to achieve the level of education of which I know she is capable. I would suggest she attend Bridmore next year and complete her schooling there to matriculation.'

Looking totally bewildered Mum stammered, 'But how? We can't afford that. From what I've heard the fees they charge there are more than me old man gives me to keep the family on. There's nothing I wouldn't do for my Emma but...'

Miss Jones put up her hand to stem the flow. 'I realise that Mrs. Jones, but what I want to suggest is that we put in an application for Emma to go to Bridmore on a scholarship. She would have to sit an entrance exam at the end of the year, a sort of an IQ test, but I am confident your daughter would win one of the scholarships. This would pay all the fees and also provide a book allowance. You'd only have to pay for her uniforms, and most of that could be purchased second hand at the school clothing store.'

I sat listening, agog at the thought of perhaps going to what was the best school in the city and wondering what Mum would say. She was silent for such a long time, taking in what Miss Jones was suggesting, that my teacher said, 'Look think about it. Talk it over with Emma and your husband and, if you agree, I'll get the necessary forms and organise for Emma to sit the exam.'

Mum knew this was a great opportunity for me but worried about how I'd fit in at such a prestigious school. Despite her concerns towards the end of the year I sat the exam and won a place at Bridmore. Thus began my seven years as a scholarship girl and while it is true I gained an excellent education during that time I suffered.

I had thick, unruly black hair and had worn glasses from the time I was eight. I knew I was nerdy-looking, and my second-hand uniforms and worn backpack marked me out as a scholarship girl. The fact that I walked home, instead of being collected at the gate by an elegant mother in a BMW, Saab or Audi, also set me apart.

I had a few good friends, mainly other girls on scholarships. We studied in the school library together and occasionally walked into town to window shop and drink coffee in the mall. We didn't visit each other's homes or have sleepovers the way the wealthy girls did. Most of us lived in small crowded houses that were totally unsuitable as places in which to entertain friends. To be honest, we were generally ashamed of our families and saw the education we were receiving as a means of escape.

Teenage girls can be the cruellest creatures on the planet, and during all my years at Bridmore I was the butt of much nastiness from the other students. The problem was that besides being a scholarship girl I was cleverer than most of my fellow pupils. This may sound like bragging but it was true. Often a teacher chose my essay to read out in class or my science project was singled out as the best. At the end of each year I was dux of my class in most subjects. Unfortunately my academic success marked me out and resulted in increased teasing as I progressed through the school.

The group most hostile towards me was led by one of the glamour girls of the school, Sonya McFee. From the time I beat her to become dux of the class in grade six Sonya made my life a misery.

I couldn't understand this hostility but knew Sonya was the ringleader and I hated her because of it. I couldn't understand why the fact that I was cleverer than she was such a big deal. As far as I was concerned Sonya had so much that I lacked including looks, wealth and popularity. She had lush auburn hair that always looked perfect, a models figure and long legs that sported a year-long golden tan. She even had the ability to make the rather daggy school uniform look okay. Her group starred in both summer and winter sports, participated in the debating team, ran the school newsletter and organised the end of year parties.

In class I sat well away from any of them and tried to avoid them in the canteen and playgrounds, but at times they sought me out. They'd snigger names like, "Geek," "Swot" and "Four-eyes" and comment on my bushy hair or too-long tunic.

Members of Sonya's group were always the ones who picked the sides for games during sport, and they deliberately always chose me last. Even though I was really quite good at both netball and softball I would be left standing with fat Sophie and skinny, uncoordinated Michelle. They would be chosen and then a team leader would say with an exaggerated sigh, 'I guess I get Emma.'

The hardest part for me was having to keep the unhappiness I was feeling to myself. I couldn't complain to Mum about the treatment I was receiving at the hands of these bitchy girls. Although the scholarship paid for my fees and books the uniforms were expensive, even when second hand, and I needed different ones for summer and winter as well as sports gear. There were also often other contributions and dues that weren't covered by the scholarship.

To pay for these extras Mum went to work, cleaning houses and running errands for the disabled and elderly in the district. Often she looked exhausted at the end of the day. To show how much I appreciated what she was doing for me I pretended a happiness I didn't feel, and enthused about how much I enjoyed my school life.

After seven long years I matriculated with excellent results, and won a scholarship to attend university where I enrolled to do a combined Arts/Law degree.

At home things were bad. Dad could no longer work, and spent his days staring miserably at the racing guide or gazing unseeingly into space. My younger brother, John, commenced an apprenticeship, but baulked at having to attend technical college and had been put off. He now mooched around the house by day and went drinking every night with his friends. Jessie, my little sister, had begun playing truant from school and sneaking out at night, although she was only thirteen. If Mum or I said anything to her she'd answer huffily, 'It's my life,' and saunter off jauntily to join her friends.

When I heard of a position as a housemother at a hostel that provided accommodation for country girls who were attending one of the better high schools I applied. Here was a chance for me to escape from my depressing, dysfunctional family. I was offered the position and moved to the hostel shortly before the start of the academic year. I told Mum I had taken the job so that I could be closer to the university, but really I saw it as my chance to escape the family bonds I now found alien and shameful.

Chapter Thirteen

Life at university was wonderful for there I felt I was among equals. There was none of the snobbishness and bullying that had haunted me during my high school years. My fellow students were there on merit, not because their parents had large bank balances, and I soon made several new friends. At times I saw Sonya or one or two others of her group around the campus, but now I could confidently ignore them if they happened to be in the same lecture theatre.

I also enjoyed my work as a housemother at the hostel. In exchange for supervising the girls every third weekend, and helping them with their homework three evenings a week, I received free accommodation and meals as well as a small wage.

Initially I went home every Sunday, but after four or five months rarely bothered. The little house looked so depressingly dreary despite Mum's efforts to keep it immaculate. I felt I had little in common with my silent father, no-hoper brother and wild little sister. I salved my conscience with a weekly phone call to Mum.

It was during one of these calls that Mum asked if she could come to the hostel to see me. I of course agreed, feeling guilty that I hadn't thought to invite her there before.

Mum arrived looking obviously distressed so I took her to my ground-floor apartment straight away. I proudly showed her the tiny kitchenette in one corner of the lounge room, and the small bedroom with its pretty doona and matching curtains and its own en suite bathroom.

After settling Mum on the couch I made tea. As I placed the cups and a plate of biscuits on a small table I saw that my mother was crying quietly into a clean white handkerchief.

I was shocked; my mother didn't cry. Neither when my brother had been expelled for selling marijuana to his mates at school, nor when she had finally dragged my sickly father to the doctor and been given the news that he was dying of cirrhosis of the liver. My indomitable little mother had helped and protected so many of our abused neighbours, and stood up to threatening bullies attempting to drag their frightened wives back home for more rough treatment. Now she sat, tiny and miserable, looking as though all that fighting strength and vitality had leaked out of her.

I pulled Mum into my arms, felt the smallness of that frail body, and was overwhelmed by feelings of love and guilt. This woman had worked such long hours to make sure I received the best education money could buy, and what had I given her in return? I had left home as soon as I could and hadn't even bothered to go to see her recently; hadn't known that something was distressing her so much.

'Mum, what wrong?' I asked anxiously. 'Is it Dad? Is he worse, or has John got himself into trouble again?'

My mother wiped her eyes and tried to control her tears but between sobs said, 'It's Jessie. She's pregnant to that there Henderson boy from down the street, and she says she's going to keep the baby.'

I was stunned thinking, 'Jessie pregnant? Why she's only a child, fourteen a few months ago.'

I had made the effort to go home for Jessie's birthday and taken her a pretty blue sweater. We'd sat in the lounge room Mum had decorated with streamers and balloons and eaten savouries and little cakes. There had been a pink birthday cake with its fourteen candles and an extra one for luck. A couple of Jessie's girlfriends were there, and the lumbering boy from down the street. What was his name? Jake or Jack I seemed to remember.

My mother disturbed my reminisces of that day by saying tearfully, 'Can you come out and try to talk some sense into her? You know I've never held much truck for abortions, at least not when married women find themselves up the duff. They should know what's what. But this is different. Jessie's only a baby herself. She don't know what she's letting herself in for. She's not thinking of what this'll do to her life.'

I promised Mum I would talk to Jessie the following weekend, and looked into organising a termination for her at the Family Planning Clinic in town.

I did try; talked and argued with Jessie for a whole afternoon. I pointed out what it would mean to have a baby to care for when she was barely fifteen, how it would destroy her chances of finishing high school and getting a good job and having a carefree life while she finished growing up.

Jessie sat silent and sullen, her hands clutched protectively across her flat stomach and finally snapped, 'You're talking about what you wanted at my age. I'm not you. I'm not clever and good at schoolwork like you were. I won't ever get what you would think of as a good job, but I can do this. I'm going to have Jake's baby, and I'm going to be a real good Mum.'

During the remainder of the year I visited home on a regular basis. I went mainly to see Mum, but also to help Jessie as much as she'd let me. Because I now owned a small second-hand car I took my little sister for her monthly checkups at the doctor's surgery, mainly to make sure she went.

This should have brought us closer together, but it didn't. I couldn't completely hide my disappointment in Jessie and my anger at her causing Mum so much worry. For her part Jessie disliked having to rely on me. She felt my critical attitude towards her, and it only made her more defensive and angry at having to accept my help.

The contrast between Jessie and her aspirations and those of the teenagers at the hostel was stunning. Several evening a week I helped the girls with their homework. I enjoyed listening to Julie's interpretation of a sonnet, or the light of interest in Anne's eyes when we worked through a maths problem together. At times I felt it was like having lots of younger sisters, but ones who were interesting and full of promise and ambition. I often thought sadly of Jessie, sitting at home day after day in that cramped front room watching soaps on television, and eating candy and crisps that were making her skin pimply and expanding her waistline at a far faster rate than the baby growing inside her could possibly manage alone.

Despite my efforts to keep in touch as the months passed I felt increasingly alienated from my family. I was enjoying my studies, and had made a few good friends at university. Life was good and I felt really happy for the first time in my life.

One Saturday night I was on duty, supervising a dozen or so girls who had not gone home for the weekend. Some were off seeing a movie. The others had turned the common room into a beauty salon and were spending a giggling girls' night in styling each other's hair and trialling makeup they had bought at a cut-price shop in town.

When I joined them they begged me to let them give me a makeover and I laughingly agreed. Julie, who had ambitions of having her own hairdressing salon sometime in the future, washed my thick unruly locks and then set them on giant-sized rollers. Another of the girls, Moira a pale, glamorous beauty, proclaimed herself the expert with makeup. She removed my glasses then proceeded to apply foundation, eye shadow, mascara and lipstick. At first I felt rather like a captive beetle as I sat in a straight-backed chair, closed my eyes and suffered the young fingers plucking at my hair and applying who knows what to my face.

I had never bothered much about my appearance. I hadn't known what to do with my hair and knew my thick glasses gave me a nerdy look. The teasing I'd suffered at the hands of Sonya and her group reinforced the low opinion I'd always had of my looks. I'd told myself looks were unimportant; that what you felt and knew was what mattered. Sometimes, though, I had thought about replacing my thick heavy glasses with contact lenses. Of course this would be more for convenience than looks.

As I felt Julie's hands gently unrolling the curlers then brushing out my hair in long smooth strokes I kept my eyes closed, now rather enjoying the feeling of being pampered. Gradually the giggling stopped and was replaced by "oohs" and "ahs."

Anne, a bubbly fourteen year old said, 'Open your eyes Emma. Look at yourself,' as she thrust a mirror at me.

I gazed at my reflection and saw big brown eyes surrounded by long curling lashes, a prettily curved crimson mouth and hair that fell to my shoulders in soft dark waves. As the girls gathered round me, saying how great I looked, I felt beautiful for the first time in my life.

Chapter Fourteen

That Christmas I shouted myself contact lenses and a set of rollers like the ones Julie had used. I went home to have dinner with my family, taking with me carefully chosen gifts for them all including a play mat complete with colourful mobiles for baby Ross who had been born at the end of November.

When I walked in the door without my glasses, and with my hair surrounding my face in soft waves Mum stared at me in disbelief and said, 'Oh my God. You look lovely Emma.'

John muttered rather gauchely, 'I wouldn't a recognised you.'

Dad, whose skinny frame and wispy grey hair made him look old beyond his years, sat at the kitchen table shelling peas. He looked at me with red-rimmed eyes, and his hazy gaze made it obvious that, despite doctor's orders, he had been drinking. I could tell from his vacant stare that he didn't quite know who I was.

Jessie came into the room, her baby clutched to her breast and rather spoils things for me by saying sarcastically, 'Look whose here. The Queen of Sheba.'

The day passed reasonably pleasantly. Mum had cooked a lovely meal, everyone liked their presents, and I had a cuddle of baby Ross who looked to be thriving and smelt clean and powdery. It seemed Jessie was coping with motherhood, although the room I had previously shared with her now looked a shambles with baby's gear and clothes piled in untidy heaps on every surface.

When I returned to my neat, compact apartment at the hostel I breathed a sigh of relief and pleasure.

Although all the girls had gone home for the long summer vacation the matron, who always visited her daughter during the break, was happy for me to continue living at the hostel. The assistant matron and the cook, both childless widows, also remained there. Occasionally we three women shared an evening meal and played cards or scrabble afterwards, but most of the time we lived our separate lives.

Because I didn't receive a wage during this time I needed to earn some money and managed to get work at a local hotel. For the first time in my life I had men ogling me, calling me "Beautiful" and asking me to go out with them. I found this embarrassing and blushed shyly not knowing how to deal with the attention in a light hearted way. For so long I had considered myself plain and nerdy-looking, as indeed I was. Now, although the mirror told me a different story, I still lacked the confidence of those women who have always known they were beautiful.

I had also never bothered much about clothes. While I was growing up Mum had only been able to afford to buy me inexpensive jeans and sweaters. During the past year I had spent little of my meagre wage and scholarship money on clothes, preferring to invest in a cheap car.

During my stint at the hotel I earned good money as many of the male customers tipped generously. For the first time in my life I felt I could afford some really good clothes.

Before the start of my second year at university I splashed out on some well-cut slacks, a couple of cashmere sweaters, some silk shirts and a fabulous pair of black high-heeled boots. Looking at my reflection in the mirror before I left for the first day back I felt great and knew I looked good.

I had enrolled to do two units with the law faculty as well as continuing with English and History. It would be a slight overload but I thought I could manage it.

The previous year I had seen few of the girls with whom I had attended Bridmore, and avoided those who happened to be in the same lectures or tutorials. I was, therefore, put out when Sonya walked into the room where the first English tutorial was to be held, sat down in the chair next to me and said, 'Do you mind if I sit here?'

I felt myself begin to blush, but took a deep breath and answered coolly, 'Suit yourself,' before turning to speak to my friend Jill who was seated on my other side.

Later, as we were leaving the tutorial, Sonya turned to me and said, 'Incidentally, you're looking terrific,' before tripping off down the stairs.

'Patronising bitch,' I muttered angrily.

Jill laughed 'Gee, what's got your goat? You do look terrific and so different. She was just being friendly Do you know her from somewhere?'

'Yes. From Bridmore, and she was one of the snobbiest, nastiest girls in the school. When I left there I thought I'd be happy if I never saw her again. Now she's going to be in this tutorial group all year.'

'Cheer up. It's only one hour a week and you don't have to talk to her if you don't want to.'

As the year progressed that tutorial actually became the high spot of my week. I was finding the law lectures very boring, the lecturers pedantic and much of the associated assignment work repetitive. In contrast the lecturers in the English department were interesting and stimulating.

An honours student, who was completing her doctoral thesis and wasn't much older than we students, ran the tutorials I shared with Sonya. This bright young woman brought to her teaching the enthusiasm of youth and encouraged everyone to participate. Under her guidance discussions were often lively and heated, and gradually we became a close-knit group. Often we all went to the refectory together after the tutorial had finished and continued our discussions over coffee and cake.

Although I hadn't expected it to happen, slowly Sonya and I became friends. We frequently found we had similar opinions about a certain text or had both particularly enjoyed the same novel or poem. At times I felt a sense of inferiority well up in me when I was around Sonya, but I told myself, 'Grow up girl. That's all in the past.'

Despite telling myself this it took a long time to get rid of that feeling.

Something happened during the year, however, that brought us closer together and cemented our growing friendship.

I had found an interesting book in a second-hand bookshop in town. It was a critical analysis of the works of Virginia Woolf, and explored the ways in which she used aspects of her own life in her fiction. I offered to lend it to Sonya and we went to the hostel together to get it.

When Sonya walked into the lounge-room she looked around admiringly and murmured, 'Oh, it's lovely.'

Her saying this about my tiny apartment when she lived in a veritable mansion made me angry and I said to her. 'Look Sonya, you don't have to patronise me. I know that compared with where you live this isn't much, but I think it's great.

She seemed sincere when she said, 'And so do I. I envy what you have here.'

'Oh come off it,' I snapped. 'You don't have to lie to make me feel good'.

'I'm not lying. I really do envy you.' Sonya gave a sigh. 'You have your independence and I'm still living at home. For God's sake, I'm nearly twenty, but if I so much as mention the possibility of moving out my mother turns on the histrionics. She carries on, and makes me feel so guilty about something I did a couple of years ago. Honestly, she won't be happy for me to ever leave home unless it's into a marriage to someone who she deems to be suitable.'

I listened in amazement to her tirade. Sonya always seemed so cool, so self-assured and in control. Why would she allow her mother to dictate to her?

Unable to hide my astonishment I said, 'For God's sake, what did you do that makes you let her rule your life to such an extent?'

Sonya answered quietly, 'I'd like to tell you about why I feel the way I do. I haven't told anyone else, not even the girls who were my friends all through school, but I need to talk about it and feel I can trust you. Perhaps you can tell me how to deal with my guilt.'

Sonya then proceeded to tell me about what had happened to her during the last few months at Bridmore. I listened in amazed silence, and when Sonya became upset I held her hand and wiped away her tears.

Later I watched from my window as she walked jauntily to her little red convertible, and turned to give a cheerful wave before getting into the car and speeding off.

Long after the car had disappeared around the corner I stood staring out at the darkening sky, and thinking about what Sonya had confided to me. What she revealed had made me realise that you never really know what is going on in someone else's life.

If anyone had told me a time would come when I would feel sorry for snooty, bitchy Sonya McFee I wouldn't have believed them. Now that was exactly how I felt, for that afternoon I learnt that behind the confident and slightly arrogant veneer Sonya showed to the world she was eaten up by feelings of guilt about taking a life and spoiling what had evidently been the happy marriage of her parents.

Chapter Fifteen

In the morning after the night out with Sonya and Jenny, I snuggle up to my sleeping husband, enjoying the warmth and feel of his strong, sturdy body next to mine. I think of our love-making of the previous night and marvel that, after thirteen years of marriage, Bruce can still excite me so with his touch and his kisses. He had been my first and only lover, so for me sex and lovemaking are inextricably bound up with the feelings I have for him.

Once, during a rather boozy evening with Sonya and Jenny, I drunkenly admitted that Bruce had been my only sexual partner.

Sonya, who has been married twice and had numerous lovers chortled, 'I can't believe it. You don't know what you are missing out on. Variety is the spice of life darling.'

Jenny said, 'Don't listen to her. I think it's lovely the way you feel about your Bruce.'

Although we had known each other for many years we three friends rarely spoke about sex. Occasionally Sonya would tell us of an erotic weekend with a new lover or laughingly refers to another as being, "Good in the sack." Jenny and I enjoyed her tales, but noted a hint of bravado behind her smiles for we knew her first marriage left her emotionally damaged.

Jenny rarely talks about Don now. During the early years of her marriage she spoke lovingly about him, of how understanding he had been during her pregnancies, of what a good provider he was and about how much time he spent with their boys. In recent years she has stopped praising him. I wonder if her feelings of powerlessness, and her distress when she mentioned never having made the important decisions in her life are indications of problems in the marriage. Whatever is wrong, that article of Sonya's and our subsequent conversation stirred up something in Jenny. Obviously she feels she has had little control of her life and something is making her very unhappy.

I try to imagine what it must feel like to have the most important decisions in your life made for you. I have been independent from the time I was eighteen, and feel I determined how my life would be from then.

As I lie in bed feeling warm and contented, I think back to those years at the hostel.

When I compared my life with what I now knew about Sonya's I felt so free and independent. I loved my little apartment and enjoyed university life. A bonus was the unexpected pleasure I felt while helping my young charges with their schoolwork, and providing sisterly advice or comfort to them when they were upset or had a problem.

Life was good, especially after what I now thought of as the "makeover" I had received at the hands of those giggling girls.

I had seen programmes on television where people were given what were touted as "extreme makeovers". The participants were whisked off to some glamorous place and had everything done to them, from plastic surgery and teeth capping, to new hairstyling and makeup. They were suitably clothed in designer outfits before returning to a gathering of their friends and family who greeted them with cheers and tears.

My makeover had been achieved much more simply, and I well-remembered the low-key reaction of my family to my new appearance, remembered my father's hazy glance and Jessie's sarcastic remark. Only my mother had enthused about my new look and been truly pleased for me.

Although my family's reaction to my makeover had been low key I now frequently received compliments about my hair or clothes from female friends. Boys who had ignored me the previous year now paid me attention. Several of them made sure they sat near me during lectures, and afterwards invited me to join them for a coffee in the refectory. My social life became a whirl of noisy parties in cheap digs where everyone danced to loud music in darkened smoke-filled rooms. There were also quieter evenings when I sat around with a group of friends drinking cask wine, while enjoying deep and meaningful discussions about everything, from the true identity of the dark lady in Shakespeare's sonnets to the notion that the wilderness is important even if no one sees it.

During that second year at university I had several light-hearted romances, and for a while imagined myself in love with a fellow student named Brad. He was tall and blonde and the stroke in the university rowing crew. I spent several Saturdays towards the end of that year watching rowing races while shivering on the shore in the weak, early summer sun. Afterwards we would go back to his room in a shared house and eat pizzas or chicken and chips and drink beer or cheap red wine. Later we lay on his uncomfortable single bed and kissed and fondled each other intimately, but I never allowed Brad to enter me. Even when we were both in a state of total arousal I pulled back, unable to give myself completely.

Soon Brad began to be angry; called me a tease and accused me of not caring for him in the way he did for me. Having seen how getting pregnant affected my sister's life I was not going to let the same thing happen to me. I didn't believe Brad's assurances that sex would be safe if he used the condoms he had so hopefully stashed away in a drawer.

At the end of the year Brad went home to his parents' property in the country. Our frustration and bickering about sex had marred whatever feeling we'd had for each other. Earlier we'd planned to spend part of the vacation together as Brad wanted me to meet his parents, but now he went alone. We said a wistful goodbye knowing our love affair was over, though neither of us said this outright.

I again spent the vacation at the hostel, catching up on lost sleep, reading books for pleasure instead of as part of a curriculum and going out with friends for the occasional evenings to dinner or to see a film. Some nights I whiled away the time with those two old companions, the assistant matron and the cook. We'd prepare lavish meals for ourselves and afterwards played board games in Cookie's little parlour which was adjacent to the kitchen.

From a sense of duty I made a weekly visit to my family home. During term time I used the excuse that I was on duty at the hostel or busy studying, but now there was no reason for not going. I hated the time spent back there and suffered pangs of guilt for feeling that way. My father continued to ignore the doctor's warnings and was always slightly drunk by lunchtime. John usually sat silently through the meal before going off to join his friends, and Jessie alternated between sullenness and almost hysterical gaiety depending on how things were between her and her latest boyfriend. Mum fussed over us all, and showed her obvious happiness at having me there and hearing about my life.

It was only for Mum that I made these dutiful visits. My mother's belief in my abilities and her constant support had been a driving force in my life, and I loved her and was grateful to her for this.

During my third year at university my life changed dramatically.

Several new girls came to the hostel, replacing the older ones who had moved into university colleges or returned home to help on the farms until they married. Amongst the new recruits to come into my care was Bella. She was only fourteen, but had completed year ten at the Area School that served her community. Her parents, recognising her intelligence, wanted her to further her education. They had enrolled her at one of the matriculation colleges and booked her a place at the hostel. She was so young, this was the first time she had ever been away from home and she felt lost, lonely and homesick.

Seeing this I went out of my way to talk to her, to cheer her up when she was looking sad, and to give her that little bit more attention during study periods. In time Bella settled in and began to enjoy the camaraderie of the other girls, but I had been there for her when she needed that extra bit of help and we remained close.

I met Bruce when he came to take Bella out. I had heard about this adored older brother who worked as an accountant in the city. Bella was a delicate-looking blonde with pale blue eyes surrounded by long white lashes. With her slim white arms and legs she reminded me a little of a young palomino colt. I expected the brother to be a male version of Bella, pale, thin and serious.

Our meeting took place one Saturday night when I was on duty. I had been told Bella's brother would be calling for her at six and would bring her home before twelve.

When I opened the door to him I blinked with surprise. He was nothing like I had imagined. For a while I just stood there unable to speak. He was gorgeous. Although only of average height he exuded an air of strength and masculinity. He wore jeans and a cable-knit sweater topped by a camel-coloured suede jacket.

As he put out his hand to shake mine he said, 'I'm Bruce, Bella's brother. And you must be Emma. I've so wanted to meet you. Bella's told us all about you and how you've helped her.'

I stared into his dark hazel eyes as I shook his hand feeling almost limp with longing.

Fortunately Bella chose that moment to come hurtling down the stairs and fling herself at her brother. If not for this interruption I think I may have stood there forever like a lovesick wimp.

Bruce gave his little sister a hug, and then turning to me said, 'I don't suppose you'd like to come with us? We're going to the Taverna for dinner and then to see a film.'

There was nothing I'd have liked more but I gathered my scattered wits together enough to explain that I was on duty as there were other girls still at the hostel.

He said self-ashamedly, 'Oh gosh, I should've thought of that. Perhaps another time.'

As he and Bella disappeared down the path I hugged myself and whispered, 'Perhaps another time.'

The next week I received a magnificent bouquet of flowers, delivered to the door of the hostel, much to the giggling appreciation of the girls. They watched me read the accompanying note, and clustered around me saying, 'Who's it from Miss?' and, 'Miss Emma's got a boyfriend.'

I laughingly fobbed them off, but later, after I had arranged the flowers in a vase and placed it next to my bed, I sat at my desk reading and re-reading the message, "You are as beautiful as these flowers. Please see me. I will ring later in the week. Bruce."

That was the beginning of our love affair. The following weekend we went to dinner and talked non-stop about books we had both read, films we had seen, politics, the environment and of course ourselves. As the night progressed I felt swamped by a desire to hold one of those strong brown hands in mine, to see what it would feel like to kiss his sweetly curved mouth and run my hands through his thick brown hair. When he suggested that we have a nightcap at his flat I didn't hesitate.

Once at the flat, I looked around curiously as he busied himself putting on a c.d. of peaceful unfamiliar music, and pouring generous amounts of a golden liquid into brandy balloons before joining me on the brown leather sofa. We sipped our drinks then kissed for the first time. It was like an instant conflagration, burning away all my previous inhibitions, and when Bruce picked me up and carried me to his bed I removed his clothes just as urgently as he removed mine.

Our coupling was frantic and wonderful; and even though it hurt a bit at the start I still experienced the most amazing feelings of pleasure.

Afterwards Bruce pulled away and said humbly, 'It didn't occur to me you were a virgin. I'm so sorry.'

I jumped from the bed, feeling both embarrassed and angry. 'Don't you dare say you're sorry. It was my choice and I thought it was wonderful. If you're going to apologise you'll ruin it.'

With that I started hunting around on the floor amongst the scattered clothes for my panties and bra, angry tears wetting my cheeks.

Bruce gathered me up in his arms and held me until I calmed down. He kissed me gently, smoothed my hair and wiped away my shameful tears before saying solemnly, 'It was wonderful and special, and I only wish you could have been the first woman I made love to. But let me tell you, my fiery one, you will be the last.'

I have never forgotten those words, nor ever had reason to doubt that Bruce has kept that promise.

Now I move closer to his back, rather hoping that he will wake up, for the memories of that night have made me feel sexually aroused. Unfortunately he is sleeping soundly and doesn't stir, not even when I move my hand across his pyjama-clad penis. I sigh, and then lay on my back remembering back to that time.

I still had my fear of an unwanted pregnancy, so the following week went to the Family Planning Clinic, this time for myself, and obtained a prescription for the pill.

From that first night Bruce and I spent every possible moment together. I stayed at his flat for two out of every three weekends, and when I was on duty at the hostel he came around and helped me supervise the girls. These were chaste weekends, because even in my little apartment there was no guarantee of privacy, and it would have set a bad example to the girls if I'd allowed him to stay overnight.

By the end of my third year at university Bruce and I were planning our future together. I had become increasingly bored with the units I was studying for my Law Degree, but could include them as part of my Arts Degree. In this way I would graduate in Arts at the end of the year. Because I enjoyed tutoring my hostel girls so much I had been thinking about teaching as a possible career. From an early age I had thought I wanted to be a lawyer and my mother had shared the dream of me gaining the qualifications to be able to help women who were victims of domestic violence. She had always been so encouraging and so proud of my academic achievements I worried about telling her of my changed plan. I felt very tentative about telling her of my decision to teach instead of continuing my studies to become a lawyer. Mum just smiled and said I should do what would make me happy. Despite this loving response I felt I was disappointing my mother.

Sonya and I both enrolled to do our education diploma and at the start of the following year met Jenny. Although we would be teaching different subjects we were all required to do certain core courses as part of our study. Jenny seemed rather out of her depth amongst the other students who had attended university together, and initially Sonya and I felt sorry for her. She seemed so shy and insecure, but once we got to know her we saw her imaginative, fun-loving side.

Before long we became a tight-knit trio. We helped each other with assignments, commiserated when practical teaching weeks went badly and shared many happy, celebratory evenings.

At the end of the year I obtained a position teaching English and Legal Studies at the only matriculation college in the area. Jenny was to teach Art at the same college.

Sonya, who had done her final month of practical teaching at our old school, Bridmore, had been invited to join the staff there as the French teacher.

Once I was earning money, and could afford to pay my share, I moved into the flat with Bruce and at the end of that year we married.

Sonya was my chief bridesmaid and Bella, who at nearly seventeen had blossomed into a gloriously beautiful blonde teenager, was my junior bridesmaid.

Jenny, who had married Don the previous June, was pregnant at the time so couldn't be part of the bridal party, but she was there as a guest. She enjoyed the wedding and was pleased to see me so totally happy.

My father stayed sober long enough to walk me down the aisle, but he later disgraced himself and his family by vomiting in the foyer of the rather posh hotel where the reception was being held. Mum supported him from the hotel and pushed him into a waiting taxi, but she told me later she had given him what for once she got him home.

Despite my father's behaviour it had been a lovely wedding. I had insisted on paying for the reception even though Bruce said it should be something we shared. I had been adamant that it was the bride's parents' responsibility, and as they couldn't afford the wedding I would pay. By now Bruce knew not to argue against my strongly held beliefs so spent lavishly on a luxurious honeymoon for us on an exclusive island in the Whitsundays.

Shortly before our marriage we had found a house we both loved and Bruce paid the deposit on it. On the return from our honeymoon we moved into it.

We didn't want to wait to start our family and by the following summer I was pregnant. Our beautiful son John was born in April, and two years later we had our second son who we named Xavier. I enjoyed my time at home with my little sons, but once they were both at school I found life as a housewife boring so decided to return to work.

As I think back over my life I feel I determined the way in which my life would be, and can't imagine any decisions I made that had a viable alternative. I feel sorry for Jenny who has had so much of her life decided for her.

Of course, after meeting Bruce, most decisions were made by us both but fortunately we have always agreed about the important things.

Our marriage seemed to both of us to be pre-ordained from the moment we met, so perhaps that wasn't a choice that could not have been made.

Other decisions were weighed more carefully. Together we planned when we would start a family and when we would have our second child. Before I returned to work I naturally talked it over with Bruce.

Thinking once more about the discussion my friends and I had the previous night, I idly wonder how many parallel worlds I may have been responsible for creating. And could there possibly be any truth in the whole wacky concept? Is there a world where I don't have my lovely sons - or another where I became a lawyer instead of a teacher? And what part does chance play in this theory of parallel worlds? Could there be a world in which chance didn't allow Bruce and me to meet? I don't even want to think of that possibility.

I hear sounds coming from along the passage. Slowly our bedroom door opens and two cheeky faces appear.

John says in a serious, artificially deep voice, 'Isn't it time you two were up?'

He stands at the door. At twelve, he is self-conscious about entering the parental bedroom. After Bruce told both boys about "the facts of life" John's mind took the unthinkable leap. He realised his parents participated in sexual activities. This has made him wary of entering the room where these acts occur.

Xavier, at ten, has not yet made this connection, so lacks the inhibitions of his older brother. He skitters across the room and plumps himself down on the bed waking Bruce.

It seems such a short while ago that the boys would come sleepily into our bedroom in the mornings and snuggle themselves down under the doona. We would lie there together, a warm tangle of arms and legs, and plan what we would do that day. I think back fondly to that time but, as I get out of bed and pull on my dressing gown, I think there really is only one thing I would like to change about my life. I wish there was something I could do to help Mum.

I love my mother dearly and know I owe her a debt of gratitude I can never repay, but I now finds the weekly visits to see her are becoming a chore. It is even harder to get the boys to go with me. They have grown up in a comfortable, spacious home and had the benefit of a good private school education. They love their Granny but are beginning to notice that she, "talks funny", and I see how they look critically around the small crowded rooms and at the now weed-infested back yard.

My father died several years ago from liver damage caused by years of drinking. Since then both of my younger siblings have caused Mum endless worries.

My brother John rarely keeps a job for more than a few months, and has spent most of his adult years on the dole.

Jessie, at thirty, is living in a housing department house with the father of her fourth child. She has not been, "a real good Mum," as she imagined she would be when she was a rebellious teenager. She tries, but will sometimes neglect her children when there is a new man in her life. Because she didn't have time to grow up before trying to take on the responsibilities of motherhood she has never quite matured. This makes her erratic in her mothering, alternating fierce loving cuddles with screams and slaps.

The years of hard work and unremitting worry have tarnished Mum's bright optimism and, although she is not yet sixty, she moves and looks like an old woman.

As I walk around my bright, sunny kitchen, putting on the grill, filling the percolator with water and listening to the cheerful chiacking of my sons, my mind returns to my earlier thoughts about parallel worlds. Wistfully I hope that perhaps there is another world where my mother is living a better life.

Pierre

Chapter Sixteen

When I return to the car, after escorting Emma to her front door, I see that Sonya has fallen asleep with her head pressed against the window at what appears to be an uncomfortable angle. I slide in and gently pull her towards me so that her head now rests on my shoulder, then I start the car.

As we pull up at her house she wakens with a start and say sleepily, 'Are we home?'

I go round to her side and help her out saying, 'Come on my sleepy princess. I think we'd better get you to bed.'

She fumbles in her bag for the keys and hands them to me. I open the door and guide her inside, then shut it behind us

Sonya clings to me drunkenly murmuring, 'Oh I feel so tired, and I wanted us to have really lovely sex.'

I lift her up and carry her to the bedroom saying, 'We will have many other times for making love, but for now it's sleep time for you my darling.'

I take off her shoes and clothes and settle her beneath the thick white doona that covers the bed. I gaze down at her enjoying the sight of her rich auburn hair spreading across the pillow and the pearly colour of a bare shoulder. She really is a magnificent-looking woman.

I turn out the light, go into the lounge room and pour myself a small brandy. Because I had planned to pick up Sonya and her friends I had not had a drink tonight. I now relax in one of the large white leather chairs that dominate the room. Having had a busy day at work organising the final details of a dinner at which my family's wines will be showcased, I too am tired. I have now been in Australia for nearly two years setting up an import/export business, and this dinner is meant to be one of my final tasks before returning to France. My father is ailing and, as the only son, I am expected to take over the running of the family company, but I don't want to leave Australia, at least not alone.

I know I am attractive to women and the fact that I come from a wealthy family is an added attraction for most women. I am now thirty-nine and have had many lovers, but had never been in love until I met Sonya. Now thoughts of her dominate my days and I can't imagine a life in which we are not together. I know she loves me too but she has, so far, refused to marry me. As the only son I am expected to produce an heir, but she is adamant she will never have a child. Although she has told me her reason for feeling unworthy of this right, I cannot understand why she allows a decision made when she was but a child to still dominate her life; how she can continue to carry these feelings of guilt. At times I wish I had the power of a priest to wipe away her sense of shame, for I love her deeply and sincerely and want us to be together forever.

Many do not believe in the possibility of love at first sight, but I know it can happen for it happened to me. From the first moment I spoke to her at that strange little wine and cheese evening organised by the local Alliance Francaise group I knew she was the one.

I had gone to it rather unwillingly. A French couple, who befriended me when I first arrived in Australia, often asked me to come along to the various functions held by this group. Until that evening I had always found an excuse for not attending.

Most of the time my excuses were genuine. I was very busy during the first year, setting up the business, obtaining the relevant import and export licences, making contacts with potential customers and organising the marketing. I only agreed to attend this time because I had recently broken up with my latest amour and was rather at a loose end.

From the time of my arrival in Australia I had led a full social life and enjoyed several light hearted romances. I love women and enjoy their company, but at no time did I plan on entering a serious relationship with an Australian woman. My familial duty is to eventually marry and produce an heir to the family name and fortune. On the rare occasions when I thought about marriage I had always envisaged I would wed a French girl, for like most men of my country I had the belief that France is the home of the best wine and food, the most sophisticated culture, the most beautiful scenery and the most attractive and sensuous women. Thus I was completely unprepared for the instant and lasting impact Sonya has had on me.

The wine and cheese evening was held in the home of the French Ambassador, a rather fussy little man who had been living in Australia for many years. I had met him on several previous occasions and found him slightly annoying, but I liked his wife Monique. She is a large handsome woman with a warm friendly personality. They seemed to me to be an ill-matched pair. I would look at them and wonder how they ever got together, let alone had a sexual relationship, but they seemed happy enough and had produced a large brood of attractive and polite children.

That evening when I arrived at the house the door was opened by a girl of about fifteen, who showed me into the spacious lounge room with a shy, 'Everyone's in there,' before skittering off in another direction.

I stood at the doorway, searching the crowded room for my host and hostess or the friends who had insisted on my attendance. The guests were gathered in small groups around the room, chatting noisily in a mixture of French and English and drinking wine, while several of the ambassador's children circled the room bearing platters of biscuits, cheeses, pates and fruit.

I spotted my friends and was heading in their direction when my eyes were drawn to a laughing group near the fireplace. They were all looking at a tall redhead who had evidently just delivered the punch line of a funny story or joke. As I entered the room, she turned her head in my direction and our eyes met. She was stunning. Her hair was the first thing I noticed. It was a rich auburn with golden highlights and fell in soft waves to her shoulders. She wore a deep purple dress that outlined the curves of her long, full-breasted torso, small waist and rounded hips.

Around her neck was draped a light silk scarf patterned in swirls of purple, lavender and gold, and when I joined the group surrounding her I saw that her eyes were the same colour as the gold in her scarf. I found the sight of her truly breathtaking

I knew some of the others in the group and Danielle, a woman whose husband was the vigneron at a local winery, greeted me effusively saying, 'I suppose you know everyone.'

I smiled at the familiar faces before turning to the beautiful woman, 'Yes I know most of these reprobates, but I haven't met this lovely lady before.'

Danielle laughed, 'Allow me to do the honours. Sonya, this is Pierre Belleau, importer of fine French wines and Pierre, meet Sonya McFee, Principal of Bridmore Girls' School. Some of Sonya's more advanced language students are here tonight to have the opportunity to practise their French.'

As we shook hands I felt an electric tingle pass between us and from the expression in those magnificent golden eyes I knew Sonya felt it too.

For the remainder of the evening I didn't leave her side. When people began to leave I of course offered her a lift to her home, but she answered, 'I have my car here, but I also have to make sure all my students get home safely. Parents are picking up most of them, but I'm driving the two boarders back to school. Give me a call.'

We exchanged cards under the watchful eyes of the students, and I was sure I heard their barely suppressed giggles and someone whisper, 'Miss McFee's making a date with him.'

I rang her the next evening and we met for drinks. From that first night I knew she was the woman with whom I wanted to share the rest of my life.

To me she is perfect, the ideal woman and companion. I love the way she looks, appreciates her intellect and has seen how she charms her staff, the students and their parents with her warm outgoing personality. She even speaks fluent French, having studied the language at university and taught it for years. The one stumbling block is that she is adamant she will never have a child. Despite this I have proposed marriage, but she refused me because she knows about my family's expectations.

When she turned me down she said, 'Let's just enjoy the time that we have. When you return to France you will find someone else; someone who will give you the children you want and an heir as your family expects.'

I finish my brandy and then go quietly to the bedroom where I undress and slide into bed, being careful not to wake my sleeping lady. She turns to me in her sleep, and puts a long bare arm across my chest and her head on my shoulder. As I lie there awake, smelling her perfumed hair and enjoying the sweet familiar warmth of her body next to me, a feeling of desperation wells up inside me. Soon I must return to my homeland, but I don't want to leave without her. Her reason for not being willing to have a child is the one thing we have argued about. How can I convince her that she did not forego the right to motherhood by her youthful decision to abort her first baby?

Sonya

Chapter Seventeen

I wake to the smell of coffee and the sounds of Pierre moving around the kitchen. I hear the whirr of the mixer and guess that he is making his specialty, the delicious cheesy omelettes he says his mother taught him to cook when he was a child. Although I feel I could do with a few more hours sleep, I get up and have a quick shower before donning navy blue track pants and top and pulling a wide comb through my hair.

As I join him in the kitchen he is pouring our coffees. He motions me to sit at the little breakfast bar that overlooks my small private back yard. He places the omelette and coffee in front of me and kisses my cheek, saying teasingly, 'And how is my sleepy beauty this morning? You promised much last night but did not deliver.'

I run my hand lovingly down his back and answer half apologetically, 'The spirit was willing but the flesh was weak. I get so tired by the end of term, and I guess we girls had a bit too much to drink.' I lower my voice to make it sound sexy and say, 'But don't worry, my darling, I will make it up to you tonight.'

Although it is Saturday Pierre has to work, so I plan to spend the day shopping, doing a few chores around the house and preparing an extra special dinner. I look forward to an evening of good food and wine and sensual pleasure. Soon he will be leaving, and I want to make the most of these last few weeks we will spend together.

After breakfast he kisses me passionately at the door, and before leaving says jokingly, 'I look forward to tonight my little temptress when you will not be so tired.'

I shut the door still grinning at his teasing remark. This past year with Pierre has been so good. Besides being a wonderful lover and a congenial companion he has a wacky sense of fun and finds humour in most situations. During these last months, though, a bittersweet element has overshadowed our times together. He knows I love him as much as he loves me and cannot understand why I refuse to marry him, or how I can continue to feel such guilt about my girlhood decision to get rid of my baby.

There is nothing more I would rather do than marry Pierre and have his babies. I have tried to talk myself out of feeling that I have lost the right to have a child, but my sense of guilt and unworthiness persists. This is the reason I have refused him, because it would not be fair to inflict a childless marriage on him or dash his parents' hope for an heir.

As I pack the breakfast dishes into the dishwasher and turn on the machine I think back to that time when I was seventeen, and how hard I'd had to fight my mother for the right to have an abortion.

I was the only child of Edward and Marjorie McFee a wealthy and highly social couple. I had a doting father and a mother who considered her lovely, talented daughter to be her greatest achievement. With such parents it's probably no wonder I considered myself superior and at times behaved like a spoilt brat. I knew I was beautiful and clever as well as being good at sport. These attributes had given me a degree of self-confidence bordering on arrogance and made me a natural leader.

Unfortunately, at seventeen, I was not very nice and inclined to use my leadership quality to encourage others in the teasing and bullying of less fortunate students. The particular butt of our teasing was Emma Williams, a scholarship girl who looked like a freak but who managed to top all our classes. I had been used to being top girl during my primary school years and was miffed that this little nobody had displaced me. I encouraged my group to make Emma's life a misery and this is something I came to regret, but at the time I simply saw it as a lark.

Apart from this rather nasty streak I was a very satisfactory daughter and my mother never ceased bragging to her friends about her amazing child. I knew this and was aware that I must not let anything spoil this illusion. From the beginning of my relationship with Harry I was very conscious of the fact that it must be kept a secret, for my mother would consider him far too working-class and common to be a suitable partner for her daughter.

Before we even met I knew him by sight because he worked as a mechanic in the local garage where my parents had their cars serviced. He rode a big black motorbike, and was notorious around the district as a wild boy. I think I found him attractive but just knew he was out of bounds.

One Saturday morning I saw him lounging outside the local pub with a group of bikers. They all wore the bikers' uniform of black leathers, black boots and wrap around shades. My girlfriend and I were on our way to the mall to do some shopping, and as we passed the men whistled. One made a rather crude and suggestive remark and Harry said to him, 'Tone it down mate.'

I felt grateful to him, but also surprised when he added, 'Sorry about that Sonya. Some of these larrikins don't know where to draw the line.'

As we walked away my friend, Elsa, giggled and asked how he knew my name.

I answered rather primly, 'I have no idea. Mum and Dad get their cars serviced at the garage where he works, so perhaps he's heard one of them say it.'

'You wouldn't think he'd remember though. Perhaps he fancies you.'

Elsa was always imagining that some boy or other was staring at us, and made a big deal of it if we so much as talked to a group of boys in town or at the library.

About a week later I was walking home alone after spending the afternoon at Gail's place where a group of us had gone for a swim in her parents' new pool. I heard a motorbike roar past and was surprised when it pulled up further down the road. When he took off his helmet I saw it was the man who had apologised for his friend's crude remark.

He waited until I was alongside then said, 'Hey Sonya, do you want to go for a ride? I've got a spare helmet.'

I knew my parents wouldn't approve of me doing this. In my head I could hear my mother's voice say, "Consorting with riffraff," and my father's more measured tones, "Motorbikes are dangerous vehicles."

I looked at Harry and ignored the voices in my head. All my life I had been an obedient daughter, but suddenly I wanted to break away from the restrictive, comfortable life I had been living. I didn't know this man, but as he sat there with a smile on his handsome face and held out to me the spare helmet I felt the urge to rebel.

I took the helmet, tied the strap under my chin and said cheerfully, 'Okay, where are we going?'

Harry laughed, pleased by my ready acceptance, 'You'll find out when we get there. Now hold on tight and lean with me in the corners.'

He took me on a wild and fast ride on the winding road that led to the top of the mountain that dominated the city. I clung on tightly, my arms encircling his waist. I enjoyed the feeling of being at one with this man and machine as we leant low around the bends and sped along the straights.

When he stopped the bike I stepped off, took off the helmet, and flinging my arms in the air turned in circles saying loudly, 'That was wonderful, wonderful, wonderful.'

Harry also removed his helmet, and stood watching me pirouetting around the large lichen-covered rocks scattered around the barren ground. When I paused for breath he grabbed me and pulled me into a rough embrace.

Tilting back my head with one large rough hand he said, 'I always thought there was a real woman hiding beneath that school-girl uniform,' and kissed me long and hard.

I had been kissed before, but only by smooth-faced boys. Theirs were shy, tentative kisses given on my parents' doorstep at the end of an evening at the movies or after a teenage party. This kiss was different. Harry's face was rough and his lips firm. I felt his tongue flickering across my lips, and then entering my mouth. I had never been kissed like that; was unprepared for the way my heart pounded and my body seemed to melt. We stood there, high on that mountain, and kissed and kissed while a high whistling wind filled the air.

I knew I would never forget the magic of that time, the warmth of his lips, the responding warmth of my body and the contrasting cold, cold wind swirling around us. Perhaps I should have seen that wind as an omen.

When the sun disappeared behind the mountain I pulled away and said, 'You'd better take me home. It'll be dark soon, and my parents will start wondering where I've got to.'

As we rode home I pushed my face into his back and my hands under his jacket so that I could feel his heart beating. Without being told he pulled into a narrow alley a distance from my house and helped me off the bike and out of the helmet. He stood there, towering over me in the twilight, looking dark and menacing, but his voice was gentle when he said, 'Look, I wanna see you again. I know your folks won't approve, but they needn't know. What do you say?'

Of course I said I wanted to see him again, and eagerly agreed to come to his place after school the next day. He told me he lived in a small flat behind the garage, and explained how I could get to it by a back lane and thus avoid being seen by nosy neighbours.

In school the next day I couldn't concentrate. Twice my teachers reprimanded me for not paying attention. I kept thinking of Harry's kisses and how they had made me feel. When the end of school finally came I pretended to my friends, with whom I usually walked home, that I wanted to see a teacher about an assignment so they would leave without me.

As I walked up the narrow lane leading to his flat I felt anxious. What if I saw him and felt differently about him? Would he turn nasty if I didn't want to kiss him?

I knocked nervously on the door, and he opened it so quickly I knew he must have been waiting for me to arrive. He stood there, looking tall and brown in a clean white shirt and blue jeans. Obviously he had showered recently for his dark hair was a mass of damp ringlets and he smelled of soap and a mild woodsy aftershave.

I hadn't known quite what to expect, and was surprised that he seemed to be as nervous as I when he said diffidently, 'Welcome to my humble abode. Would you like a beer or a white wine?'

I had drunk the occasional glass of wine at parties and with my parents on special occasions so said I'd like a wine. As he poured wine from a bottle that was already open I looked around the room. It was sparsely furnished with a couch and an armchair both facing a large television set. At one end of the room was the kitchenette that contained a stove, small fridge, a sink and a few cupboards. It certainly wasn't fancy but everything looked clean and tidy.

He handed me the glass of wine saying, 'Cheers to us,' and we clinked glasses while staring solemnly into each other's eyes.

I drank the wine slowly, delaying the moment when we would kiss, but my whole body was tingling with anticipation. Harry moved closer along the couch. I could feel the warmth of his body and clean male smell of him as we sat sipping our wine trying to make small talk.

'So you didn't have any trouble finding the laneway?' he asked.

When I said I hadn't he asked me how long I could stay. I didn't know what to say. If I said a couple of hours it might make me look too keen, but if I said I couldn't stay long he might be put off.

With a coyness that was alien to me I smiled, and said in a deliberately seductive voice, 'How long do you want me to stay?'

He took my empty glass and pulled me into his arms saying, 'I want you here for as long as possible, now let's not waste any more time.'

We kissed for a long time as he fondled my breasts through my thin school blouse. I had never been aroused in this way, and when he removed my blouse and bra and touched and kissed my bare flesh I clung to him frantically, wanting more. He picked me up and carried me to his bed where he continued to kiss and stroke me while he removed my clothes. When he undressed I stared in fear at his erect penis and cried out in pain when he entered me, but I so badly wanted him to do it.

Afterwards he was very loving and said, 'I thought you'd be a virgin. I hope I didn't hurt you too much. Next time I'll wear a rubber.'

I was such an innocent I didn't even know that by a rubber he meant a condom, and so uncaring I hadn't even thought of the possibility of becoming pregnant. All I wanted was to have him kiss and touch me forever.

That was the beginning of our affair.

I went to his flat every day during what was my last week at school. The next two weeks were swot vac, a time to be spent studying for and then sitting the matriculation exams. As I could no longer drop into his place on my way home from school I became devious. I lied to my parents that I needed to visit the library or was studying with friends, and then ran the four blocks to Harry's flat. As soon as I arrived I'd fling my books onto the table and myself into his arms. We didn't talk much, but spent the evenings making love.

Afterwards Harry always escorted me home along the back streets, and we'd kiss desperately in the dark laneway where he had dropped me off after our first exciting date.

During the day I tried to study, but thoughts of Harry and of what we did together filled my head. I found it difficult to concentrate on English texts and French translations. Although I had very good internal marks, I knew I must do well in the exams to achieve the results both my teachers and parents expected of me.

By the time the exams were over I felt drained, both emotionally and physically. I hadn't heard much from my friends during swot vacation, because we were all busy studying. The only times I'd seen them were before each exam when we'd chatted briefly and nervously together. Now, with our studies out of the way, they were ready to party.

My best friends, Gail, Elsa and Jemma, were constantly on the phone, wanting to go shopping or to the beach or a movie, and I went along with their plans. If I didn't they would want to know why; might notice a change in me. I felt as though I had moved into a totally different world, one in which the only time that mattered was that spent with Harry. My friends and their girlish chatter annoyed me, and I found it difficult to share their fervent planning for the Leavers' Dinner.

Before I'd met Harry I had bought my dress for this occasion. Gail and I were being escorted to the dinner by Ralph and Anthony, boys who attended a private boys' school nearby. We had met them at a social organised by the two schools, and until Harry came on the scene Anthony had been my "sort of" boyfriend. We had gone to the movies and the odd party together, and he had phoned me a few times during the study time leading up to the exams. I'd cut these calls short using the excuse that I was busy, but now the exams had finished he began calling me again and asking me out.

A month ago I had quite liked him, but now I couldn't care less if I never saw him again. He seemed so juvenile. Even his voice sounded high and girlish when I compared it with Harry's, which was deep and masculine. My problem was I needed Anthony as my escort for the dinner, so I finally agreed to go to a movie with him.

With the exams over, I could no longer pretend to be studying at the library or with friends, so I began sneaking out at night after my parents were in bed. I'd climb out my bedroom window, creep across the side lawn, scramble over a fence, and then run down the back streets to Harry's place. We'd make love for hours, and then he'd escort me back before the early summer sun rose in the sky.

I hadn't mentioned the Leavers' Dinner to Harry or who my date would be because I thought it would create a problem and I was right. When I told him Anthony was to be my escort for the dinner, and that I was going to the movies with him the following Saturday night, Harry became very angry.

We were sitting close together on the couch and he pushed me away saying, 'Why do you have to go out with the dipstick? If it comes to that why can't I take you to the dinner? I can hire a penguin suit as easily as the next bloke.'

I hadn't quite known what to say. I'd thought he understood my parents would never approve of him. How was I to explain that they would be appalled at me associating with him, not only because he was a man of twenty-three but also because of his working-class background?

I stammered, 'My mother and father wouldn't let me go out with you. I thought you realised that.'

Harry pulled me to him saying angrily, 'Yer, I guess I did. I'm just your bit of rough, not good enough to be seen with you in public.'

Before I could say anything to smooth things over he ran one hand over my breasts and then down between my legs and said hoarsely, 'But I'm good for this aren't I Baby?'

I leant limply against him as his fingers explore my vagina until I was frantic for him to enter me. That night we made love so often I felt quite sore as I walked home with my lover in the early morning mist.

After that evening Harry seemed to accept that I would have to lead a double life and pretend to be the normal, sociable teenager I had been before we met. He found it difficult to hide his jealousy though, when I went out with Anthony or with my girlfriends instead of spending the night with him.

On the evening of the Leavers' Dinner he even hid across the road and watched me being escorted home, watched the chaste kiss I allowed Anthony to give me at the front door. Later he knocked on my bedroom window and I let him in. We made passionate love on my schoolgirl bed, but I was so afraid my parents might hear us I failed to orgasm.

We had been carrying on our secret affair for nearly two months when I missed a period. I had always been very regular from the time I first started menstruating so was instantly worried. I told myself I couldn't be pregnant;

except for that first time we had always been careful and condoms are safe, aren't they?

During the next month of the summer vacation I continued my double life, spending time with my girlfriends and double dating with Anthony and Gail and Ralph. By the time I had missed a second period I was really concerned, and cried on Harry's shoulder until he promised to buy a pregnancy kit to allay my fears.

The next evening he handed it to me as I walked in the door, and I went instantly to the bathroom to take the test. When it showed I was pregnant I stared at the little strip in horror before falling in a crumpled crying heap on the floor.

Harry picked me up and carried me to the bedroom. He was so gentle, wiping away my tears as if I were a child, rocking me in his strong arms saying, 'Don't worry Baby. I love you. I'll look after you. I'm earning good money, enough to rent a nice house for you and the bub.'

I couldn't believe what he was saying and stared at him in horror before yelling, ' I don't want a baby, 'I'm not ready for that. I'm going to university this year. You'll have to help me get an abortion.'

Harry pulled away so suddenly I fell backwards on the bed and lay there awkwardly as he said in an ominously quiet voice, 'I won't help you get rid of my kid. I've told you what I want to do. I'll marry you and we'll have the baby, but if you think I'm not good enough for you that's it. If you want an abortion you're on your own.'

I ran crying from the flat and Harry made no attempt to follow, nor did he try to get in touch with me again.

For the next two weeks I spent hours in bed, feeling sorry for myself. At times I felt so angry with Harry, blaming him for what had happened to me. He had said condoms were a hundred percent safe. When had it happened? Perhaps it was that night when he was jealous about me going to the Leavers' Dinner with Anthony. We had certainly made love a lot of times.

At other times I missed him and wanted to be back in his arms, wanted him to love me still. I missed his warmth and adoration and the excitement I had felt being with him, but really I knew our brief and frantic affair was over. Despite my confused feelings I was sure of one thing; I definitely did not want to have a baby. Every day I was conscious of it growing inside my body like some cancerous growth, and all I felt was panic. If I didn't do something soon it would be too late, but I didn't have the money to pay for an abortion, or even know how to go about finding a doctor who would do it.

Finally I told my parents.

We were eating our evening meal when my mother said impatiently, 'You're just picking at your food Sonya and I made that casserole because it's one of your favourites. You haven't been eating very well these past weeks. Aren't you feeling well?'

This was enough to cause me to burst into tears and blurt out between sobs, 'No, I'm not feeling well. I'm pregnant.'

Both of my parents stared at me with shocked looks on their faces.

My mother recovered first demanding, 'Who's the father? Surely not Anthony. He's such a nice boy.'

With tears streaming down my face I sobbed, 'No it's not Anthony. You wouldn't want to know who the father is, and that doesn't matter anyway. I want an abortion. I just want to get rid of this thing that's growing inside me. Mum, Daddy, you've got to help me.'

My mother stared at me coldly, before saying in her iciest voice, 'Don't talk about a baby in that way. And don't think for a minute your father and I will help you kill a child. No, we'll have to think of a way for you to have it so that no-one will know.'

I screamed hysterically at her, 'Didn't you hear what I said. I want an abortion. It's not a child inside me, it's a foetus, and I want it gone. If you don't help me I'll kill myself.'

With that I ran to my bedroom where I lay sobbing on the bed until the doona was soaked and I fell into an exhausted sleep.

Later I was woken to a gentle tap on her door, and my father came into the room.

Without switching on the light he made his way to the bed and pulled me into his arms saying, 'Oh my precious, I'm so sorry this has happened to you.'

I snuggled into him as I had as a small child, feeling the love and comfort he had always given me.

'We'll find a way to work things out. Your mother feels very strongly about abortions because she had so many miscarriages. She can't understand how anyone would willingly destroy a potential life.'

I had known in a vague sort of way my mother had lost babies and that was why there were no brothers or sisters. I even half remembered being woken late one night, and a fast ride to the hospital with my mother groaning in the front seat. Because I had only been about eight at the time I hadn't really understood what was happening. A few days later my mother returned from the hospital, looking frail and pale. Dad told me that I must be very good because my mother was sad about losing another baby.

Remembering this I understood a bit why my mother was so against abortions, but surely I could make my father understand that my circumstances were totally different

I pleaded desperately, 'But this is my body, not hers. She wanted babies and I don't, certainly not yet. Please Daddy help me get rid of it.'

He held me closer before saying, 'Your mother's idea is for you to go to France for a year. She has an old school friend living in Provence. You could stay with her until the baby is born and then have it adopted. We would tell everyone you are having a gap year to improve your French and see a bit of Europe.'

I listened patiently although there was no way I was going to go along with my mother's plan. I knew I could manipulate my father if I stayed calm. He had always been so doting, and we were close, but could I convince him to go against my mother?

Taking a deep breath I said with calmness I wasn't feeling, 'Daddy, I do understand where Mum is coming from, but I'm not her. I don't want to sneak off to France to have a baby. I'm only seventeen and my life's just beginning. I want to go to university, not hide away in some French village getting fat and out of shape while I wait to give birth to a baby I don't want. Please Daddy, help me to have an abortion.'

He patted my hand saying, 'I'll see what I can do,' before kissing my forehead, gently easing me back into bed and covering me with the doona.

For the next few days my mother barely spoke to me, and Dad was very quiet in the evenings when he came home from work. My parents usually never argued, but one night I woke to hear raised voices coming from their bedroom.

In the morning my mother said to me in a cold, hard voice, 'Well Miss, you're getting your own way. Your father has made an appointment for you to go to a private clinic so you can have done what you want. He'll have to go with you though, because I certainly won't.'

A few days later my father accompanied me to the clinic where a genial white-haired gentleman examined me.

Afterwards he said cheerfully, 'It's early days yet so there shouldn't be any problems.'

I was then taken into another room by a friendly plump nurse who handed me a blue hospital gown to change into and helped me up onto a narrow gurney. The nurse wheeled me into a stark white room where a man put a needle in my hand and told me to count backwards from ten.

When I woke I was lying on a bed in a small bright room and my father was seated by the window.

As soon as I opened my eyes he came over to the bed, an anxious look in his kind blue eyes, 'How are you feeling precious?' he asked.

I smiled at him, 'A bit sore down below, but I suppose that's to be expected. The main thing I'm feeling is relief that it's over. Thank you Daddy. I know this has been hard for you.'

He kissed my cheek saying, 'I really do think it's for the best, but your mother certainly doesn't feel that way. I reckon we'll both pay for this.'

His words proved to be prophetic. From that time my mother behaved less affectionately towards my father, and she never let me forget what I had done. In many subtle and not so subtle ways she made me feel I had let her down; was no longer the daughter of whom she had been so proud.

She made me feel so bad about what I'd done I spent the next years trying to please her; trying to make amends for having gone against her wishes by aborting the baby.

I know people who met me during those years saw someone who had it all. I was good-looking, clever and popular, the only daughter of wealthy doting parents, but I felt I was living a charade. I lived constantly with feelings of guilt about disappointing my mother, and also for causing the coolness that now existed between my parents, for Mum never forgave my father for going against her wishes. Sometimes I even felt badly about the haughty way in which I had treated Harry's genuinely loving proposal. I knew he had really cared for me, and was sad about the way our love affair had ended.

Although initially I felt nothing but relief after aborting the baby, or the foetus as I chose to think it at the time, my mother's attitude led me to see what I had done in a different light. Instead of decreasing, my feelings of guilt about the abortion increased, fuelled by my mother's unrelenting disapproval. At times I wished for a more independent life away from my mother's watchful eyes, but the need to regain my mother's approval was strong. Outwardly I was once again the perfect daughter, but inwardly I longed for escape. Often I thought how comforting it must be for Catholics who could confess their sins and be forgiven.

I have taught at Bridmore all my working life and progressed from teaching French throughout the school and English to the senior girls, to Vice Principal, and now to Principal.

Initially I accepted the invitation to teach at this exclusive girls' school to please my mother who had said, 'If you must teach, at least there you will have pupils who come from good homes, girls who should know how to behave.'

I couldn't help but feel there was yet another sting in this remark: a reminder of my poor behaviour.

During the years I actually discovered that as much emotional cruelty and neglect can take place behind the doors of mansions as those of poorer houses. My girls can face the same problems as those from lower socio-economic backgrounds. After teaching at the school for so long I know every one of the three hundred and fifty girls in my charge; have watched over them as they change from shy little preps to vibrant young women.

Over time I have developed a sixth sense for knowing if any one of them is troubled. When this happens I call them into my office for a quiet talk. They trust me, and through the years I have provided comfort and support to many girls who are unhappy because they are being bullied or rejected by their classmates. When I hear of incidences of bullying I talk quietly to the guilty parties about showing kindness and consideration to others. The girls leave my office suitably chastened and invariably change their ways. Since becoming friends with Emma she has never alluded to the way in which my gang and I made her life a misery by our constant bullying, but I know it took a long time for her to forgive me. Because of my own past behaviour I am constantly on the lookout for any incidences of bullying in my school, and deal severely with the culprits.

I have also had girls come to me seeking help on how to break the news to parents about an unwanted pregnancy. In this latter situation I go to the home of the girl to help her tell her parents what has happened and to hopefully lead the way for a practical and calm discussion of the problem.

Sometimes one of the more senior girls will come to my office, seeking advice on how to cope with a situation involving a boy; will admit to wanting to have sex or to having "gone all the way". My affair with Harry has given me an understanding of what they are going through so I don't preach at them. I do tell them in a matter of fact way about the importance of having self-respect, of behaving in a way that is true to oneself. I assure them I understand how strong these feelings seem to be, but that sexual desires should be controlled until a relationship based on companionship and trust develops. Most important of all the girl should do what she knows is right for her, and not what the boy in question insists on.

At times I know, even before the girl leaves the room, that my words have fallen on deaf ears, but on other occasions I think and hope I have had an influence.

After these sessions I think about my brief time with Harry and sometimes wonder if anyone would have been able to convince me I should have stopped seeing him and not had sex with him. At the time I was so totally besotted I rather doubt anyone could have talked sense into me.

Chapter Eighteen

My affair with Harry and the resultant pregnancy had aroused other emotions besides those of guilt. Our lovemaking had awakened my body to pleasures and feelings I hadn't previously experienced.

When I returned to the clinic a week after the abortion for a check-up the genial old doctor gave me a clean bill of health.

He then wrote me out a prescription for the pill saying cheerfully, 'We don't want to see you back here again, do we?'

Although, at the time, I had felt mildly insulted by the doctor's comment as the months passed and I began dating boys who I met at university I had the prescription filled.

During the next few years I had a few brief affairs, but none of them gave me the pleasure or excitement I had felt with Harry. Although he had called himself my "bit of rough", he had never been a rough or violent lover. He had been tender and adoring as well as very passionate and experienced. Compared with him, the boys I now dated were often gauche and awkward and failed to arouse or pleasure me in the way he had. At times I thought wistfully about the times we'd spent together and wondered how long our affair would have lasted if I hadn't got pregnant. Realistically though I knew it would have ended because the worlds we came from and our expectations from life were just too different.

I met David at the end of my third year at university when he came home from ANU for the holidays. His parents had moved into their enormous mansion six months earlier.

During the previous months everyone in the neighbourhood had watched the house slowly rising from the ground and marvelled at its size. It spread across the top of the hill that overlooked our leafy, secluded suburb. All of the nearby houses were large, built on one or two acre blocks and surrounded by well-maintained gardens, but they did not compare with this new addition either in size or opulence.

Rumours concerning the identity of the owners ran riot for months. Some said it was being built for a popular Australian singer, while others had heard that it belonged to a certain film star who planned to use it as a base when she was not in Hollywood. Nearest to the truth was the one that the occupants were Indians of royal blood who had made their wealth by importing spices into Australia.

When big Barney Phillips began making regular trips to see how the house was progressing he often stopped at the local hotel for a beer before making the trip to the airport. The rumour mongering stopped. Everyone knew about Barney. He and his beautiful Indian wife frequently appeared in the social pages of newspapers and magazines, and his generosity towards several charitable causes was well known. He owned the biggest haulage fleet in Australia, and was known throughout the country as a highly successful self- made man

Once the house was completed Barney and his wife moved in, and he immediately joined the local golf club, the tennis club and Rotary. Although he was a slow-moving, heavily-boned man he was deceptively effective on the tennis court because he analysed his opponents' play and anticipated where they would put the ball. He also had a killer serve. On the golf course he was equally effective, and in Rotary was always the first person to volunteer to help with any proposed fundraiser.

In a very short time he became a popular and familiar figure in the community.

The same could not be said of his wife. She didn't accompany her husband either to golf or tennis. Barney said his wife was "not into sport." According to the grapevine she was either recovering from a nervous breakdown, of royal blood and therefore very snobbish, or simply not very outgoing.

Sometimes she and Barney were to be seen at The Pines, a very expensive restaurant overlooking the bay. She came with him to the social events organised by Rotary looking gloriously exotic in beautiful silken saris, but seemed withdrawn and shy. Apart from these occasions she was rarely seen in public.

In a short time my father, Edward, and Barney became good friends. Both men were members of Rotary and also keen golfers. Often Barney came back to the house with my dad after a game of golf, and they shared a beer while recounting each hole and the mistakes that either one or the other had made.

My mother, an inveterate snob, longed to get to know the so-called princess, and eventually prevailed upon my long-suffering father to invite Barney and his wife, Indira, to dinner. Mother was jubilant when they accepted and made sure all her friends knew about this social coup.

The evening went well. During the meal Barney told of how he and Indira met. She had come to Australia to visit her sister and brother-in-law who had immigrated two years earlier to manage the Australian side of his family's import business.

Barney laughingly said, 'She was meant to go back and marry some bloke who her parents had picked out for her. The minute I clapped eyes on her I knew she was the one for me. I wooed her until I wore her down.'

Indira smiled shyly and said, 'He certainly would not take no for an answer. My parents were very upset, but in time they agreed and it has been right.'

She looked lovingly across the table at her big, beaming husband.

He grinned, 'Yep, we've been married for over thirty years and to me she's still the most beautiful woman in the world.'

As the evening progressed Indira relaxed and talked fondly of their two married daughters in Sydney and of their son David, who was studying economics at the university in Canberra. When Marjorie asked why they have chosen to move to Tasmania Indira seemed uncomfortable, and looked to her husband to answer.

'We wanted a bit of peace and quiet, away from the hurly burly of Sydney,' Barney explained. 'I'd been in this neck of the woods on a couple of fishing trips. It seemed like a good place to grow old in, and I can run my business from anywhere.'

The conversation turned to business and of how computerisation had simplified so many aspect of commercial life. Barney explained how computers were now used to determine routes and timetables, besides the more obvious task of working out the pay cheques for his numerous full-time and part-time drivers. Because of this technology he could keep his finger on the pulse of his vast empire from a distance. He only needed to return to Sydney for the occasional meetings with his management team, and Indira would accompany him on these trips to catch up with their daughters.

I came home from an evening out with friends to find my parents and their guests chatting away happily.

My mother looked happily flushed and said, 'Ah, here's our beautiful daughter. You know Barney, and this is his wife Indira. Sonya's in her final year of an Arts Degree.'

As I held Indira's small brown hand in mine I looked into her luminous dark eyes and saw sadness lurking there despite the smiling mouth. I wondered if the rumours about her having had a nervous breakdown could be true and, if so, what could have caused it.

After that evening the two couples began to dine regularly together, either at one of their homes or at a restaurant. Occasionally the two women met for coffee, and my mother introduced Indira to friends in the neighbourhood. She was charming and gracious in their company but declined invitations to join the bridge and tennis clubs. She seemed to prefer to keep to herself, and many of the women thought her snobbish. My mother, who enjoyed the kudos of being Indira's only real friend, said she was just shy.

Indira and Barney's son David was due home a few days before Christmas. They invited my parents and me to their place to meet him, and to join them for a barbecue and swim.

We were all out the back of the house, seated in the gazebo overlooking the enormous green pool that curved around large boulders and had a waterfall at one end.

I'd been for a swim, and was wrapping a sarong around my wet body before joining the others for a drink when I heard the back door slide open. Standing at the door was a slim brown young man dressed in jeans and a red shirt. His shiny black hair almost reached his shoulders and framed a beautiful face. Clearly this was Indira's son for he had the same luminous eyes, small straight nose and curved mouth.

He looked towards me and put a finger to his smiling lips before walking quietly to the gazebo. From the side of the pool I saw him creep behind his mother and put his hands over her eyes, before bending to kiss the top of her head.

Indira turned, a look of pure joy on her face. She stood to embrace him before saying, 'Marjorie, Edward, this is our son. Sonya come and meet my David.'

After David had shaken hands with us all Barney lumbered to his feet and gave him a bear hug before declaring, 'This calls for champagne. Sit down son and I'll go and get it.'

He soon returned from the bar area at the back of the gazebo with a magnum of champagne and glasses. We sat around toasting David's return, Christmas, success for both David and me in the exams we had both just completed and good health to everyone.

While we talked and drank Barney cooked steaks and jacket potatoes on the barbecue. Indira brought out a huge bowl of salad and we ate around the table in the gazebo, drinking a second magnum Barney had insisted on opening.

By the time the evening was over we were all more than a little drunk, so my parents and I opted to walk home and collect dad's car in the morning. Years later I still remember enjoying that walk down the hill and along the dark streets; my arm linked in my father's and my mother on his other side. It was the first time we had felt like a family again, the way we had when I was young, the way we had been before the abortion. Unfortunately this feeling didn't last because my mother never forgave me for having the abortion and continually made remarks that made me feel guilty about my decision. I didn't really regain my mother's approval until I married for the first time and even then it was only temporary.

That summer David and I became close friends. I took him along to the tennis club and introduced him to my friends. We were both good players, and soon became an unbeatable pair when we partnered each other in the friendly competitions that were held at the club throughout the summer.

When not at the club we spent lazy afternoons around his parents' pool, swimming, drinking, talking and reading. Other days we drove to scenic places David had heard about but never seen. We'd stop on the way for lunch in little country pubs, or buy bread and cheeses and pates and have picnic lunches beside a creek or in a rainforest.

I had never known anyone quite like David. I was fascinated by his strangeness, by how different he was from any of the other boys I had met. At the same time I sensed that he was familiar. He felt this too, and we joked that we had known each other in another life; perhaps we had been brother and sister or husband and wife.

During that summer I told my mother I had enrolled to do a Graduates Diploma in Education. I had been putting it off because I knew my mother wanted me to do something more glamorous and high-profile than teaching.

I waited until Dad was at golf so he would not be drawn into the argument I was anticipating. We were sitting on the sunny verandah that overlooked the garden drinking a mid-morning cup of tea when my mother gave me the opening by asking about my plans for the coming year.

Tentatively I said, 'I've enrolled to do a Diploma of Education so that I can teach French at one of the high schools. I absolutely love the language and would enjoy sharing it with other young people.'

My mother raised a well-shaped eyebrow and said, 'What! You plan to become a teacher? You don't even like children.'

I said defensively, 'What makes you think that? I like kids. I've enjoyed tennis coaching with some of the young ones at the club and I get on well with them.'

'What a facile thing to say. Of course you don't really like children. Anyone who could get rid of a child doesn't really value them.'

I had been expecting this sort of answer but still felt tears filling my eyes and turned away from my mother's baleful stare. When would she stop reminding me? And more importantly why did I continue to let her disapproval affect me so much? I wiped away the tears. I knew I could try to explain as I had so often before that to me it wasn't a child, but a thing that would have ruined my life but I was tired of going over and over the same ground. As I stood to leave I said, 'No matter what you think I'm sure I'll be a good teacher and that's what I'm going to do.

Always determined to have the last word my mother came back with, 'Well you didn't think you were fit to be a mother so I don't see why you think you're cut out to be a teacher.'

The day after that argument with my mother about my plan to teach, I was still upset. When David asked me what was wrong, I finished up telling him about the abortion and how it changed my relationship with my mother and also damaged my parents' marriage..

He was very sympathetic and said, 'Oh I know what you are going through. I too did something that upset my mother, and since then I feel so responsible for her happiness. We are both adults and shouldn't let them make us feel this way, but it's hard not to. It's hard to lose the approval of a parent when you've had it all your life.'

I felt that sharing these feeling had brought us even closer together.

As the summer progressed and vacation time was coming to an end I began to dread the thought of not seeing David for many months. He was returning to ANU to do a Master in Business Administration, and would not be back again until the following summer.

After he left I cried in my bedroom. He had promised to ring me regularly and we would see if we could catch up during the year, but I didn't think we would. I told myself that ours was a good friendship, not a love affair. Of course I would miss him, but would see him again next year.

My problem was I felt I was in love with him, even though nothing sexual had taken place between us. I had wondered at times why David never showed anything more than a brotherly sort of affection towards me, for sometimes he had looked at me with desire in his beautiful dark eyes. Could his reticence about close physical contact be because of his Indian parentage and upbringing or was he simply shy. Perhaps I should have kissed him passionately when he had given me a brotherly peck on the lips after a night out, or signalled in some other way how much I wanted us to be more than friends. I consoled myself that the year would soon pass and I would see how things worked out when we met again.

That year I worked hard and enjoyed the weeks of practical teaching. I knew from my experience in front of a class that I had chosen a career for which I was suited, despite what my mother said.

During the year, Emma and I became friends with Jenny who had completed her degree at the art school. The three of us studied together in Emma's little flat, and commiserated with each other about various problems we encountered in the classroom during practical teaching weeks.

At the beginning of the year we went out together every Friday night, but soon Jenny wasn't able to make it sometimes if Don had other plans. Emma's boyfriend Bruce was more understanding about the need for girls' time, and often came to take us home after our evening out.

Despite my quiet yearning for David I had a couple of affairs during that year. One was with a married professor, but I ended that abruptly when he started talking about leaving his wife.

The other was with a man who I met at a pub. Something about him reminded me of Harry. Later I thought that might have been why I was attracted to him, for one's first love does leave an imprint. His name was Bob, and he was big and dark and powerful looking. As with Harry, the sex was exciting, but I was now twenty-two not seventeen, and expected more from a relationship than just sex. He didn't read, only went to horror or action movies, and his conversation was limited to what had happened on the building site at work or what we would eat when we went out to dinner.

When I broke up with him he became threatening. I was glad we had only always met at bars or his flat so he didn't know where I lived.

During the year David and I spoke fairly regularly on the phone. We talked about our studies and of shows and films we had seen. At times we made plans about what we would do the following summer.

I didn't tell David about my two lovers. In a strange way I felt almost as though I had been unfaithful to him. Even though there was nothing between us but friendship I very much hoped that, in time, this would change. I didn't want to say anything to put him off and looked forward to seeing him once the university year ended.

Chapter Nineteen

It was the end of the academic year and I was sitting in the back garden reading when he suddenly appeared around the side of the house. He was dressed in white chinos and a white shirt. As he walked across the lawn the sight of him almost took my breath away. During the months we had been apart I had forgotten just how beautiful he was.

He pulled me to my feet and held me in a long embrace saying softly, 'Oh, I have missed you. Seeing you again makes me realise just how much.'

I lifted my face to his and we kissed, really kissed, for the first time.

That summer we were inseparable. We did all the things we had done the previous year, but now when we picnicked in quiet and beautiful places we made love slowly and passionately in the sunshine. After dinner at the club or in a restaurant we often had uncomfortable sex in his car, and laughed together about the discomfiture of these couplings.

David was to spend the next year in Sydney to gain first hand knowledge of his father's business. We bid each other a tearful farewell, promising to meet as often as possible during the year.

Shortly after David moved to Sydney I took up my position at Bridmore. There I was to teach English in the senior school and French to all grades from threes to matriculants. It was the first year French was to be taught to juniors and proved to be a very heavy workload.

During the year David made three brief visits home, and I flew to Sydney on several occasions, often to partner him at social functions to which David had been invited. For the first time we could make love in a comfortable bed, as David now had a very nice apartment overlooking the harbour. On Sunday mornings we would lie in bed kissing, fondling and stroking each other for hours ending with a final frantic coupling. Our weekends always ended with a rushed trip to the airport and a sad farewell.

Those weekends were the happiest times of that year for me and I missed David when I returned home, but I had a lot to keep me occupied. Although I was enjoying teaching, there was so much work involved in preparing lessons for such a wide age range and a considerable amount of marking. I also spent many happy evenings with Jenny, Emma and Nina discussing the bridesmaids' dresses we would wear at Jenny's wedding in June, and later attending fittings before going out for dinner or drinks.

When Emma married Bruce at the end of the year his little sister and I were the bridesmaids. Jenny was pregnant so felt she could not be part of the entourage. By the time of the wedding she was beginning to show so wore a colourful floaty gown to hide "the bump."

Amidst much jostling and hilarity I caught the bride's bouquet.

I heard one of the old aunts say, 'It's just as well she caught it. You know what they say. Three times a bridesmaid never a bride.'

I smiled to myself about the remark, but that night as I lay in bed I wondered if David would ever propose marriage. He constantly told me he loved me and felt I was his soul mate. Despite these protestations I always had the feeling he was holding something of himself back, that there was a part of him I would never know, could never touch.

That Christmas a tragic event occurred.

Barney and my father were playing golf when Barney complained of a headache.

Jokingly Dad had said, 'Are you going to use that as an excuse when I beat you?' Then he'd looked at his friend's face and said anxiously, 'Gee mate, you're not looking too good. I think we'd better get you to the clubhouse.'

He was half carrying his heavy friend across the greens when Barney slumped to the ground, seemingly unconscious. Dad immediately rang for an ambulance on his mobile phone. The paramedics, who arrived promptly, placed his friend on a stretcher, muttered something that sounds like "stroke" and sped off, sirens wailing.

Dad followed the ambulance, but lost it in the busy traffic. By the time he had parked his car and walked to the hospital Barney had disappeared into its labyrinthine depths. It took him over an hour, and several conversations with receptionists and nurses, before he managed to see the admitting doctor.

When he asked about his friend the rather harried doctor replied curtly, 'Mr. Phillips has had a stroke that has paralysed one side of his body. He is currently receiving treatment that will hopefully lessen the effects of the stroke. It is too soon to tell how he will be in the long term. We need to have his wife sign some papers, in case we have to perform any further medical procedures, so if you could notify her of what's happened and bring her in it would be appreciated.'

Dad drove up to the big house on the hill, dreading what he had to do. He knew, from the odd things Barney had told him that Indira had a nervous breakdown the year before they moved, and that she was still not very strong emotionally.

As soon as she saw him she guessed something was wrong with her husband.

He told her what had happened straight away, assuring her Barney was getting the best possible treatment. She sobbed, shaking in his arms, and he wished he had stopped on the way to get my mother. She would have known what to do. He led Indira to a couch, poured two large brandies, and explained to her the little he knew while encouraging her to drink. He quickly finished off his own drink, finding the warming alcohol helped steady his own shaken nerves.

Later he drove Indira to the hospital, and stayed with her while she filled in the innumerable forms that were presented to her. They were allowed to take a quick look into the room where Barney lay, still and silent, looking as white as the hospital sheet that covered him. The nurse quickly shushed them out and told them to come back in the morning.

On the return trip this time Dad collected my mother. She soothed Indira's fears, helped her to bed and stayed with her until she slept. My father then phoned David and the daughters to tell them what had happened, and offered to meet them at the airport once they knew their flight times.

The following morning my mother took Indira to the hospital, and I went with Dad to the airport to pick up David and his sisters, who had all managed to get on an early flight from Sydney.

I hadn't ever met the sisters, but knew that one lived in the Blue Mountains with her husband and two children and the other was a highly qualified nursing sister working in Sydney. David had never actually described them to me, but I had imagined they would look something like Indira. As I watched the three siblings walking across the tarmac I almost laughed in surprise to see David flanked by two tall blonde women who were female versions of Barney. Obviously he inherited his mother's genes and they their father's.

They both also had their father's easy warmth, and hugged my father and me before asking anxiously about their father. As we drove to the hospital Daddy filled them in on what had happened.

After listening carefully to his description of the event Rose, who is the nurse, said comfortingly, 'It sounds as if you got medical help quickly, and that's very important with a stroke. And Dad's basically as strong as an ox. I'm sure he'll be right again in no time'

When we arrived at the hospital and were shown to Barney's room we were relieved to see that Barney was awake, but were all shocked by his appearance. On the left side of his face his eye and mouth drooped, giving him an evil, slightly devilish look. When he tried to speak his words were slurred and difficult to understand, but he smiled lopsidedly at the sight of his big blonde daughters and slim dark son.

Rose's early assessment proved to be overly optimistic. In a short time Barney's face returned to normal and he could speak clearly again, but it took six months of fairly intensive therapy before he had regained the full strength in his left hand. It was even longer before he could walk properly without dragging his left leg. David moved back from Sydney and took over running the business from his parents' home.

Shortly after his move back David asked me to marry him, and, of course, I accepted happily. Together we found a delightful house on a large bush block some distance from town and the homes of our parents. David had enough for the deposit and his father lent him the remainder.

All of our parents were thrilled that we were getting married but more particularly my mother. For the first time since the abortion I felt I was doing something of which she approved.

Indira was equally happy and gave me an exquisite diamond and ruby necklace saying shyly, 'It is the custom in my family for the mother of the groom to give a gift of jewellery to her future daughter-in-law. I am so pleased you and David are to wed. I am sure all will be well for you two.'

She looked so intense I felt my shy little future mother-in-law was almost willing happiness upon us.

My mother and Indira spent months discussing possible venues, deciding on the menu and selecting musicians for the reception and flowers for the church. David and I were happy to let them arrange it all for we could see how much pleasure it was giving both mothers.

I would have dearly loved to have had Jenny and Emma as my attendants, but Emma was pregnant and Jenny still breast-feeding and feeling out of shape. Neither felt they could look sufficiently glamorous to be part of my wedding party. They assured me they would be there to wish me well from the sidelines.

In the end my bridesmaids were girls with whom I had gone to school and whose mothers were part of my mother's social set. David's best man and groomsman, Josh and Alex, had been fellow students at ANU. They are both big good-looking bachelors who set hearts fluttering among the local girls during their brief stay before the wedding.

David and I only had time for a short honeymoon on Norfolk Island. For me the school year was due to commence and David was needed to help his father. Barney hadn't yet regained his full vigour and confidence so was still very reliant on his son.

We promised each other we would have a belated honeymoon at the end of the year, perhaps in Europe or India. Neither of us had travelled, and during that year together we spent many evening reading various guidebooks, trying to decide where we would go.

I now prefer to forget that year. Sometimes little things will spark a memory of that time, and I feel again the same confusion and hurt I experienced then.

Initially all seemed to be wonderful. At last David and I could spend every evening together. It was a novelty for me to finally be living away from home, away from the critical eyes of my mother. Although David had lived in college housing in Canberra and an apartment in Sydney, this was the first time he had owned his own home. We both gloried in the freedom and privacy we now had, and the lack of neighbours nearby increased that feeling.

During the week we cooked exotic meals together, laughing over the strange dishes we invented. We rarely invited friends to join us at weekends, preferring to spend our mornings lying entwined in bed until noon, wandering hand in hand over our small acreage, and then cooking the evening meal together before luxuriating in the hot tub on our deck and drinking champagne.

I was completely and utterly in love with David and thought he felt the same way about me. We had always been so comfortable together, had felt a kinship and familiarity with each other from the time we first met, and this remained unchanged. What did change were my expectations with regard to sex. I had thought we would make love frequently once we were married and could share a bed every night. In this I was disappointed. Most nights David kissed me and ran his hands over my body lovingly, but then said a fond goodnight and fell asleep leaving me aroused and frustrated.

Although I was nearly twenty-five I wasn't very experienced sexually; had only had three long-term lovers. Both Harry and Bob had wanted sex every time I'd been with them. Even the professor, who was an older man, had made love to me at least three times a week.

I began to wonder if there was something wrong with David or was I just oversexed? I certainly couldn't discuss this problem with my mother, and my best friends and I had never talked much about sex. Eventually I decided I wouldn't let this one thing spoil our life together.

During that year Barney's health continued to improve, but he had developed a fear that he might have another stroke. As a result of this he was unwilling to fly, fearing the vulnerability of being distanced from quick medical assistance. Because of this David continued to make the monthly trips to Sydney for meetings with the management team. Occasionally I went with him and we'd have dinner and see a show or catch up with some of David's friends. Usually David went alone, saying he had business meetings lined up and I would be bored.

Once he returned from Sydney with several dark bruises on his body. He told me he and his friends had been set upon by a group of thugs. I was naturally concerned and asked if they had reported the incident to the police, but David answered evasively, 'No, we were just in the wrong place at the wrong time. It won't happen again.'

Something about the way he looked when he said this bothered me, but I didn't question him further as he obviously didn't want to talk about it. I thought he and his friends were probably at some strip joint or one of those places where they have lap dancers, and he knew I wouldn't have approved.

We had been married for nearly a year, and planned to spend the six weeks' vacation I would have from school travelling around Europe. Our flights to Paris were booked and accommodation arranged for four nights in one of the most expensive hotels in the city. We had also booked a hire car in which we planned to travel where the spirit took us. We spent many happy evenings pouring over maps and working out distances.

Shortly before the end of the year Alex phoned to say he would be in the area, and would like to catch up with us. David was delighted, as he hadn't seen him since the wedding, and I thought it would be nice to get to know this friend of David's better.

Together we aired out the guest bedroom and made up the bed. This would be the first time we had had a guest to stay, and we both felt quite excited about it. David said Alex was a big eater so we shopped for huge steaks to barbecue, a chicken to roast and lots of vegetables and fruit as well as cheeses and several bottles of really good wine.

Alex's plane was due to arrive at one thirty and he had organised to pick up a hire car at the airport. When I got home from school the two men were already ensconced happily on the deck drinking wine and eating biscuits and cheese.

As I walked up the steps Alex stood and came towards me saying, 'Lovely to see you again Sonya. How's married life with this ruffian been treating you?'

I had forgotten how tall he was, and was conscious of him towering over me as we shook hands before I said, 'Life's good and it's nice to see you again. You'd better hide out though. You left a couple of broken hearts behind last time you were here.'

He grinned wickedly, 'I don't know about broken hearts, but there was one girl who got my phone number and called me for months. I finished up getting it changed to get rid of her?'

I smiled, 'Well don't blame me. I didn't even know your number. Perhaps David gave it to her.'

David protested his innocence then changed the subject saying, 'Alex is here in search of oil. He'll tell you all about it while I get the steaks ready.'

He left us after pouring a wine for me and topping up their nearly empty glasses.

Although I had scarcely got to know Alex during those hectic days leading up to the wedding I now found him easy company. When David returned with the marinated steaks, a big bowl of salad and a crusty French loaf we were engrossed in a conversation about the impact of mining on the environment.

Hearing the tail end of their conversation David interjected, 'I hope she's not giving you too hard a time about damaging the environment. Sonya's a greenie from way back. If she had her way there wouldn't be another tree chopped down on this fair island.'

Alex winked at me. 'I think you're being a bit hard on her there. We actually agree that there are some spots in the state where mining could be carried out, without being a threat to the forests. Fortunately the places where oil is most likely to be found are fairly barren areas in the central highlands, or others of sparse sclerophyll forests on the east coast.'

The evening continued pleasantly. The conversation flowed easily and Alex was complimentary about the meal and admiring of our house. After we said goodnight to him and went to our room David surprised me by making long, passionate and very satisfying love to me.

When I thought about this later I remembered how I had foolishly thought that perhaps the presence of another man, who obviously enjoyed my company, had made David jealous.

The next morning I woke with a dull ache between my eyes. I felt quite out of sorts as I waved goodbye to the two men, then drove the twenty odd kilometres to my school.

Before the first lesson for the day I went to the staff room and took a couple of painkillers, but by the end of class I knew this was not an ordinary alcohol-induced headache. I was beginning to experience the flashing lights and zigzags which I knew were the precursors to a migraine, and if I didn't go home soon I wouldn't be able to drive. After giving a hurried explanation to the Principal, who assured me she would reorganise her classes, I drove home.

I had expected to see the men on the deck, but they weren't there. When I opened the front door the house was silent so I assumed they must be somewhere outside. I walked into the bedroom to be confronted by the horrifying sight of David spreadeagled on the bed with Alex on top of him. Both men were naked from the waist down.

I screamed in disgust at the sight of Alex abusing my husband and rushed to David's aid screaming, 'Get off him, get off my David,' while I swung my handbag at his head.

Alex pulled himself away, but I continued to hit him yelling all the while, 'You filthy animal. What were you doing to him?'

David turned over and said simply, 'It's all right Sonya.'

I stared at my husband in horror, not quite able to take in what I was hearing, but knowing my world was falling apart.

With tears streaming down my face I stumbled out of the house and ran blindly into the bush, unmindful of branches scratching my arms as I battered my way through a thicket. My one thought was to get away, to escape from what I had seen and the implications behind David's quiet acceptance of what was being done to him. Eventually I came to a clearing where I threw myself down on the hard ground, and sobbed until I felt as dry and withered as the leaves on which I lay.

David found me there; tried to touch me, but I cringed from him screaming, 'Don't touch me you dirty animal. How could you do that? I thought you loved me.'

He sat on the ground a short distance from me, looking totally distraught, totally lost and totally beautiful as he whispered, 'I do love you. You are the only woman I will ever love.'

I interrupted sarcastically before he could say anything else, 'But I suppose you could love plenty of men. What's wrong with you? Why did you marry me if you want to have sex with men? Have you used me to hide the dirty secret of what you're really like from your family and the rest of the world? Did you have to steel yourself to make love to me? Has it all been pretence?'

I had worked myself into a fury at the disgust I was feeling and couldn't stop crying.

David looked at me and tears filled his dark, luminous eyes as he said quietly, 'I'm so sorry to have hurt you Sonya, but let me say the way I feel about you was never a pretence. I have loved making love to you, loved the smoothness of your body, the feel of your hair tangling across my face, your woman's smell and your softness enfolding me. From the moment we met I felt you were my soul mate, but I held back from showing my love because there is a sickness in me.'

Despite the loathing and bewilderment I was feeling I found myself being swayed to listen to him. He seemed so intense and so sincere, but how could he explain away his behaviour?

'What do you mean by "a sickness" in you?' Is that your way of saying you're homosexual?'

'No, it's not as simple as that.' He sighed deeply before continuing. 'I have always been attracted to women, and I love you in every way a man should love a woman.'

I wanted to interrupt, but stayed silent as he continued. 'The first time with a man it was rape. He was a friend of my father's and he threatened to kill me if I ever told. The next time was at school. My maths teacher offered to give me extra tuition, and I would go to his office after school. I really liked and admired him, and was grateful to him for the extra time he was giving me. When it happened that time it was not really rape. I didn't fight him, and in fact felt a peculiar enjoyment from the feeling of being powerless, of being forced into something over which I had no control.'

'How could you?' I asked, feeling totally bewildered by the things he was telling me.

I knew I must have a looked of disgusted because David answered in a quietly determined voice. 'Please don't judge me Sonya. This is something I don't really understand myself. All I know is that at times I feel an overwhelming need to be dominated in this way.'

He paused as though not knowing how to proceed then continued. 'I told you I had done something that made my mother very unhappy. There was an incident at university, and a faculty member knew of it and informed my parents. It was hearing of this incident that caused my mother to become so depressed she nearly had a complete nervous breakdown.'

I felt anger welling up in me again and sneered 'So you have pretended to be normal, and used me as a front to convince your parents you are.'

He shook his head sadly, 'I know I shouldn't expect you to understand this, but please believe me I didn't use you as a front. I really thought my love for you would help me overcome this sick need that I have'.

I stood up and said savagely, 'Well I can't understand it, and I'll never be able to forget the sight of you and Alex together on our bed. All I feel is disgust for you both.'

With that I turned and walked away, and when I returned to the house thankfully Alex had gone.

That night I slept on the couch in the lounge room. I couldn't stand the thought of using the guest room where Alex had slept and I certainly didn't want to share a bed with David.

In the morning I pretended to be asleep while David moved quietly around the house before leaving early for work. After ringing school to say I had a full blown migraine, which was true, I lay in the darkened room trying to come to terms with all that David had told me. While I could feel sorry for the young David, who had been raped by one predator and manipulated by another, I knew I would never want him to touch me again. I remembered the time he returned from Sydney bruised from what he had said was a fight. Had he been with someone then, someone who had taken advantage of his powerlessness to inflict cruelty as well as lust on him? It all seemed too disgusting to think about.

My migraine lasted three days, and I spent the time on the couch with the curtains drawn, only getting up to make myself the odd cup of tea and to take another tablet. I would hear David return from work each day and hear him moving quietly around the house, but I avoided seeing him.

By Saturday morning the migraine cleared. I felt almost light-headed with relief from the pain and strong enough to face David once more. When I walked into the kitchen he poured me a coffee.

I muttered a perfunctory thank you before sitting on a stool at the breakfast bar and saying, 'We've got to talk.'

David remained standing, looking awkward and uncomfortable.

I blurted out, 'Look David, there's no way I can forget what I saw or forgive you for what happened.'

He said quietly, 'I thought you'd feel like that. I'm so sorry I've hurt and shocked you. I know I can't expect you to really understand, but please believe me; I do love you. I'll make this as easy as possible for you.'

I felt my scarcely controlled anger building, threatening to engulf me like a tidal wave, so took a deep breath before saying sarcastically, 'And how to you plan to make it easy for me? How do I live with this, let alone explain to my parents and friends that you couldn't resist having it off with the occasional man?'

'Look, I know how I've hurt you, but I've talked it over with my father and he's suggested…'

He didn't get any further before I interrupted because I was stunned that he'd discussed this horrific incident with Barney. I screamed at him, 'What! You've talked over what's happened with your father? How could you worry that poor dear man? What did he say?'

David looked distressed, 'Naturally he was upset, but he's known about my problem since that time at university. Back then he sent me off to a psychiatrist and it came out about his friend raping me, so he's been pretty understanding. I think he felt guilty he'd put me at risk. Anyhow I know you won't want me hanging around. Dad's suggested I move back to Sydney and we get a quiet divorce later. We can say we were apart too much.'

'Well that all sounds nice and convenient for you.' I couldn't keep the sarcasm out of my voice and didn't really try.

'It'll be better for you too, and you can keep the house. Dad said he'll give you clear title to it. The main thing he's concerned about is Mum finding out about why we are splitting up and the affect it would have on her.'

I answered furiously, 'So I'm to be bought off. Look, I'll go along with your plan, as much for my parents' sake as for Indira's, but I want no part of this house. As soon as you've moved I'll find somewhere to rent.'

We spent the weekend together, moving around each other quietly like visitors in the sickroom of a terminally ill patient, the sorrow we both feel etched on our faces.

On the Monday morning David put a hand on my arm, but I pushed it away as though I could be infected by his touch.

He said sadly, 'This is the last thing I wanted to happen.'

I answered coldly, 'Well you're the one who destroyed us,' before striding to my car and driving away. I barely made it round the first bend before I had to pull over. I couldn't see the road for the tears streaming down my face.

Chapter Twenty

After David returned to Sydney I moved into a small rental property close to the school. I told family and friends I felt too isolated and lonely in the house David and I had shared. Six months later I filed for divorce, much to my mother's disgust.

'You should have gone with him to Sydney,' she said angrily. 'You'll regret giving him up so easily.'

My father intervened saying, 'Leave the poor girl alone.'

He gave me a long comforting hug after my mother had left to go home, and it occurred to me that possibly he knew the real reason for the break up; that perhaps Barney had confided in him about his son's problem.

Barney visited me shortly after I'd moved into the rental property. Over a cup of tea he talked about David; of what had happened after Indira and he were told about the incident at university.

Shaking his head like a big bewildered bear he said, 'I should have looked out for him better. He was such a beautiful trusting boy, and that made him a vulnerable target.'

It was hard for me to watch this big loving man blame himself for his son's problem and for my unhappiness. I was feeling too raw and angry to want to hear excuses being made for David's behaviour and said angrily, 'You can't blame yourself for how he is now. He's a grown man.'

Disregarding my comment Barney continued, 'I destroyed the man who raped my son, and would have gone after the teacher but found out he had committed suicide the year before. Sonya, I was so eaten up with hatred for those creatures that warped my son my main thoughts were for revenge. Because of this I didn't give either David or Indira the support they needed at the time. I should've made sure David had more counselling, and been there more for my wife."

'Don't beat yourself up,' I told my father-in-law. 'You did the best you could and David's lucky to have you.'

He dropped in often during the following months. We'd have a cup of tea or share a bottle of wine. These were sometimes uneasy visits, but I made him welcome for I knew he was genuinely concerned about me.

Shortly before I filed for divorce Barney offered to organise the sale of the house, and deposit the proceeds into an account for me.

I refused saying, 'I don't want that, and I also want to return the necklace Indira gave me.'

He sighed heavily. 'I think I understand where you're coming from regarding the house and I respect your independence, but please keep the necklace. It would hurt Indira so much if you gave it back.'

Because he looked so sad I bowed to his wishes but locked the necklace away in a box with the marriage certificate. Later I added the divorce papers. From that time the box was left unopened, hidden away in the back of my wardrobe.

Chapter Twenty-one

I met Jeff the year after my divorce was finalised.

A new subdivision was opening up not far from the school. When the agents held an open house of the first one built on the estate I was impressed with the workmanship and very taken with one of the designs, so signed a contract on the day.

During the year I saved rigorously, and my father gave me a few thousand dollars towards the deposit. I moved in at the end of the school year, and was looking forward to having the six weeks in which to buy furniture and start the garden. I had taken nothing but my clothes from the house David and I had shared and had been renting a furnished house. My only possessions were a bed, a television set, some cookware and crockery.

On the first night in my new home I stepped into the shower, looking forward to an early night and a read in bed. The water pooled in the shower base and continued over the lip and onto the floor before I could turn off the tap. I planned to get in touch with the contracting plumber in the morning, but when the toilet overflowed on flushing I rang him straight away. Jeff was the plumber. He came that night, assessed the problem as being caused by builder's rubble blocking an outlet pipe and worked under lights until it was cleared. I was so grateful at having it fixed so promptly I offered him a beer.

He declined saying, 'Better not drink on an empty stomach,' and then I felt badly for having kept him from his dinner. I made him a big pile of toasted cheese sandwiches that he ate with obvious relish, while we sat on my small front deck chatting happily until quite late.

As he is leaving we shook hands and he said casually, 'If you run in to any other problems just give me a call. I'm pretty handy with other things besides plumbing.'

The next week I met him at a nursery where I had been buying some lavender bushes I planned to grow as a front hedge.

While he was helping me load them into my car he asked casually, 'Would you like a hand with getting these into the ground?'

Of course I accepted his offer and we spent a pleasant afternoon planting the shrubs.

Afterwards I cooked us a quick chicken stir-fry while he sat in the kitchen drinking red wine and discussing further possible plans for the garden. We ate the meal sitting side by side at the breakfast bar as I still hasn't bought a dining setting. Later we sat on the deck finishing off a second bottle of wine. He was easy company, talked humorously about problems he had encountered as a plumber but also seemed interested in my work as a teacher. When he said goodnight we shook hands. I liked the feel of his big, firm hand in mine and wondered briefly if he'd try to kiss me.

He pulled away first with an almost shy, 'Well, goodnight. See you around,' before sauntering off down the path.

As I watched him walk away I thought, 'Oh, he's so nice; and he has a lovely bum too.'

This was the first time since the debacle with David that I'd felt even the slightest interest in another man.

A few days later I almost bumped into him as I was leaving the hardware shop. I was loaded down with pieces of timber with which I planned to try and make a bookcase.

He stood before me, his blue eyes crinkling with laughter, 'And what're you going to do with that lot?'
I grinned back, 'Well I seem to remember a friend of mine making quite a passable bookcase out of bricks and boards. I'm in desperate need of somewhere to put my books so I thought I'd give it a go.'

He surveyed the timber critically before saying, 'That's a pretty temporary way of shelving books. Tell you what, I'll come round on Saturday and make you a decent bookcase in exchange for dinner.'

I laughingly agreed and spent the next two days planning what I would cook, surprised by how much I was looking forward to seeing him again.

He arrived early in the afternoon and set himself up in the back yard, after giving me strict instructions I was not allowed to peek until it was finished. I busied myself in the kitchen, cooking a tasty beef casserole and an apple crumble to be served with custard. I had picked him as a man who would like hearty old-fashioned food.

At the end of the afternoon he called me outside to see his handy-work. He had made a really lovely piece, consisting of four shelves separated by gently curving ends.

He had even had time to varnish it although he warned, 'It's still wet but it should be dry enough for us to move inside after dinner.'

Unthinkingly I put my arms around his neck and kissed him before saying, 'Thank you. It's beautiful.'

He mumbled, 'I'm glad you like it,' but I could see the kiss has unsettled him and wondered if I had done the wrong thing. Since the horrible break-up from David I lacked the easy confidence I used to have with regard to the opposite sex.

I had placed a centrepiece of flowers on my new dining table and set it with my best china and some recently acquired crystal glasses. While Jeff was washing his hands I carried the steaming casserole and a platter of vegetables into the room.

He stood at the door, looking down at his slightly grubby jeans and shirt, and then running his hands through his short fair hair as though to tidy it said, 'Gee this is lovely. I feel like a pillock in my work clothes. I should've bought something to change into.'

Seeing his distress I grabbed his hand and pulled him towards the table saying, 'I think you look perfectly lovely. I wouldn't expect you to be Mr. Immaculate when you've been working so hard for me all afternoon. Now sit down, and see what you think of my cooking.'

He enthused about the casserole and said the apple crumble was as good as his mother's. We laughed about culinary failures we'd both had, and he described the disaster he made of the first meal he'd ever cooked for a woman.

'I thought I'd cook roast lamb. I'd watched Mum do it stacks of times and she made it look easy, far easier than it is. Anyhow I finished up with undercooked meat, burnt vegetables and lumpy gravy.' He finished his story with a deprecatory grin. 'Come to think of it that was the last I saw of her.'

I said teasingly, 'Well that's one way to get rid of a woman. I don't think I'll let you cook for me. I'd be looking for some hidden message if the gravy was lumpy or the vegetables burnt.'

'Now I won't ever be able to invite you to my place for a meal in case I mess it up and you get the wrong idea.'

I was enjoying the easy banter, the promise behind our words that we would be seeing each other again. There was a growing feeling of sexual tension between us when our hands touched lightly as I refilled his wine glass.

I hadn't realised how late it had become until Jeff said, 'I think we'd better get that bookcase inside. It should be dry by now, and you wouldn't want it to get rained on. Even light dew could affect the finish.'

We carefully manoeuvred it through the doorways and into the lounge room, and then placed it against the wall where I'd planned it would fit. As I stepped back to admire how it looked I tripped over his foot. He caught me and pulled me towards him. When he kissed me I felt my whole being respond and returned his kiss with a passion that surprised us both.

From that night we spent every weekend and several nights a week together. He took me to his shack in the highlands and introduced me to his favourite sport of fishing. I donned huge waders and cast beside him in the icy waters, trying hard to share the pleasure he felt, but I found it cold and boring.

He came with me to plays and orchestral concerts, but I knew he was frequently bored despite him saying he had enjoyed them.

Although we didn't enjoy the same pursuits, sex between us was amazing. I hadn't been with a man since David and frequently his lovemaking had left me feeling frustrated. He had treated me more like a beautiful work of art to be fondled and caressed than a woman to be possessed.

Sex with Jeff was totally fulfilling and often quite compelling. There were times when we had been out together to see a movie or for drinks with friends, when we barely made it into my house before tearing at each other's clothes and having sex on the floor. Other times we lay in bed making love for hours until we finally slept with his penis still inside me.

Sometimes I thought it was the sex I loved rather than the man himself, but I really did like him. He was kind and capable, and seemed to be comfortable in his own skin in a way David had never been.

After we had been seeing each other for about six months he proposed.

At first I refused, saying it was too soon after my divorce, but he persisted until I finally accepted. I enjoyed being with him so much and thought we would be happy together. He was, after all, so totally different from David.

He bought me a pretty diamond engagement ring and took me to meet his family. They had been told of the engagement and put on a celebratory barbecue where I met his parents, brother and three sisters, as well as the various in-laws and children. I instantly liked his sweet-faced mother, big cheerful father and his older brother who worked as a bricklayer with their father and looked like an older version of Jeff.

His two older sisters were both rounded matronly women who spent much of the afternoon making sure everyone was fed, and that their children behaved. I liked them well enough, but my favourite was Jeff's younger sister Bethany who he introduced as, "the maverick" She was tall like her brothers and father and wore a long cheesecloth dress that showed off her deep tan. She had recently returned from six months in India, and earnestly told me of her plans to train as a mothercraft nurse and then go back to help the poor and orphaned children in that country. It was a happy afternoon and they all made me feel welcome.

The same couldn't be said of the reception Jeff received when I introduced him to my parents and told them of the engagement. My father was great, relaxed and affable, but my mother was very stiff. She questioned Jeff about his work and his family as if he were applying for a job as a servant. She served a formal afternoon tea in the drawing room, using her finest bone china on her best damask cloth with accompanying napkins. I was convinced she had deliberately set out to make Jeff feel uncomfortable, and was proud of the way he remained charming in the face of what I considered my mother's rudeness.

As we drove away Jeff said, 'I really liked your father, but your mother struck me as a hard nut to crack. She made it pretty clear she doesn't see me as a suitable partner for her daughter.'

'Fortunately she doesn't have any say in the matter,' I laughed and felt an unexpected sense of freedom. Had I finally reached the stage where I no longer felt such a strong need to please my mother?

It was a quiet wedding, or at least as quiet as it could be with Jeff's big and boisterous family there. I hadn't wanted another church wedding, so we married at the registry office and had the reception at the golf club. We honeymooned at Cradle Mountain where Jeff enjoyed the fishing, I enjoyed the spa and we both enjoyed the walks, the food and making love in front of a roaring fire while a cold winter wind whistled round outside.

Jeff moved into my house and Bethany moved into Jeff's to keep an eye on things, and to escape the watchful eyes of her parents who didn't approve of her India acquired practices of burning incense and smoking marijuana.

During our first year together we both tried so hard to please one another. Jeff had lived with a woman for several years, but they had broken up three years earlier and since then he had lived alone. Both of us were used to having the freedoms that solo living brings, freedom to eat when hungry, sleep when tired or read in bed for hours without having to worry about disturbing a partner.

Our work patterns were also very different. I worked regular hours, and was used to coming home from school, cooking myself an early dinner and then having the evening clear to catch up with marking or preparation, to watch television or read.

Jeff's working days varied. Sometimes he finished a job early. When this happened he raced home to shower and change before preparing the evening meal and welcoming me home with a warm kiss and a cool white wine.

Other days he might not finish a job until late. He rarely phoned to say he'd be late, but would arrive home tired and dirty and apologetic. I would heat up the meal I had prepared hours before, and worry that it was spoilt.

We both made adjustments, he by trying to work more regular hours and I by working hard during my few free periods so I didn't need to bring work home.

At weekends we compromised. We spent alternate weekends visiting friends, taking trips out to the country and lunching at wayside restaurants or pubs, going out to the theatre or the movies and relaxing round the house on the Sunday.

The other weekends we'd go to Jeff's shack where he spent the time fishing. Initially I had tried my hand at it, mastered the art of casting, and waded alongside him in the icy river. Eventually I gave up trying to share this pastime with Jeff. Instead I prepared big pots of soup or stew to warm him up when he came in cold and happy, then spent the day huddled up to the fire reading. Often I'd think of how much more comfortable I would have been at home.

By the end of that first year the constant need to compromise had become onerous to us both. We began to snap at each other over small things that previously we would have ignored.

One evening I kept the dinner waiting for several hours and when Jeff started explaining about the plumbing problem he'd had I snarled, 'I don't want to hear about another blocked drain or flooded toilet. It's such a bore.'

Jeff responded, 'What you mean is I'm such a bore. I know I'm not as entertaining as those spoilt brats you spend your days with.'

That night we made up in bed but our lovemaking had a desperate edge to it, a desperation fuelled by the growing feeling we both had that it was all too hard.

We stayed together for another year, but had really given up trying to make the marriage work. I no longer went with him on his fishing trips and he no longer accompanied me to events we both knew he wouldn't enjoy. Instead I went with friends and told them Jeff was working late or had been called out on an emergency.

Eventually we sat down, drank a bottle of wine and talked about our life together. I said, 'It seems pointless to continue. We really don't seem to want to spend time together any more. We're two very different people, living separate lives.'

Jeff gave me his lopsided grin I'd always found so appealing and replied, 'Sonya the differences were always there. I always knew you were out of my league, but thought we had enough going for us to make that unimportant.' He shrugged his shoulders and sighed, 'It hasn't worked out. I could never really fit into your life any more than you could fit into mine.'

We opened another bottle of wine, and drank it before going to bed and making passionate love for one last time.

I will always think fondly of Jeff. He really was such a nice man, and although I regret we couldn't make our marriage work my time with him left no emotional scars.

This can't, however, be said of my time with David. I didn't hear from him once he returned to Sydney, but over the years I have seen the occasional photo of him in the social pages of newspapers or women's magazines. For a long time the sight of him looking elegantly handsome with his arm around some glamorous girl filled me with an overwhelming sense of sadness. I would wonder if he had ever sought further help to overcome his "sickness", or had continued to show a false face to the world and the women he squired.

Chapter Twenty-two

As I speed along the road in my little red sports car that I love so much I sing along with the tune playing on my radio. I have spent the morning thinking of the past and made myself thoroughly miserable, but am determined to cheer up. Perhaps I'll buy some new sexy underwear, something black and lacy to please Pierre.

As I turn into the parking area behind the mall I see Jeff's utility driving out. He gives me a wave and a smile and I wave back. I am pleased we have remained friends. Although we don't see each other often we still chat easily when we happen to meet, and one time he introduced me to his wife and their two little boys.

Since meeting Pierre I thought I had put all memories of past loves behind me. Dredging back over the past as I have been doing today is unusual for me. I mutter under my breath, 'It's that damned article that set me off.'

As I push open the heavy glass door I breathe in the subtle perfume that pervades the air in the boutique where I hope I'll find something really glamorous to wear for Pierre tonight. Lately he has seemed a little sad, not quite his usual ebullient self, and I know this is because of my refusal to marry him. I have let Emma and Jenny assume Pierre and I have had problems because of his womanising, but this has not really been fair to him. I preferred to have them believe this of him rather than to try and explain why I refuse to marry him. Neither of them would understand how I can allow my irrational guilt about having an abortion to haunt me still. They know I don't have a very close relationship with my mother so would wonder why I let this woman, who I no longer love or respect, still affect me? My problem is that the guilt she made me feel about having an abortion has stayed with me. I can't get rid of the feeling that because I got rid of one child I don't deserve to have another.

A smartly dressed assistant approaches her, says in an artificially precise voice, 'Can I help you madam?'

I wave her away with what I hope is a winning smile and say, 'I'm not sure what I want, but I'll know it when I see it.'

I look through racks of lace-trimmed teddies, diaphanous negligees, colourful bra and panty sets, not quite sure what I'm looking for, and then I see it. It is rather like the old-fashioned corsets from an earlier era when women forced unwilling flesh into tight undergarments to achieve curves that were not nature endowed. This confection, however, is not designed to torture but to enhance. It is black satin with an overlay of lace and green ribbon lacing down the front. When I try it on and look at myself in the two-way mirror I know it is just what I was looking for. It is outrageously sexy, a little bit tarty, but it flatters my long curvy body and I know Pierre will love it. It will be a nice surprise for him when he undresses me later tonight.

After I have made my purchase I shop for the evening meal. I buy a free-range chicken, beautiful fresh asparagus and strawberries, baby carrots and rich dark cooking chocolate. In the bottle shop I choose a sauvignon blanc to serve with the chicken and a sauterne that I know will complement the chocolate mousse I will make for dessert.

As soon as I arrive home I prepare the mousse, pour it into two elegant crystal bowls, and put them in the refrigerator. I plan to serve them topped with whipped cream and strawberries. It is too early to start cooking the chicken, but I rub it with olive oil, lemon juice and salt and puts slivers of garlic beneath the skin. Later I will stuff it with more garlic, slices of lemon and some thyme, but for now I set it aside.

I want to make this a special evening for Pierre, want to cheer him up. He is being pressured by his family to return to France but he's been putting it off, hoping to get me to change my mind and go with him as his wife.

With the food preparations complete I wander into the lounge room and settle myself on the couch with a book. On the coffee table lies the magazine containing the article that has disturbed me so. I put my book aside and reread the article, trying to understand why I found it so interesting.

I find the part that struck such a resounding cord with me. It is in the last paragraph, put there almost as a tease. It reads, "Sometimes there is a crossover between two worlds. It may be as fleeting as a moment of déjà vu, a feeling of familiarity when meeting someone for the first time or may come in a dream that is particularly memorable."

For many years I had vivid nightmares of being with David in an unfamiliar house sharing a meal with him and a friend. In the nightmare I leave the room and return to see David and his friend mounting the stairway with their arms entwined. For a long time I thought those dreams was my subconscious mind reliving what had been a traumatic event in my life. Now I wonder if these nightmare were actually glimpses into another reality; one where I chose to stay with David and tried but failed to help him overcome his problem.

I have had another recurring dream over the years in which small, demanding children surround me. Instead of waking with a feeling of relief I am sad, and overwhelmed by a sense of loss, for in the dream I have felt happy and fulfilled.

Long ago I also experienced a strange incident, the one I alluded to when talking to Jenny and Emma. It was not a dream but something that occurred one day when I was sitting in a park. I was suddenly with Harry and our children in a park. At the time I felt as though I wasn't just watching that family but had actually moved into that life. I sat on a bench watching while Harry pushed a small boy and girl on a double swing. As I watched the girl called out excitedly, 'Look Mummy, I'm nearly up to the clouds.'

Harry looked across at me, a big loving grin on his handsome face. I smiled back as I smoothed a hand over my rounded stomach and felt the baby kick.

Suddenly I was alone, sitting on a park bench, watching an empty swing move slowly in the breeze.

This incident occurred when I was very unhappy after my break-up from David and at the time had often felt lost and confused. I had been so frightened by the strangeness of that event I deliberately tried to forget it, fearful I might be having some sort of mental breakdown.

The article has reminded me of that incident and those vivid worrying dreams. It has also made me really analyse myself and the decisions I've made in the past.

I remember telling Jenny and Emma I didn't feel my marriages to both David and Jeff were my decisions, but of course they were. I just hadn't been willing to own them because they represented failures. Jenny said I was a strong-minded woman, and really I always have been. Because of the memories the article has evoked I now accept that I have been responsible for all the major decisions in my life. Some of them have been good and some disastrous, but they have been mine.

Now I am facing the most important decision of my life and I am unable to act decisively. I want to marry Pierre and be with him for the rest of my life. Only the foolish way I feel about having a baby stands in the way of our happiness, and I can't seem to let it go; can't make a decision to forget the past and forgive myself.

I think once more about the article. Nowhere is chance mentioned, and surely it is an important element in everyone's life. What part does it play in the creation of parallel worlds? Perhaps I should let chance take over. Tonight I'll stop taking that little white pill, and see what happens during the last few weeks Pierre and I have together.

Will there be one world where we bid each other a sad farewell, and he returns to France to marry some suitable French woman who is willing to have his babies, and another where I get pregnant "accidentally" and go to France with Pierre to become his wife.

Another World

Chapter Twenty-three

Phillip Radcliff puts his head in his hands and rubs his weary eyes. He sighs deeply and looks at the wall clock. Six-thirty, and he has been working since eight-thirty with just a short break for a quick coffee and sandwich at lunchtime. In the next room he can hear Marcia moving quietly around, tidying the waiting room, closing the filing cabinet and turning off switches. She has been here since nine and he feels guilty about the long hours she is working while her assistant is on holidays, but it was impossible to get a replacement. More precisely it was impossible to get a replacement who would meet Marcia's high standards; someone who she could trust to keep her files in order, as well as provide proper care for the patients and assistance to him.

He is thinking that he probably takes advantage of her willingness to work so hard and of her loyalty to him when she pokes her head around the door, and says cheerfully, 'Time to call it a day Chief. You must be feeling as buggered as I am.'

He grins at her colourful language. Of course she doesn't swear in front of the patients, but out of hours Marcia reverts to the speech and mannerisms of her youth. She grew up in a house full of brothers, and still has the tough tomboyish ways she developed then in order to fit into their masculine world. Although she is a little overweight she is rounded in the right places and has a pretty face topped by a mass of dark curls. Many men have found her attractive, but she treats them all as brothers. They find themselves confiding in her about their problems instead of making a pass.

Phillip and Marcia met when he was doing his internship, and she had completed her degree and was experiencing her first year on the wards as a fully qualified nurse. During that first year they were often rostered on together and became close friends. When he met Emma, Marcia was the one he confided to about his feelings for this gorgeous young lawyer who he had met at a celebratory lunch with his older brother.

She had watched the way Phillip's face lit up as he talked about this girl, and pretended to be happy for him. For nearly two years she had nurtured the silent hope that a time would come when he would love her in the way that she loved him, but now she knew this was never going to happen. She decided he definitely would never know of her true feelings.

She had kept that promise to herself throughout the years they have worked together, but when she sees him sitting behind his desk looking so tired and worn out she wishes she could give him a hug.

Instead she puts on her bossiest voice and says, 'Okay mate, time to get yourself out of that chair and get home. No point in hanging around here like a worn out dishrag.'

As she is talking there is a loud banging on the surgery door and she turns saying angrily, 'Damn, don't people know that we've finished for the day?'

When she crosses the room and opens the door she sees a tall woman supporting a slim teenage boy and two frightened young faces peering round from behind them. Marcia's face takes on a look of consternation when the little group enters the brightly lit room. She sees that the woman has a deep cut over one eye from which blood is oozing, and the boy has his arm wrapped in an icepack.

Before she can ask them anything Phillip comes from the next room and says in a falsely hearty voice, 'Mrs. Mills, what's been going on? You two look as if you've been in the wars.'

The woman answers haltingly, 'I think John's arm might be broken doctor.'

The boy flinches as Phillip Radcliff gently removes the icepack and examines the boy's swollen arm.

He says quietly, 'Yes, I think it is broken, but he'll need to go to the hospital to have it X-rayed and then reset and plastered. The icepack was a good idea, but I'll also put on a sling so that young John here isn't tempted to try and move it around.'

The boy grins at the silliness of this suggestion as the doctor had hoped he would.

After Phillip has made the boy as comfortable as possible he turns to the mother saying, 'And now, let's take a look at you.'

She looks embarrassed, 'It's nothing, just a little cut. John's the one I'm worried about.'

Putting his hand under her chin, Phillip peers at her face, 'It is actually a nasty cut and you'll need a few stitches in there. You've also got the beginnings of a pretty bad black eye. You need to be patched up and put to bed. Is there anyone you can call to take young John here into hospital? It could take a long time, and I don't think you're up to it.'

Phillip has deliberately not suggested the husband because the injuries of his two patients bear all the hallmarks of a domestic violence incident. He plans to enquire further into how the two acquired their injuries when he has the mother alone.

His guess proves to be correct because the woman doesn't mention the husband but instead says, 'I'll call my father. He'll come and take John to the hospital for me, and then I can take the two younger kids home and get them to bed.'

Marcia, who has been standing by, says to the children, 'You kids all take a seat, and I'll see if I can rustle up some Milo and biscuits while Doctor Radcliff takes care of your Mum.'

After seeing her children settled and making the call to her father Sonya Mills follows the doctor into his surgery. He waves her to a chair as he pulls on sterile gloves and then positions a bright light so that it shine onto her face.

While he cleans the wound preparatory to stitching it up he says, 'Did your husband do this and the damage to John's arm?'

She and her children have been his patients for the past six years, ever since he opened his solo practice, so he knows them quite well. He has treated the children for several minor ailments, Lisa when she had an allergic reaction to a jack jumper bite and Frank for warts on his hands, as well as the usual coughs and colds. Mrs. Mills has always impressed him as a sensible, loving mother and her children are well cared for. He has never met the husband, but there have been no previous signs of ill treatment of the children or of violence towards the mother.

The woman is silent for a while as if marshalling her words before she blurts out, 'He didn't mean to. He was tired and something I said upset him so he lashed out. John tried to protect me and Harry just pushed him aside.'

'Going by the state of your son's arm it was a very violent push, and he hit you very hard to cause this damage. It also looks to me as though he punched you more than once. You have quite severe bruising on your cheek as well as this cut.'

She sits silently while he works on her face and Phillip wonders, not for the first time, why women are prepared to take this sort of treatment from the men who are supposed to love them.

As he finishes stitching the wound he looks into the tear-filled golden eyes of the woman in front of him and says kindly, 'You don't have to put up with this sort of thing you know. If you notify the police we can get a restraining order put on your husband.'

'Oh, I wouldn't do that to him. Harry is really a good man. He hasn't been himself lately. I'm sure it won't happen again.'

Phillip has heard this sort of thing before, only to have the woman return later with even more severe injuries.

He fears for this woman and her children so asks, 'Would you like to talk about this with another woman? My wife's a lawyer, and has had a lot of experience working with women who have suffered from domestic violence. Let me give you her card, and perhaps you might like to make an appointment to see her.'

He sees the look of doubt in her eyes and says half jokingly; 'Look even though she's my wife I can assure you without bias that she's a good listener, and an easy person to talk to.' Seeing the doubt still there he adds, 'It won't cost you anything.'

At that moment they hear a loud knock on the outside door and the woman pushes the card hurriedly into her bag and says, 'That will be Daddy.'

She reaches the door before Phillip and falls into the arms of a tall, stooped white-haired man.

The man holds her and then tilts her face up to his, 'What's happened precious? You said something on the phone about John having a broken arm, but you didn't mention your face. Harry didn't do this to you two did he?'

She says defensively, 'He didn't mean to.'

Edward McFee almost bellows, 'Didn't mean to? Well how did it happen if he didn't mean to? And where is the blighter now? I'll kill him when I get my hands on him.'

Seeing his patient's distress and the worried faces of the children Phillip steps forward saying, 'I'm glad you're here. Young John needs to be taken to hospital to have that arm X-rayed and probably reset and plastered. I'm pretty sure it's broken. Your daughter should get herself to bed with a couple of pain killers as soon as possible, and she's worried about the other children being up too late so you're a Godsend.'

Not to be deterred from his harangue Edward McFee turns to Phillip, 'Has she told you how it happened or where Harry is now?'

Rather taken aback by the arrogance of the man's tone Phillip answers rather tetchily, 'Look sir, I'm sure your daughter will tell you all about it later, but at the moment it's important that you get your grandson seen to. He's being very brave, but he's in quite a lot of pain, and the sooner he's seen to the better. I'll ring the hospital so they'll be expecting you.'

After seeing them on their way and Sonya and the two younger children out Phillip and Marcia give each other wry looks.

Marcia says, 'Who'd have thought she was married to a wife basher? She's always seemed kind of superior to me; not the sort of woman who'd let herself be pushed around.'

Phillip answers thoughtfully, 'I certainly haven't seen any signs of either Mrs. Mills or the children being injured before. She told me her husband is a good man, but that he hasn't been himself lately. I wish I could've got a bit more out of her, but she didn't want to talk to me about him.'

'Perhaps she will when she comes back to get the stitches out,' Marcia says as she pulls on her coat and begins switching out the lights.

Phillip answers doubtfully, 'She might, but she certainly didn't want to say anything against her husband tonight. I gave her one of Emma's cards; suggested she make an appointment with her to discuss any problems she's having with him. You never know, she may be more inclined to open up to another woman.'

Marcia, who despite her feelings for Phillip has a lot of admiration for Emma says, 'Well I'm sure Emma will find out what's going on if she gets the chance. Now I'm off for a quick microwaved dinner, a hot toddy and bed. See you in the morning.'

As he watches her drive away he thinks how lucky he is to have her. It's now seven-thirty, and she has put in a ten and a half hour day, but still manages to look cheerful and alert while he feels old and tired, "like a worn out dishrag," as Marcia had so aptly put it.

Chapter Twenty-four

As Phillip pulls into his driveway he looks at the clock on the dashboard. It is nearly eight o'clock, and he remembers that this morning he'd promised to be home in time to help Simone with her maths. He sighs at the thought that once more he has let down their daughter. Either Emma or he try to be home by six so they have time with Simone, and he had known this was one of the two nights a week Emma would be working at the Women's Shelter.

He takes his bag and gets out, locking the car as he walks slowly to his front door. While he is putting the key in the lock Emma's car turns into the drive. The headlights blind him temporarily as he turns to watch her park her car next to his in the carport. He waits for her, and when she joins him on the step they kiss hello before she says, 'Goodness darling, I thought you would be home before this. You must have had a very busy day.'

'I would've been home earlier, but we had an emergency just as Marcia and I were ready to shut up shop. I'll tell you about it later, but right now I must make my peace with Simone. I promised I'd be home in time to help her with some maths homework.'

'Yes, we'd better go in and face our disgruntled daughter. She was saying to me the other day that she sees more of Grand than she does of us.'

When they walk into the brightly lit kitchen Simone is eating her dinner and Mrs. Murray sits opposite her drinking a cup of tea. She has been their housekeeper for six years but steadfastly refuses to share an evening meal with them, saying she prefers to eat alone. They are fairly sure she enjoys a quiet tipple with her evening meal, but she is such an important part of their household they turn a blind eye to the crushed down wine casks that appear regularly in the recycling bin.

As they enter the room she stands and says, 'Well, I'll be off. There's lasagne still hot in the oven and salad in the fridge. See you all in the morning.'

She rinses her cup in the sink before walking slowly down the passage to the back door and outside to what they jokingly call her "Granny flat."

Phillip bends to kiss his daughter's cheek, but she jerks her head away saying crossly, 'You said you'd be home in time to help me with my maths homework.'

'Sorry darling, I got held up at the surgery. Do you want me to help you after dinner?'

'It's too late now. I've done it and it'll be your fault if I get it wrong.'

She pushes back from the table and carries her plate to the sink.

Emma goes to hug her saying, 'Oh Baby, don't give your Dad a hard time. He's had a busy day.'

Simone moves away from her mother's outstretched arms, 'You're just as bad. Neither of you is ever here for me. You just rely on Grand looking out for me all the time. Anyhow, I'm off to bed.'

They listen to her quick footsteps on the stairs and to the loud bang of her bedroom door.

Phillip says wearily, 'I feel badly about letting her down, but I really couldn't help it.'

'I know you'd have been here if you could.' Emma gives him a comforting pat on his shoulder as she passes him to get to the oven. 'She's been so moody lately, and I don't know why. Perhaps it's hormonal.'

She serves them each a helping of lasagne and puts the bowl of salad in the middle of the table before sitting down and saying, 'Tell me about your emergency. Was there a car accident?'

While helping himself to salad Phillip answers, 'No, not a car accident. Something more up your alley. One of my patients came in just as we were leaving. Her son, who's about fifteen, had a broken arm and she had bruises on her face, a black eye and a nasty cut above the eye.'

'The husband did it I suppose,' Emma says matter-of-factly. 'Is she going to have him charged?'

'I don't think there's any chance of that. When I suggested it she stuck up for him. Said he was a good man and hadn't meant to do it.'

Emma snorts derisively, 'The usual from the sound of it. I can't understand why women make excuses for these brutes.'

Phillip answers thoughtfully, 'No, I don't think this fits the usual pattern. They've been my patients for six years. In all that time, I haven't seen any sign of the mother or the children being abused. I haven't ever met the husband, but she said something that got me thinking.'

Emma helps herself to more salad as she asks, 'And what was that?'

'Well she was adamant this behaviour was unusual. She said he hasn't been himself lately. I don't know if he really has changed or if she was just making excuses for him. What I do know is she needs to talk about the problem with someone, but she clammed up with me. I gave her one of your cards and suggested she make an appointment to see you. You don't mind, do you?'

'You know I don't mind when you do this sort of thing. I think it's great if we can work together to help someone. I just hope she gets in touch with me. It sounds from what you've told me this is the first time her husband has behaved violently. Perhaps it's a one off, but it could be the start of abusive behaviour. Whatever, I'd like to talk to her.'

As she says this she collects their now empty plates and begins loading the dishwasher.

Phillip stands wearily and says, 'I'm so tired. I think I need an early night.'

Emma turns from what she is doing saying, 'I won't be far behind you darling,' and blows him a kiss.

When he comes level with his daughter's bedroom door Phillip pauses then opens it slowly, not wanting to wake Simone if she is asleep but needing to see her because he feels badly about letting her down. He is expecting to see her in bed, either asleep or reading, but instead she is hunched over the computer.

She is concentrating so intently on the screen she doesn't hear him until he says, 'I thought you'd be in bed.'

She turns abruptly, a flushed look on her face. 'You could knock you know.'

Taken aback by the hostility in her voice Phillip mumbles, 'Sorry darling. I just wanted to say I'm sorry for being home too late to help you with your maths. I thought you'd be in bed. What are you doing up still?'

As he takes a step into the room Simone turns back to the computer and quickly logs off. 'If you must know I was checking my e-mails.' She turns away from him and says pointedly, 'And now I am going to bed.'

Feeling he has been dismissed Phillip says quietly, 'Goodnight then sweetheart,' and leaves the room.

As he begins to undress Phillip thinks about how close Simone and he once were, of how she would run to the door when he came home in the evenings and greet him with hugs and kisses. During the weekends she had been his little shadow, helping him get Mummy's breakfast, and afterwards following him around while he mowed the lawns or tidied his shed. He hadn't realised until tonight, when she looked at him so coldly, just how much their relationship has changed. He knows he can no longer take his daughter's love for granted.

He lies in bed thinking about what Emma told him earlier. She said Simone's recent mood swings may be hormonal, and this could be the case as she recently started menstruating. He still thinks of her as his little girl. It's hard for him to realise she will soon be a young woman. But are hormonal changes the cause of her moodiness, or is it that she feels neglected? Tonight she said they aren't there for her, and perhaps this is a fair criticism. Both Emma and he work long hours, and have come to rely more and more on Mrs. Murray as their workloads have increased. They so rarely spend relaxing time together as a couple and never as a family. It is no wonder Simone is feeling neglected.

Emma comes into the room quietly. She doesn't turn on the bedroom light, and he listens to the soft swish she makes as she undresses, hears her flush the toilet in the en suite, the sounds of her cleaning her teeth. As she slips into bed beside him he pulls her to him. He would like to make love, if only for the comfort it would bring, but sex has ceased to be an important part of their relationship. They both work such long hours in emotionally demanding jobs. He resists the urge to move his hands from her waist to her breasts, knowing she will be too tired to respond to any overtures he might make. She has spent two hours at the Women's Shelter after a full day at the office so needs to sleep.

He would also like to talk about Simone; share the hurt he felt at her curt dismissal of him, but he remains silent.

In no time he hears Emma's breathing deepen and knows she is asleep, but he lies staring into the darkness, thinking about their little girl. He makes a silent promise to try to spend more time with her.

Chapter Twenty-five

Sonya sits at her kitchen table, a cup of tea held tightly between her hands, and waits. Doctor Radcliff had given her some tablets to deaden the pain and help her sleep, but she hasn't taken them yet. She wants to be awake when John and her father get back from the hospital. Lisa and Frank are asleep.

Fortunately Deirdre was at a sleepover at a girlfriends house so didn't see what happened. Sonya is thankful for this because Harry and their firstborn daughter have always been close. She doesn't know how Deirdre would have coped with the sight of her beloved father screaming abuse, and then attacking first her and then John.

Until the past few months Harry had always been a loving husband and father. When they married she was already four months pregnant, and had just turned eighteen. They had to wait until her birthday because her parents wouldn't give their permission for the marriage. Her mother wanted to pack her off to France, have the baby adopted, and then pretend it hadn't happened. Sonya wanted an abortion, but both Harry and her father refused to help her. Faced with the prospect of having the baby she gained a certain amount of pleasure from shocking both of her parents by moving in with Harry and marrying him as soon as possible.

He had been wonderful from the start. During the months before Deirdre was born she often behaved like a spoilt brat, bemoaning the fact she was fat, uncomfortable, unhappy and tired of living in the cramped flat. Despite her behaviour Harry was patient and loving during the pregnancy, telling her how beautiful she was, and promising that they would soon move to somewhere more spacious. When the baby was born he held his tiny daughter gently in his big arms and gazed at her with adoration.

After they returned home from hospital he took the responsibility for bathing Deirdre, and it had been Harry who fed her when she woke in the night.

Sonya hadn't been a good mother with her first baby. She refused to breast feed Deirdre, insisting she be put onto a bottle straight away. Because of this, and the fact that she hadn't wanted a baby in the first place, it took her a long time to bond with her firstborn. She has never felt quite as close to her as she does to her other three children, but Deirdre hasn't missed out. She had the unconditional love of her father from the minute she was born, and has always returned that love. Even lately, when he has been irritable and moody, she has managed to cheer him up.

Sonya hears a car pulling up in the driveway and hurries to open the door. She puts her arms around John, being careful not to knock his arm that is now in plaster.

She kisses his cheek then asks anxiously, 'How are you feeling darling? Did it hurt much getting it reset?'

John mumbles, 'Not too much. It feels better now it's plastered.'

Edward McFee beams proudly at his grandson. 'He was very brave. They let me stay with him while they reset it and there wasn't a peep out of him.'

Sonya's father sounds chirpy, but she can tell by his pale strained face that this has been hard for him. He recently turned seventy, and tonight looks very much his age.

John says, 'I'm off to bed Mum. The doctor gave me some tablets to help with the pain and they've just about knocked me out.'

Sonya looks at her tall slim son with loving eyes. At fifteen he is as tall as she and still growing.

She says rather helplessly, 'Will you be able to get undressed by yourself?'

He manages a grin. 'Well, I certainly don't want you taking my clothes off Mum. See you in the morning. And thanks Gramps for taking me.'

He kisses them both before leaving the room.

As soon as his grandson has left Edward turns to his daughter, 'How are you feeling precious?'

She puts on the kettle before answering, 'Not too bad Daddy. I've got a bit of a headache, but I'm worried about Harry.'

'What are you worried about him for?' Edward splutters. 'Look what he's done to you and John. I've always thought he wasn't too bad, despite what your mother says, but this is unforgivable. You should notify the police and get him locked up.'

Sonya pours them both a cup of tea and says tiredly, 'Sit down Daddy and calm down. Look, you know what Harry did tonight is out of character. He's never laid a hand on either me or the kids before, but I think something is happening to him.'

'What do you mean happening?' Her father looks bewildered.

'He's been having a lot of bad headaches lately, and he's been irritable with the kids. It's not like him. If I try to talk about it he just says he's okay; that I'm making a fuss about nothing. But now I'm worried about where he is and what he's doing.'

'What do you think he's doing?'

'I don't know Dad. When he saw what he'd done he ran out of the house and drove away like a mad thing. I'm afraid he might've had an accident he was in such a state.'

Edward Mc.Fee gets slowly to his feet and moves around the table to put a comforting hand on his daughter's shoulder, 'Oh precious, he's probably sleeping somewhere in his car. I bet he'll be back before long, full of apologies. Now you need to get to bed. I'll pop around in the morning to see how you all are.'

As Sonya stands at the door watching her father drive away she feels such love and gratitude for him. Although she has been totally alienated from her mother since her marriage to Harry, her father has always been there for her. He visits her and his grandchildren regularly, and has even become quite friendly with Harry over the years. Tonight will put an end to that, unless she can find a reason for her husband's changed behaviour.

She shuts the door and leans against it with her eyes closed. Her head is pounding. She must take those tablets and get to bed. Tomorrow she'll need to take care of John, reassure the younger children that everything's okay, explain to Deirdre what happened and hopefully be able to sit down with Harry and talk things out.

Chapter Twenty-six

Marcia carefully removes the stitches before saying cheerfully, 'It looks really good. You'll only have a fine white line. If you just wait here a minute Doctor Radcliff will be in to look at it.'

She turns off the bright light that has been shining on Sonya's face and leaves the room.

Sonya sits gazing around the small room that is adjacent to the waiting room. It contains a narrow bed, the chair on which she is sitting and some cupboards with a bench in the middle of them. On the walls are various pieces of exciting reading which include a poster on the procedures to be followed with a patient suffering a heart attack, another on care to be taken to avoid the spread of influenza germs and a rather lurid chart of a skeleton with the names of the various bones listed down the side with arrows leading to the relevant body part.

Her eyes wander back to the first poster, and she wonders idly why a doctor would need these instructions on the wall. Surely how to care for a heart attack patient would be one of the first things taught in medical school.

As she is desperately searching for something more entertaining to read Doctor Radcliff hurries into the room, turns on the light again, and peers closely at the results of his workmanship.

'That looks fine,' he says briskly as he turns off the light and moves away. 'And how is young John? The arm was broken wasn't it?'

As she stands Sonya answers, 'Yes, you were right, but once it was plastered he said it was much less painful. He's coping pretty well with one hand.'

'And your husband. Has he come back?'

She looks uncomfortable and mutters, 'Yes, he came back the next day.'

To try and make it easy for her, Phillip says, 'Look I know this is difficult for you, but you really do need help in a situation like this. Have you given any thought about having a talk with my wife? She does a lot of counselling work in cases like yours, and she could help.'

Sonya assures him she will make an appointment and hurriedly leaves the surgery. Slowly she walks to her car and slides inside, but instead of starting the engine she sits for a while thinking over the past few days. Deirdre had returned home the following morning, and been shocked to see her mother's face and John's arm in plaster. She was even more shocked when she learnt her father was responsible for their injuries. Then she angered them both by asking what they had done to cause her father to behave in such a way.

John answered crossly, 'The old man went at Mum for no reason, and when I tried to stop him he knocked me over and broke my arm. We didn't give him a reason. He just went off his head.'

Deirdre retorted, 'That doesn't sound like Dad. Mum must've done something to rile him,' and walked from the room.

Later Sonya heard her daughter crying in her room and felt sorry for this dear loyal daughter. She too feels there must be a reason for Harry's behaviour, but he won't talk to her about it.

He came home the next night, after the children were in bed, and wept when she told him John's arm was broken. He'd held her damaged face in his big hands saying over and over, 'I'm so sorry Sonya. I'm so sorry. I don't know what got into me. It's these headaches I've been having. They make me so irritable.'

She tried to talk him into seeing the doctor but he refused, saying all he needed were some good painkillers.

During all the years of their marriage Harry has never gone to a doctor. His mother died as a result of a bungle following what should have been a straightforward medical procedure. From that time he developed an intense distrust of the medical profession; was even wary of the doctor who delivered their babies. Fortunately he has always experienced very good health so his phobia has not been an issue, but it is now. Sonya is convinced there is a medical reason to account for the change in her husband. She had hoped to be able to talk to the doctor about Harry today, but because the waiting room was full she hadn't liked to take up more of his time.

She searches around in her bag and finds the card the doctor gave her six days ago. As soon as she gets home she'll make an appointment to see the doctor's wife. Perhaps she can advise her on what she should do to help Harry.

It is three days later and Sonya sits nervously in the lawyer's waiting room. It is a rather dreary-looking room with dull fawn walls and a cheap patterned carpet on the floor. The receptionist was very friendly though. She smiled brightly and offered to make her a tea or coffee while she waited. Sonya declined feeling she was too on edge to concentrate on holding a cup without spilling the contents. Except for when she and Harry had signed the papers when they bought their house Sonya has never been to a lawyer, and she isn't sure what to expect. She also thinks it is medical help that's needed rather than legal advice, but she'll see what this woman has to say.

A door opens and a rather dowdy little woman comes out followed by a smartly dressed woman with wavy, shoulder-length blue-black hair and an attractive face.

She smiles encouragingly across the room and says, 'Would you like to come in Mrs. Mills?'

When Sonya enters the room the lawyer is looking at a sheet of paper on her desk. She looks up and puts out her hand saying, 'Hi, I'm Emma Radcliff.'

As they shake hands she has a puzzled look on her face. The woman before her is tall and solid. Her auburn hair is streaked with white and pulled into a rough chignon. She has none of the style of the girl who Emma remembers with hatred, but the golden eyes look the same.

She stares intently at Sonya before asking, 'You aren't related to a Sonya McFee by any chance?'

'Actually that was my maiden name. Why do you ask?'

'You may not remember me, but we were at Bridmore together. My maiden name was Williams.'

Emma sees a look of discomfort on Sonya's face and feels a faint stab of satisfaction at the thought that the snooty bitch, who made her school life miserable, has now come to her for help and advice. She dismisses this thought as unprofessional and says encouragingly, 'I understand your husband has begun to show violent tendencies and injured you and your son.'

Sonya stands up, 'Look, I can't do this. I'd find it embarrassing enough with a stranger, but I couldn't possibly ask you for advice.'

Emma allows a slightly superior tone to enter her voice, 'Why ever not? What happened when we were at school is in the past, and I'm happy to help you in any way I can. Now sit down and tell me what you think the problem is.'

Sonya stares as though mesmerised. She can't believe this smart, sophisticated woman is nerdy-looking Emma Williams. Where have the glasses and the bushy hair gone?

Once her children started school, and had come in for the occasional bout of teasing, she had felt ashamed of the way she had behaved when she was at school. She feels she should now apologise to this woman, but can't find the words.

Seeing the quandary the other woman is in Emma says softly, 'Look, we've all done things we regret, but there's no point in dwelling on them. What's important is the future. Now tell me about your husband. I believe this was the first time he's been violent towards you or any of your children. I think you told my husband he is a good man.'

Sitting down again Sonya says intently, 'He is. Harry and I have been married for eighteen years and in all that time he's been a wonderful husband and father. The kids all adore him, or at least they did until a few months ago. Now they're more wary around him. He has headaches, then gets irritable and yells at them.'

Looking intently at the woman opposite her Emma says seriously, 'Sonya, I really want to help you. From what I understand Harry isn't normally a violent man. I work all the time with women who've been abused or had their children harmed by their husbands or partners. Generally there is a pattern of violence in the relationship. This hasn't been the case here so we need to look for reasons for this sudden change. What do you think could be the cause? Has he started drinking? Does he have business problems that could be causing him to be stressed?'

'No, it's nothing like that. Harry's never been a drinker and his business is going very well. Just recently he put on another apprentice. He runs a service station and garage.'

'So if we can rule out drink and money worries as a cause for this change in your husband we need to look at his health. Very often when a person changes fairly dramatically, and especially if they are experiencing headaches, are moodier or more irritable it can be caused by some physical problem.'

'What sort of physical problem?'

'Well this is more my husband's field than mine. Clinical depression is one, but as Harry has evidently not shown previous signs of that it could possibly be a brain tumour.'

Sonya stares at Emma, a look of fear in her eyes, 'Do you mean he could die?'

Seeing the look Emma answers, 'As I said, this isn't my field, but I do know that most brain tumours are benign and completely curable. I think from what you've told me your husband needs to have a thorough physical check up.'

Sonya looks at her, tears misting her golden eyes, 'I know there's something wrong with him, but I can't get him to see a doctor. Years ago his mother died after some minor operation, and since then he doesn't trust doctors.'

Seeing how distraught the other woman is becoming Emma gets up from her chair and comes to stand near Sonya's chair.

She touches her shoulder in comfort and says, 'I'll help you convince him. You know despite what happened in the past I think we're meant to be friends. Now let's sit over there on the couch and I'll get Justine to make us a coffee. You can fill me in on this man of yours.'

Sonya is still feeling uncomfortable about the situation and says tentatively, 'I don't want to take up too much of your time. You must be very busy.'

'Nonsense,' Emma answers briskly, 'Actually you're my last case for the day so I'll get those coffees and let Justine go, then you and I can have a good talk. Catch up on the last eighteen years.'

After Emma leaves the room Sonya sits on the couch feeling slightly awkward about being called a "case." She's also not sure how this woman can help her; that she can somehow show her how to convince Harry he needs to see a doctor.

In a way it is rather funny how their lives have panned out so differently. Nerdy little Emma Williams is now an attractive lawyer, and she's just a housewife and mother, a far cry from the glamour girl she was at school. She's glad she wore her good suit, but wishes she'd spent more time on her hair. She is smiling to herself about this small vanity when Emma comes back carrying the two cups of coffee.

'I'm pleased to see you're looking more relaxed. I really meant what I said. When you walked into my office today and we shook hands I had the strangest feeling you and I should be friends.'

Emma hands Sonya her cup of coffee and sits next to her on the couch, 'Now tell me about Harry. What sort of man was he before these problems began?'

Sonya smiles, 'It seems so odd to be talking to you about him. Not because you're you, but because you're a lawyer. I thought perhaps I'd be told of some way Harry could be made to see a doctor, some legal mechanism that could be used to insist he seek help because of his violent outburst.'

'I don't think that will be necessary. From what you've said I gather he hasn't shown signs of violent or erratic behaviour during the eighteen years you've been married until recently.'

'No, he's always been so stable; he's been my rock.' Sounding close to tears Sonya takes a deep breath and continues. 'As you undoubtedly heard at the time, I had to get married. I was in such a state about getting pregnant I really felt I had no other choice. Neither my parents nor Harry would help me get an abortion. I guess I married Harry to spite my mother and because I was desperate.' She gives a self-conscious laugh. 'Not the best reasons for getting married. Anyhow, I wasn't the easiest person to put up with during the first couple of years. I moaned about being pregnant, about the flat we lived in, and wasn't much of a mother to our first baby Deirdre. I behaved like the spoilt brat I was, but Harry was wonderful. He put up with my childish tantrums, cared for our baby much better than I did and worked and saved hard to get a deposit for our home. I guess eventually I grew up and realised how lucky I was to have him. He really is a lovely man, has always been great with the kids and a wonderful husband and I love him so much.' Here Sonya pauses.

Emma, sensing that the other woman may be finding it hard to keep her emotions under control says, 'It sounds as if there must definitely be a physical reason for the change in him. It's imperative that he undergoes a complete check up, and you're going to need to be tougher than you have been so far.'

'But how? I've pleaded with him to see a doctor about the headaches, but he absolutely refuses.'

'I know you're going to find this hard, but my suggestion is this. First find a time when he is feeling well and none of the kids are around. Try asking him again to make an appointment to see the doctor. If he refuses use emotional blackmail. Say you're afraid of him becoming violent again. If this fails you'll need to threaten him with the law. You know he could be made to seek medical assistance because of his violent behaviour, but I don't think it will come to that. From what you've told me I think he'll see reason, if you make him feel badly enough about what he did to you and John.'

'Suppose I manage to talk him into this, what sort of doctor should he see?'

'He'd need to see a G.P. first and then be referred to a specialist. I can't tout for customers for Phillip, but it might be easier if he sees him. That way he won't have to go through all the background as to why he's there.'

Sonya stands and puts out her hand, 'I feel so much better after talking to you. Thanks so much Emma.' She pauses as though working out what to say. 'And I really am so sorry for being such a bitch to you back then.'

Instead of just shaking hands Emma holds on and grins, 'Apology accepted. Now you make sure you get back to me and let me know how things pan out. I want you to realise that I'm here for you if you need me.'

The women let go their hands and are walking across the room when a perky face topped by a cap of blonde hair peeps around the door, and a voice says, 'Hi. I wasn't sure whether or not you had someone with you. I'll wait outside.'

'It's okay. We've just finished. Let me introduce you. Jenny this is Sonya, an old school friend, and Sonya meet Jenny, interior designer extraordinaire. Jenny designed and oversaw the refurbishment of my office years ago, and we've been friends ever since.'

Sonya gazes around the dreary space that looks as if it was last decorated in the fifties, and wonders what to say. It doesn't appear to be the work of an exceptional designer.

Seeing the look on her face Jenny says laughing, 'Not this office Sonya. I don't think this place has had a cent spent on it since it was built. No this is only where Emma hangs out when she's slumming. Her real office is very upmarket and posh.'

Emma fears Sonya may be offended by her friend's reference to "slumming," and is glad she introduced her as a friend instead of as a client.

She says, 'We're going for a quick drink. Would you like to come too?'

'No thanks. I should be off. The kids will be home from school.'

As she walks towards the door Emma calls, 'Don't forget to keep in touch.'

Sonya turns and smiles, 'I will. I'll give you a ring if I get results.'

Chapter Twenty-seven

Emma and Jenny sit in a small alcove in the pub opposite the building where Emma works two days a week. This isn't a particularly salubrious suburb, but the hotel is clean and not crowded at this time. Later it will be filled with young people who flock here on Friday and Saturday nights to hear the live bands that are a regular feature of this pub, but this is late afternoon. There are only a few men at the bar and some couples in the other alcoves.

As they sip their wines Jenny says, 'I thought your friend looked familiar. Would I have met her with you some time?'

Emma doesn't want to discuss something she thinks Sonya would rather remain private so simply answers, 'No, not with me. Actually I hadn't seen her for years until today, but we were at school together.'

'I'm sure I know her from somewhere; she seemed so familiar. Anyhow enough of that. You said you were worried about our girl. What's wrong? Not boy trouble already surely.'

'No. At least I don't think so, although she does spend an inordinate amount of time on her computer, and who knows what she's getting up to there. She told us she needed it for her homework, but seems to spend quite a bit of time e-mailing friends. I don't know if it was a good idea to let her have her own computer in her bedroom.'

'Oh, come off it. All the kids do now. It's part of the age. But that's not the main thing that's worrying you, is it?'

'No. It's that she has become so moody lately. You know what a sunny little girl she's always been.' Jenny nods before Emma continues. 'Well now she's forever in a glum. She's started saying how Phillip and I are never there for her, and that we don't care what happens to her. I thought at first that it was probably hormonal, but now she's got me wondering if perhaps we are neglecting her a bit and relying too much on Mrs. M always being there.'

'Well if you feel that way perhaps you should cut back a bit on the extra work you do. You can't be home much, what with your work at Radcliff's, your pro bono work and a couple of evenings a week at the Women's Shelter. If I had a daughter I'd make her my priority, and you don't seem to do that anymore. I can quite believe Simone is feeling a bit neglected.'

Emma grins across the table at her friend, 'One thing I know is that I can always rely on you for an honest answer. So you really think I don't give her enough attention?'

'Quite frankly Emma I don't see how you could. But I also think you are running yourself ragged with all the extra work you do. What are you trying to prove?'

'I guess I've always felt I was so lucky to land the job at Radcliff's straight out of university, and then to be made a partner when I was still so young. Because of that I feel I owe society for all the luck I've had. The other thing is, from the time I was quite young the reason I wanted to become a lawyer was to help disadvantaged women.'

'Whoa there. I seem to remember you landed the job at Radcliff's because you topped your year at university, and you earned your partnership, so that wasn't luck. And I know that most of your paying customers are spoilt biddies who expect you to screw the guys who they are divorcing for every dollar you can get for them. I work for a lot of the same women and know what they're like. I can see why you'd want to help more needy women, but surely your pro bono work should have been enough to salve that working class conscience of yours.'

'But the problem is the work at the Shelter has kind of escalated. When I first started there I thought it would only be an hour or two a week, but it's a lot more than that and those women really need me.'

'It seems from what you've told me Simone is telling you she needs you too. If you want my advice I'd say cut back on the pro bono work and limit your time at the Shelter. It won't be very long until she doesn't want you around, and then you'll regret the lost time. Once she's fourteen or fifteen she'll be glad that her parents aren't watching her every move.'

Emma reaches across the table and takes her friends hand, 'Oh Jen, you talk such sense. How is it you're so wise about kids when you don't even have any of your own?'

As soon as she has said this Emma realises she's been tactless, for Jenny has told her about her ectopic pregnancies and of how distraught she had been about not being able to have children.

She knows she has stirred up unhappy memories when Jenny says wistfully, 'No, I don't have kids of my own, but I so wanted at least one. I've always felt I was meant to be a mother.'

'I'm sorry Jen if I've upset you. And you would have been a wonderful mother. I've seen what you're like with Simone. She adores you, but also respects you. When I see you two together I sometimes feel quite jealous. You seem to be on the same wave length.'

Suddenly the wistful expression on Jenny's face is replaced by an impish grin, and she looks about sixteen as she says, 'Yeh , I guess I'm still a kid at heart, but I've also got lots of nieces and nephews who confide in me when they think their parents' are being a bit heavy. I've learnt from them how the young ones think.' She pauses to sip her wine. 'By the way some of them are coming for a swim and barbecue this Sunday. How about you three join us?'

'That'd be lovely. Now I must be off. Phillip was hoping to be home by five-thirty today so they'll probably be cooking an early dinner. See you Sunday, and thanks for the advice.'

During the drive home Emma thinks back over her day, and about what Jenny said about her need to cut back on her work and spend more time with Simone. While she sees the wisdom in what her friend has said, she can't really see how she can do it.

She has seen twenty women today, all in need of help and advice. Their problems have included everything, from how to deal with abusive husbands and unreasonable landlords to a plea for her to represent an obviously no-good son who has been caught selling amphetamines to his schoolmates. Her days doing this pro bono work are so different from those spent at Radcliff's.

There, each of her clients is allocated an hour. She listens patiently to these "spoilt biddies" as they explain why they should get the lion's share of their estranged husband's worldly goods. Some of the women have a genuine right to a fair share, having worked beside their husbands during lean years and borne their children only to be discarded for younger models. Emma is sympathetic with these women.

There are many others, though, who obviously only married for money in the first place, and are determined to take as much as possible of it with them when they go. She has less sympathy for them, and sometimes finds it difficult to listen patiently and advise them on the best way to ensure they get all they feel they deserve.

After five years of this sort of work she began to feel she was wasting her time and training, but also not really contributing; not helping women who really needed her help. These feelings led her to working in the rundown office she has been in today doing pro bono work with women who really need her help. This is also why she took on the advisory work at the Women's Shelter.

If she is to salvage some time to spend with Simone she should probably cut back on her work at "The Firm", which is the family term for Radcliff's, but she would feel she was letting down Phillip's brother Craig. He gave her the opportunity to work in one of the top legal firms in the city when she was straight out of university, and mentored her through those early years when she was learning to relate all she had learnt during the years of study to the problems of her clients.

She had been a little in love with Craig. She knew he was happily married, had met his charming wife Julie at office functions and seen photos of his little son and two daughters. Despite this, and the fact that he never treated her as anything but a colleague and friend, she nurtured this feeling; loved it when they worked together on a case and glowed when he praised her.

When she became a fully-fledged lawyer Craig took her to lunch to celebrate. He said it would be a double celebration as his brother Philip, who had just completed his internship, would be joining them.

It was a lovely lunch. Both she and Phillip were in celebratory mood, and Craig had been a generous host, toasting them both with the best champagne then ordering a banquet, the specialty of the restaurant.

There was an instant rapport between Emma and Phillip. They talked about their years of study, and their dreams of how they would use their knowledge. When Craig quietly excused himself they were so engrossed in their conversation they barely noticed him leaving. Often over the years they have joked about Craig, the matchmaker, and he just smiles benignly.

Jenny had never felt much love or any respect for her weak drunken father who died from liver failure during her first year at work. After meeting Phillip she realised her love for Craig had been that of the love of a daughter, and she still sees him as a kind and wise father figure. When she and Phillip were planning their marriage it seemed the most natural thing in the world to ask him to give her away. She loves him dearly as a brother-in-law and colleague, and throughout the years he has always been supportive. He offered her the partnership when old Mr. Grange retired, and later acceded to her wish to spend more time on pro bono work. She really can't see how she can cut back on her time at "The Firm" for she knows Craig relies on her to deal with the more difficult female clients that come their way.

As she pulls into her drive she is pleased to see Phillip's car already there. He told her he would be home early tonight so that he could spend time with Simone, but sometimes he gets held up as he had a couple of weeks ago with Sonya and her son.

Now that was a surprise! Who'd have thought she would have finished up as a housewife with four children and married to a mechanic? Sonya assumed Emma had heard about her early marriage, but in fact she hadn't. They'd always lived in different parts of the city, and she hadn't known anything about Sonya after the end of the school year. If she'd thought about her at all it was with relief that she didn't run into her at university.

The funny thing about meeting her again was that, after an initial feeling of antipathy, she felt she could really like her, almost as if they should be friends. She hopes Sonya can get her husband to see Phillip, and that she lets her know what's happening.

She lets herself in the front door and goes straight to the kitchen where Phillip is sitting at the table cutting a bright red capsicum into thin slices. Beside him is a platter of neatly prepared vegetables, celery sticks, onion triangles and mushroom slices. When she walks into the room he looks up and smiles hello.

She walks to him and kisses his upturned face before asking, 'Where's Simone? I thought she would be helping you prepare the stir fry.'

He sighs. 'That's what I'd hoped for. We used to have fun getting the dinner ready together when we knew you were going to be late home. Tonight, as soon as Mrs. M. left, Simone said she was going to do some work on her computer. When I said I'd thought we would cook the dinner together she said quite snappily, "I'm sure you can manage it on your own," and flounced out of the room. I don't know what's got into her lately. She's certainly not my Sunny Simone anymore.'

'I know. I was telling Jenny how much Simone's changed lately, and she virtually told me that I neglect her. She said I should cut back on the pro bono work or the time I'm at the Shelter, and spend more time with our daughter.'

Phillip turns from the stove where he is frying chicken pieces in a wok, 'Don't take all the blame darling. I'm not here enough either. I don't think I realised just how much I was taking on when I changed from the group practice to working by myself. I really should think about getting a partner to share the workload. That way I could be home early on the days when you're working late. And perhaps you could take on a bit less work.'

He turns from the stove and looks at Emma who is sitting slumped in a chair, 'You look so sad Sweetie. Why don't you open a bottle of wine while I dish out? We'll drink to a more leisurely life and more time with our girl.'

As he is saying this Simone walks into the room, and hearing his words says sarcastically, 'What are you planning now? Are you working out how to fit me into your busy schedules?'

Emma snaps, 'There's no need to talk to your father in that tone of voice. And you could have helped him with the dinner.'

As soon as she has spoken these words Emma regrets them. It isn't how she wants to speak to her daughter, but so often lately this sort of thing happens. At times she feels she is turning into a nag, but Simone's attitude riles her. The closeness they had until a few months ago seems to have slipped away, and she doesn't know how to get it back.

As the three of them begin eating Emma turns to her daughter and asks, 'What homework have you been doing?'

Simone mumbles, 'Just some English.'

From her answer she makes it clear she has no interest in discussing her schoolwork with her mother.

Emma is determined she is not going to let Simone see how her abrupt answer has affected her so turns to Phillip saying, 'Sonya Mills came to see me today.'

'She's a nice woman, isn't she?'

Emma smiles. 'Do you remember me telling you about Sonya McFee who made my life a misery when I was at school?'

'Yes, of course I do. You're surely not going to tell me that it's her?'

'None other, but you know what? She does seem nice now. I really liked her.'

'Did you manage to get her to open up about what she thinks could have caused her husband's violent behaviour?'

'I asked her the usual questions; whether he had started drinking heavily or if he had financial or work problems that could be stressing him out. Evidently there's nothing like that to account for his recent moodiness. She did say the change has been recent, and that he's been getting terrible headaches that make him irritable. Did she tell you that?'

'No. All she told me was that he hadn't been himself lately.'

'When she mentioned the headaches and mood swings I suggested that he should have a thorough physical check up, but it seems he has an intense dislike of the medical profession. I think I rather overstepped the mark though. When she asked what physical condition could cause really bad headaches I said it could be a brain tumour.'

'That was rather jumping the gun Love. There can be any number of things that can cause quite severe headaches including depression, or even something simple like a disc out of place in the neck. Anyhow, do you think she'll be able to convince her husband to see a doctor?'

'I hope so. From what she told me, up until recently he was a wonderful husband and father, so something must've brought about this change.'

Simone, who has been sitting quietly eating her meal, pushes back her chair and takes her plate to the sink.

She glowers at her parents, 'Well, I'll leave you two to sort out other people's lives. I'm going to my room. Not that you'd notice.'

Phillip says, 'Oh honey, I'm sorry. We didn't mean to ignore you.'

She shrugs her shoulders. 'Don't worry. I'm used to it.'

As they listen to their daughter's feet running up the stairs and the slam of her bedroom door they look at each other sadly across the table.

Chapter Twenty-eight

Simone lies in her bed but she is not sleeping; she's too upset. She's had another argument with "them". Well not really an argument, but she knows they'll also be upset and she doesn't care. At least that's what she tells herself.

Sometimes she wishes she could be Auntie Jenny's daughter; she's so cool, with her great clothes, red Ferrari and that gorgeous house. Uncle Byron's old, but he's pretty cool too. Even though he has white hair and quite a lot of wrinkles he's handsome, a bit like an older George Clooney. When Simone visits them he doesn't talk to her much, but that doesn't matter because she and Auntie Jenny always have plenty to talk about. She's almost like an older sister, a really nice one. When she's with her she gives Simone all her attention. Once she almost told Auntie Jenny about Joel.

She's not like her mother and father. They're always chatting away together, and only half listen when she tells them something. When she's talking to them she knows their minds are somewhere else. Her father's always worrying about one of his patients, and with her mother it's a case she's preparing or some woman she's met at the Shelter. Whatever it is neither of them really listens to her so she's given up trying to talk to them about things that bother her.

Nanna always listens and she really, really loves her, but she wouldn't understand about Joel. She doesn't even understand about computers, or how you could meet someone on them. This is funny when you think of it, because it was at Nanna's house that Simone first learned how to get into chat rooms and how to send people e-mails.

Her cousin Ross showed her. He's cool; although he's eighteen he doesn't talk down to her, and he's clever and funny and kind. Even when she was only little he'd let her play in his fort in the back yard, and made sure his friends didn't tease her.

The house Nanna and Ross and the rest of their family live in is pretty cool too. It's not modern like her parents' house, but it's big and rambly and has lots of hidden corners. Sometimes she plays hide-and-seek there with her two little girl cousins. They're only seven and five, but they're really cute and they love her too.

At times she feels that Nanna's house is full of love. Her mother told her once how Nanna bought it with money she won in a lottery, so perhaps the luck stayed with it.

Nanna also bought the florist shop with the lottery money, and Simone knows that her mother worked there sometimes while she was going through university

Auntie Jessie and Uncle Richard do all the work there now, but sometimes they let her help them on Saturday mornings. She likes the shop. It smells divine and sometimes it's just full of flowers. The shop isn't open on Saturdays, but that's usually the day when they have wedding flowers to do. When she works there she helps make the posies that go on the ends of the pews in the church and even the buttonholes for the men.

Auntie Jessie's really good with flowers. She makes wonderful bridal bouquets and ones for the bridesmaids, but Simone likes her dried arrangements best. Auntie Jessie can take a few pieces of driftwood and some leaves and berries or a couple of flowers and make them look like something an artist would be proud of. These are put in the shop and they always sell quickly.

Simone once asked her how she learnt to make them and Jessie showed her the books. Some of them had dirt on the pages or raggedy covers, but she could tell her aunt loved them.

She said that day, 'These are my treasures. When Mum bought the shop neither of us knew much about flower arranging, so I went out and bought all the books I could find on it. Some were new, but others I picked up in second-hand bookstores. When it was quiet in the shop I'd go out the back and read them, and then practise what I'd seen.' She'd laughed like a young girl. 'I found I was quite good at it. Until then I'd thought I was only good at being a Mum to Ross. The books and the flowers showed me I could be good at something else.'

Like Nanna's house the shop is full of love, a happy place to be. Uncle Richard works in the shop too, and in the potting shed out the back. He told Simone once how he and Auntie Jessie met when he delivered some plants from the nursery where he worked.

He'd said, 'Your Auntie Jessie was the prettiest sight I'd ever seen in my life. She was standing behind the counter, her hair a mass of curls around her face and her cheeks a match for the pale apricot-coloured roses she was holding in her hands. I fell in love with her on the spot.'

Simone can tell he still loves her. When they work in the shop together he touches Auntie Jessie's hair or pats her bottom as they pass each other. Simone has even seen them kissing out the back when they think they're alone. With anyone else she'd think this was a bit of a gross way for married people to behave, but it seems okay with those two, even though they've got three kids.

At times Auntie Jessie doesn't look old enough to be Ross's mother. Simone thinks she must have been very young when she had him, but she doesn't know her age so she can't work it out. Even though she gets on well with her aunt and they talk a lot about clothes and flowers and films Simone doesn't think she would understand about Joel. She's always telling her to enjoy being young, and not to bother with boys until she's grown up.

Joel wants to meet her, but lately Simone's not sure she wants to meet him. Sometimes he gets really impatient for them to meet, but she's put him off. At first she just wanted to wait until after she had turned twelve before he saw her. That seemed so much older than eleven, and she'd thought her breasts might have rounded out by then.

They have been e-mailing each other for about three months after meeting in a chat room. Simone thought she loved him, but she's not sure how she feels now. He said he loved her, but he thinks she's fourteen. He might feel differently if he knew she wasn't quite twelve.

He sent her a photo of himself and he looked so cool. He's seventeen and in the photo is wearing board shorts and nothing else. He's brown and slim with blond hair nearly to his shoulders and blue eyes. In the photo he's at a beach and holding a surfboard. When she first saw the photo she felt like swooning. She'd printed off a copy and slept with it under her pillow every night until recently.

When he asked for a photo of her she'd panicked for a while. Most of the shots she'd had taken recently were with her little cousins at Nanna's or with her mother or father. Finally she found one in her camera. She thinks it was taken by Ross and in it she was in her new bathers. They're bikinis and the top has a bit of padding so they make her look curvier than she is. She's just starting to develop a bust but they're really only little peaks, although her nipples have grown bigger. At times when she looks at them in the shower she thinks they look a bit gross, but she supposes they have to go through this stage to get to be real ones. In the photo they look real; not big but nicely rounded and her face looks pretty, so she sent that one to Joel.

He said she looked beautiful. No one except her Nanna and her father had told her that before. When Simone was younger her mother used to call her Little Doll so she must have thought she was pretty then. She's stopped calling her that since Simone grew about three inches last year.

Now she says, 'You're lucky you got your father's looks.'

Simone looks at her father's thinning hair and tired face and thinks her mother must be joking. It's hard to tell with her though; she's so serious most of the time. In fact both of her parents are so serious most of the time. They don't seem to get much fun out of life. Her mother isn't at all like her sister Jessie who seems happy all the time, or her best friend Jenny whose life is absolutely fabulous.

Now Jenny tells Simone she's beautiful. Sometimes when she goes to stay with her she lets Simone put on her makeup and does her hair in different ways. She even lets her dress in some of her clothes that nearly fit Simone because Auntie Jenny isn't very tall and she's slim. After they dress up they make pretend cocktails and drink them beside the pool. She's always saying how she wished she had a daughter like Simone.

It was on one of those days that she almost told her about Joel. She began by asking Auntie Jenny how old she was when she first had a boyfriend.

She'd laughed and said, 'That's so long ago my darling; let me think. Gosh I had lots of boys who were friends at art school and one or two at high school, but my first real boyfriend was a bloke called Don. I met him when I was twenty.'

Simone persisted, 'But what about when you were at high school? You're so pretty you must have had lots of boys chasing you.'

Auntie Jenny answered, 'No, I wasn't really interested in boys then. All I wanted to do was paint and draw and hang out with my best friend Nina. I had three older brothers who'd either bossed me around or ignored me so I didn't even like boys much.' She paused then looked enquiringly at Simone. 'Have you got boys chasing you at the moment, or is there someone who you're keen on? You can tell me.'

But Simone knew she couldn't. Auntie Jenny had obviously not felt as she had, had not had feelings that stirred her up and kept her awake at night. Obviously she hadn't known what it was like to be going on for twelve and thinking you were in love, and then having doubts.

The grownup who she spends the most time with is Grand, but she's the last person in the world she could talk to about Joel. Most of the time they get on well together, but if Simone says something cheeky, or doesn't do what she's told, Grand puts on an angry voice and says, 'You're behaving like a little miss,' as if she's still about six.

She loves Grand and thinks Grand loves her, but she doesn't show it the way Nanna does. Nanna kisses her and hugs her and calls her "My Little Princess". Grand always calls her Simone, and only gives her a hug when she's been very good. She supposes this is because she's not a real grandmother like Nanna and Grandma Radcliff.

It took a while for Simone to realise the difference because she was only five when they moved in to this house. When they first looked at it she remembers her mother saying, 'The Grannie flat will be handy.'

A few days after they moved in Grand arrived, and began living in the flat. Simone thought she was a replacement grandmother because Grandma Radcliff had moved away to a place called Noosa with Grandpa.

Once she was about six she understood Grand was really Mrs. Murray, and not related to her. She still thinks of her as a Grannie though and loves her, but they don't get on as well as they did.

Simone knows it's her fault because she doesn't talk as much to Grand as she did. After school they used to sit together in the kitchen, and Grand would have fruit and cheese and biscuits set out really pretty on a plate. It would be more like a party than an after school snack. While Grand prepared dinner Simone would tell her about what had happened at school.

This changed once she met Joel. For a while all she wanted to do was get to her computer to see if there was a message from him. She'd grab a piece of fruit and cheese and head up to her room, leaving Grand alone in the kitchen. Often she'd stay in her room writing to him or just thinking about him until dinnertime. She thinks she probably hurt Grand's feelings, but at the time she didn't really care that much about anyone except Joel, not even her mother and father.

Now she's not sure how she feels about Joel. He's changed and is frightening her, and she doesn't know what to do about it.

Chapter Twenty-nine

Jenny drives into the garage, and hears the swish of the automatic door closing behind her as she reaches for her handbag and gets out of her car. While she walks up the internal staircase that leads to the living room she is thinking about Simone. She had sensed there was something troubling her on her last visit, but something stopped Simone confiding in her.

They had spent an enjoyable day together, but then Simone asked her about something. Obviously the answer Jenny gave hadn't been what she wanted to hear because Simone clammed up.

As she puts a frozen dinner into the microwave and pours herself a glass of wine, Jenny tries to remember what they had been discussing. Had it been to do with dating boys? She stares out the windows at the view of the pool surrounded by lush gardens and beyond to the sea, sparkling in the setting sun. She sips her wine, enjoying the peace and beauty of her home, then suddenly recalls her conversation with Simone.

In answer to Simone's question about dating boys Jenny had told her, truthfully, Don had been her first real boyfriend, and that she had been the ripe old age of twenty. This was obviously not the answer Simone had been expecting because after hearing it she changed the subject.

Apart from this as yet undivulged problem she is evidently feeling neglected by her parents. Simone has hinted as much to her, and to hear Emma verify this tonight shows it's becoming a problem in their household. Tonight she told Emma what she thought. She does think her friend has taken on more work than she can handle, and still give her daughter the attention she needs and deserves.

As she watched this problem escalate Jenny has, at times, felt cross with her friend. She can't really understand how she can put the needs of her clients before those of her daughter, but in recent years this is what she's done.

Jenny loves her own work, and gets an enormous amount of pleasure and satisfaction from creating beautiful homes for her clients. She knows though, that if she'd been fortunate enough to have had a child, he or she would have taken precedence over everything else.

The microwave pings and Jenny removes her dinner from the oven, pours herself another wine, and then sits at the long chrome and glass table that is positioned near the floor to ceiling windows. From here she has a different view, one of the headlands overlooking the gently curving beach and its backdrop of wild bushland. Byron designed the house to sit comfortably on the land, but also with the aim of incorporating the land into the house. Every room has a view, and the outside is an important element of the internals. In keeping with this idea Jenny decorated all the rooms in shades of blues, greens and whites to harmonise with the views of sea, sand and trees.

Byron bought the land many years ago, but when his first marriage ended he gave up the idea of building on it. His divorce was expensive, and he paid generous child support while his sons completed their degrees. It wasn't until he and Jenny had been married for a couple of years, and her business was doing well, that they began planning the dream house they would build in this beautiful spot.

It was here he proposed marriage to her. When she happily accepted his proposal he promised her that, one day, he would design for her the most beautiful house, to be built on the place where she agreed to become his wife. It had all been very romantic, and made up for the years of angst she had experienced because of her love for him.

She had met Byron when she enrolled to do the Interior Design Course after having completed her Degree in Fine Art. Her father had not approved, saying he wouldn't support her while she did another airy-fairy course, and her mother suggested she become an art teacher.

For the first time in her life Jenny felt let down by her mother. She had always been there for her, providing love, understanding and encouragement. Now Jenny thought her mother's suggestion, that she train to become a teacher, showed how little she really understood her need to work in a field where she could use her love of colour and texture to be creative.

Determined to become an interior designer she found employment working in a bottle shop four evenings a week in order to pay for the course and be, at least partially, financially independent.

She loved the lectures and the practical assignments, and enjoyed the company of her fellow students. Many of them had studied with her during the previous three year, but her best friend Nina continued to study painting, completing her Master's Degree, before going off on an extended painting trip with a fellow student.

Her favourite lecturer was Byron Solange, a well-known architect who taught part-time at the college. In many of his lectures he stressed the importance of melding architecture and interior design. He considered it vital that architects and designers work closely together to produce a pleasing creation. The students loved him for the importance he placed on what was to be their chosen profession.

From the first time Jenny saw him he had fascinated her. He was very handsome, but his appeal to her was his colouring. He had dark greenish-hazel eyes, soft brown hair with golden highlights and a year round tan that suggested time spent out of doors away from lecture theatres and offices. He always dressed in browns and fawns and sage greens, colours that blended to create a harmonious whole.

Unlike many handsome men he did not use his looks to charm, but rather seemed aloof and a little sad. Several of the girls had crushes on him, and many flirted outrageously with him, but he seemed impervious to their charms. It was rumoured around the college that some time ago he'd had an affair with a student. His wife found out about it, and the bitter divorce that followed had resulted in her obtaining a very generous alimony and in him having limited access to their two sons. It was also rumoured that the student had attempted suicide when it all came out.

During the first year at college Jenny was going with Don Fielding. They had met at the break up party held at the Art School when Don came along with the sister of one of the other art students. He had contacted her some weeks after the party and they began dating.

Compared with the college boys Don had seemed so sophisticated and wise. He said he was in love with her. For a while, Jenny thought she was in love with him, but gradually she saw a side of him she didn't like.

Initially she had been so besotted she had wanted to please him in every way. She had also been slightly in awe of him because of his sophisticated tastes and confident manner. Because of this she accepted his suggestions about almost everything, from the clothes she wore to where they went and with whom.

As the year progressed she felt as though she was being forced to change, moulded into some preconceived idea of what he wanted her to be. He even complained about her working in the bottle shop, quite disregarding the fact that it was a necessity. Gradually she became tired of his rather domineering ways. It occurred to her that in some ways he was rather like her father. She certainly didn't want to end up in a marriage like that of her parents; didn't want to become as pliant and subservient as her mother.

Shortly before the end of that year she broke up with him.

At the party to celebrate finishing the first year of the interior design course she was feeling light hearted and free to be herself. Until she was apart from Don, she hadn't realised quite how stressed she had become from trying to change to fit his vision of who she was.

Byron was at the party, and for the first time she had a chance to really talk to him. Actually he sought her out and they spent much of the evening together. Feeling the strong attraction between them she thought he would definitely ask to take her home. She has never forgotten the terrible disappointment she felt when he said a generalised goodnight and left.

One of the other girls said, 'I thought you were going to get off with him.'

Another had asked, 'Didn't he ask to take you home?'

She laughed it off, but found it hard to hide her disappointment.

From the beginning of the second year she lived for the times she would see him at college. Usually it was only in the lecture theatre, but sometimes he would join a group of the students for a coffee. When he did he always seemed to make sure he sat next to her, and she thought he must think she was special. Afterwards she would think about how he looked at her and what they had talked about, trying to find some significance in their conversation.

During second year some of his assignments involved working on models of buildings he had designed. Jenny loved this because it gave her a chance to really talk to and spend time with him.

She thought about him constantly, and looked forward to the two days when he was at the college.

During the final weeks of the course the three top students were each given the task of selecting the colour schemes, fittings and furnishings for houses designed by Byron. It was also their responsibility to oversee the work involved in completing the houses, and a panel of professional interior designers would assess their work.

Jenny was one of the chosen students, and worked tirelessly to ensure that her house was perfect.

At the dinner, to celebrate the end of the course, Jenny was presented with a Certificate of Excellence, which was the top award.

Afterwards Byron joined her table and said to her, 'You have real talent. Let me know once you're in business. I can probably put some work your way.'

Because of the award Jenny received offers of employment from two of the most prestigious firms in town, but from the start she was determined to have her own business. She knew she couldn't expect financial backing from her father but her brother, Steve, had a successful IT business, and he had been the only one in her family who encouraged her to follow her heart. He backed her financially, and within a year her business was booming and she was able to pay him back.

During that year she worked on office blocks and a new hotel as well as numerous houses. She hoped she would hear from Byron, but as the year progressed he hadn't contacted her.

Towards the end of that year she read an article in the newspaper about a new subdivision that was opening up on the outskirts of the city. All the houses were to be designed by Byron.

Remembering what he had said to her on the evening of the dinner she sent him her business card, and a short note expressing her interest in working with him. She was thrilled when, a few days later, he phoned her and arranged for them to meet to discuss the project.

That was the beginning of what has been a successful business partnership, but it was some time before it developed into anything else. When they poured over plans together or inspected a finished house Jenny felt the tremendous chemistry between them. Despite this Byron always maintained a level of aloofness. He treated her in a paternalistic way, although sometimes she would catch him looking at her, an expression of longing in his dark hazel eyes. She knew he felt the attraction between them that she did, but for some reason he held himself apart from her.

Eventually Jenny decided to seduce him. She invited him to what was to be a working dinner, dressed in her most glamorous outfit and plied him with good food and wine.

After the meal she served coffee and brandy in her lounge room then sat close to him on the couch. Earlier she had dimmed the lights and put some soft music on the player. It had seemed the most natural thing in the world when he encircled her with his arms and kissed her passionately.

She was returning his kiss eagerly when he pulled away abruptly saying, 'Ah, I shouldn't have done that.'

Stunned Jenny cried, 'Why ever not? I've wanted to kiss you for so long, and I think you've felt the same way about me. Why do you see a need to put up this barrier between us?'

He answered ruefully, 'I'm nearly old enough to be your father. I'm forty-two and you're only in your early twenties. I have a son who is close to your age.'

She said, 'As if that matters. I've been in love with you for years and I'm sure you have feelings for me. Why does the difference in our ages matter?'

For the first time since she had known him Byron looked awkward. 'You probably heard the rumours around college. I had an affair with one of my students, and when my wife found out she divorced me.'

Jenny nodded, but couldn't refrain from blurting out, 'For goodness sake, what's that got to do with us?'

He continued. 'Please, let me explain. My wife was hurt, but also totally appalled. She accused me of not only betraying her, but of using my position of trust to seduce a mere girl. She was very bitter about the whole thing and almost turned our sons against me. The student also took it badly when I broke up with her and attempted suicide. I felt so guilty about the heartache I'd caused I promised myself I'd never get involved with anyone so young again.'

'But you're not married now and I'm not your student.'

'No, but compared with me you are so young; too young to tie yourself to an old man like me.'

'Nonsense,' she giggled, 'I love you, wrinkles and all, and I'm pretty sure you love me too, so come here and kiss me again.'

That was the beginning of their life together, and they have often joked about how she seduced him. They have now been married for nearly eleven years, and their life has been great. Jenny's business has been tremendously successful and they frequently work together. Their dream house, designed by Byron and decorated by Jenny, won an Australian award and featured in several architecture magazines. This resulted in an increase in commissions for both of them.

Jenny's one sadness has been her inability to bear a child. She'd always wanted to have at least one child, but when she broached the subject with Byron he hadn't been keen. He had been close to his boys before the divorce, but his ex-wife's bitterness had driven a wedge between him and his sons. During their years at university they rarely made time to spend with their father, although he had paid for their tuition and given them both a generous allowance. They both now work in different cities, and he has little contact with them. As a result of this experience he had a rather jaundiced view of parenthood.

During the first few years of their marriage she was content to wait. She was busy with her business, and Byron and she were happy just being a couple.

They had been married for four years when she celebrated her thirtieth birthday. Their beautiful house had just been completed, and they held a combined birthday and housewarming party. After their guests left Jenny and Byron were having a nightcap sitting on the deck overlooking the spot where they planned to build a swimming pool.

She said dreamily, 'It is all so lovely. Now all we need is a little person to share it with us.'

Byron reached for her hand smiling, 'I know I haven't been willing to talk about us having a family together. At times I've felt just too old to start again on the whole fatherhood thing. But that's not been fair to you. I know that. Actually, now the house is finished, I wouldn't mind having a son or daughter to share it with us. It's a great place for kids, and I think I'd like to be a dad again.'

When Jenny conceived she was jubilant, but by the second month she experienced breakthrough bleeding and severe abdominal pains. An ultrasound revealed she was having an ectopic pregnancy. She was rushed to surgery, where the tiny embryo was removed and the fallopian tube repaired.

She was heartbroken. When she returned to her doctor for the follow-up appointment she asked him why this had happened to her. She had always been so healthy.

He shook his head sadly, 'In most cases an ectopic pregnancy is the result of a previous surgical procedure or infection that predisposes the patient to problems of this kind.'

She had interrupted him, saying tearfully, 'But I've never had any surgery or any sort of infection. I've always been so fit.'

'I know that from your records,' the doctor said sympathetically. 'But I note you have been on a low dose birth control pill for a lengthy period of time. That could have been a contributing factor to this sort of thing happening.'

'Gosh, I didn't know that,' Jenny had blurted out. 'So could it happen again?'

'I can see no reason why you shouldn't have a normal pregnancy in the future, although there is an increased risk once you have had one ectopic pregnancy of it happening again.'

She left his surgery with strict instructions to wait at least three months before trying to conceive again, and to contact him if anything untoward happened.

Five months later she missed a period, but within a few weeks she bled slightly and experienced severe abdominal pain. Byron rushed her straight to the doctor who verified another ectopic pregnancy. This time, because it was very early, it could be treated with a drug to terminate the pregnancy.

When she returned to the doctor some weeks later he strongly advised her against attempting a further pregnancy, as it could be life threatening if not diagnosed in time.

For a while Jenny grieved. At odd times, through the day and night, she would find herself crying for the child she could never have. In her misery she blamed Byron for making her wait so long before agreeing to them trying to have a child.

Sometimes she shouted at him, 'If I hadn't been on the pill for so long this wouldn't have happened.'

Throughout her grieving period Byron remained calm and loving, in spite of her often-unreasonable behaviour, but a rift was developing between them. She felt he didn't share her regret that they would never have a child together.

Some weeks after her second failed pregnancy she wandered into the room they had planned to be the nursery to find Byron staring out the window. When he turned she saw, clutched in his hands, the small pink bear he had bought when she was first pregnant. She also saw the tears streaming down his sad handsome face and had run into his arms to comfort and be comforted.

Slowly she resigned herself to not having a child.

It was shortly after this that Jenny met Emma, who had recently been made a partner in the law firm for which she worked. She had been allocated the rather fusty office of the retiring partner and wanted it decorated to suit her taste.

She contacted Jenny and the two women liked each other immediately. During the time they worked together planning the redecoration they became good friends, and that friendship has deepened through the years.

Shortly after they met, Jenny invited Emma and her family to a party she and Byron were giving to celebrate the completion of the swimming pool. It was then that she had met Simone for the first time.

Simone had just turned six and was a beautiful, dainty little girl with long blonde hair and clear blue eyes. Jenny doesn't know whether it was because they met at the time when she was coming to terms with never bearing a child or simply just that Simone was so adorable, but she loved her immediately. She has nieces and nephews, of whom she is very fond, but Simone has always been special to her, and Emma has happily shared her daughter.

Jenny hopes she can find out what is worrying Simone when they come for the barbecue this weekend.

As she is putting her plate and glass in the dishwasher the phone rings.

She answers it and it's Byron saying, 'Hello darling. They loved my plan and have given me the go-ahead to start organising the builders. It's going to mean I'll have to spend a bit of time in Sydney, but it will be a beautiful house.'

'Congratulations darling. I'm so pleased for you. I know how happy you were with your design. But I can't wait for you to get back. I miss you so much when you're away.'

'I miss you too. Perhaps next time you could come up with me. Anyhow, I'll see you tomorrow. I'm on the four-thirty flight, but I'll get a cab from the airport.'

'Looking forward to it. See you tomorrow my love.'

'I love you darling. See you soon.'

When she hangs up the phone Jenny has a smile on her face. After all these years just the sound of Byron's voice can make her feel happy. She loves him so much. Except for the fact that she has been unable to have a baby her life is perfect. It would have been wonderful to have a child to love and cuddle, to teach to swim in the pool and to wander with on the beach.

She sighs, 'I guess it just wasn't meant to be.'

She plans an early night and a read in bed. As she gets ready for bed she remembers the woman who she met in Emma's office. It was odd how familiar she seemed, although Emma said they hadn't met through her.

Jenny is sure that she isn't one of her own past clients. Going by her clothes and her hairstyle she wouldn't have the money to afford the prices she charges for her work. She thinks how snobbish that sounds, but it's true. Sonya didn't look to be very well off, and she could certainly make a lot more of herself than she does. That hair of hers would look wonderful with a rinse through it. Perhaps she'll suggest it if she meets her again.

Chapter Thirty

Sonya idly turns the pages of the magazine, but she can't concentrate on the words. Harry has now been with the specialist for over half an hour, and as the minutes tick slowly by she feels herself becoming more and more nervous.

It had taken her a couple of weeks to convince Harry he should see Doctor Radcliff, and during that time he was in almost constant pain from headaches. He also vomited a couple of times and had numbness in one hand. She was so relieved when he finally agreed to see the doctor, but then it took a month to get this appointment with the neurosurgeon.

Sonya is wondering just how much longer it will be when Harry comes out of the doctor's surgery. He is holding a slip of paper in one hand and Doctor Middleton is saying, 'I'll get nurse to arrange a time for you to have a MRI scan, and once we have the results we'll see what we need to do.'

After the nurse has made the appointment for the following week Sonya takes Harry's arm and says in a falsely cheerful voice, 'Let's shout ourselves a coffee and cake at that nice little café I saw on the way in.'

'Sounds like a good idea. I feel like I've been pulled through the wringer, what with being poked and prodded and asked endless questions. He seems to be very thorough though.'

This is praise indeed, coming from Harry, who dislikes doctors, and Sonya is happy that the visit seems to have gone well.

Once they are seated and have given their orders she asks, 'Did the doctor tell you what he thinks might be the problem?'

'Not in so many words. He said we'd have to see what the scan shows, but he was pretty keen to make sure that it's done as soon as possible. He seems a nice bloke. I guess he didn't want to worry me unnecessarily. When I asked him if my symptoms showed that I could have a brain tumour he said it's a possibility, but not to get too uptight about it until we know more.'

'Anyhow I'm just glad that we're finally getting it seen to. You really haven't been yourself for some time now.'

Harry took her hand. 'I know I've been like a bear with a sore head for months and you've been wonderful. I'll never forget the way you forgave me for hurting you and John. I feel so terrible about that, but you and the kids have been great. I don't deserve you all.'

Sonya squeezes his hand. 'Oh Sweetie, we've known there had to be a reason for the way you've been. You've always been such a good dad to the kids, and they all love you very much. We all just want to see you get better, and back to being your old self again.'

A week later Sonya is once more sitting in a waiting room, but this time it is at the hospital. Harry has been whisked away into the room where she glimpsed the cylindrical machine in which he must lie while the scan is being done. It looked quite scary to Sonya, but Harry had been eager to get this procedure completed. He wants to know what has been causing him so much pain.

At last he comes through the door looking pale and shaken.

He had laughed when filling in the questionnaire about surgical implants and claustrophobia saying, 'I can certainly say no to all the questions about previous surgery, and I think I'd know if I was claustrophobic. When I did my apprenticeship the old guy was too lousy to install a decent hoist so we did a lot of work under the cars in the pits.'

As he joins her now he looks tense and drained. 'Let's find somewhere to have a coffee. That was terrible.'

Sonya takes his arm and leads him down the endless corridors until they come to the hospital canteen. The smells of reheated food and weak coffee that permeate the air are not inviting, but Harry looks as if he needs something quickly. She gets them each a coffee, and when she returns is pleased to see that he has some of the colour back in his face.

After a few sips he sighs, 'Ah that's better. I don't think I knew what to expect.'

Sonya, who had actually read up on the procedure asks, 'Was it very noisy?'

'It sure was, but that wasn't the worst part. I'd thought being in such an enclosed place wouldn't bother me, but it was quite scary. They give you something you can push to signal with if you begin to feel claustrophobic and I came damn close to pushing it. The only way I could calm myself was by closing my eyes and pretending I was somewhere else.'

'Well at least that's over and done with.' She pats his hand in a comforting gesture. 'Did they tell you how long it would be before you get the results?'

'They said they'd send them to Doctor Middleton, and I've got an appointment to see him next Tuesday so I guess we find out then.'

During the next few days Sonya can feel the tension building in Harry, but he tries hard to hide it. Since the terrible night, when he attacked her and John, he has tried to be calm and happy. She knows how difficult this has been for him because of the pain he's in, and now there is the added anxiety of not knowing what is to come.

The children catch her concern and talk quietly together and turn down the television when Harry comes into the lounge room. There is none of the usual noisy bantering filling the house.

On Sunday morning she and the four children are all in the kitchen. The girls are making pancakes, but the boys are eating them as soon as they are cooked and buttered

Deirdre turns from the stove and moans, 'You're both being pigs. Leave some for Lisa and me.'

Just then Harry comes into the room. In the silence that follows all the children look shamefaced, and Frank puts back the last pancake he had taken.

Harry looks around the room at the worried faces of his wife and children and shouts, 'Look you lot, I'm not a bloody ogre or an invalid. I want my normal, noisy family back. I know I've been hard to live with lately, but you don't have to creep around me like scared little mice.'

Deirdre, who has always adored her father, puts her arms around his neck and says, 'We love you Dad and are just trying to make things easier for you. We know our noise makes your headaches worse.'

Harry hugs his tall daughter, 'You've all been trying so hard that it's making me feel as if I'm not part of this family any more. What say we go for a drive to the Salmon Ponds, feed the fish and have lunch somewhere along the way?'

This has always been an outing the children have enjoyed and they all happily agree. Sonya thinks how most of Deirdre and John's friends would no longer be willing to go on a Sunday drive with their parents. Despite their rocky start she and Harry must have done something right because the children still want to do things together as a family.

As they hurry off to get coats and put on their shoes Sonya gives her husband a hug and whispers, 'You're the main part of this family.'

She thinks briefly about Harry's impending appointment with the doctor and of what may follow, but pushes that worry from her mind.

Chapter Thirty-one

It is three weeks later and Sonya looks at the still, white face of her husband. His head is swathed in a large bandage and he looks puffy around his eyes, but he is breathing quietly and regularly. He had been conscious briefly, but then slipped back into anaesthetised sleep. The doctor told her all went well, and that he was able to remove the entire tumour. He will know in a few days whether it was benign or malignant, and whether further treatment will be required.

She kisses Harry's mouth, hating to see her big strong husband looking so defenceless and vulnerable. Watching him as he sleeps she remembers the many times during the past six months when she has been angry with him.

At the time it had seemed to her he was just being bad-tempered and moody. Now she knows the reason for his changed behaviour she feels guilty. He has been her rock for so many years, and she loves him so much. As she leaves the room she looks back at him one last time before walking wearily down the long, echoing corridor and out the glass sliding doors.

The air is chilly, but she breathes deeply, loving the feeling of the cold pure air going right down into her lungs after hours of being in the stale, overheated atmosphere of the hospital. The operation took many hours, and she now realises she was breathing shallowly all that time.

When she gets into her car she looks at the clock on the dashboard and is surprised to see it is almost midnight. No wonder she is feeling so exhausted. Apart from the tremendous strain of wondering how the operation was going she has been awake since five o'clock this morning and at the hospital for sixteen hours. In all that time she has hardly thought of her children except to ring them once the operation was over, when she talked to her father and then to Deirdre.

Before the day of the operation her older daughter had said she would be quite capable of looking after the younger kids, but Sonya's father insisted on, "holding the fort," as he put it. When she had talked to Deirdre it sounded as though she'd been glad to have her grandfather there with them. He isn't a very good cook though; will have probably ordered in takeaways for their dinner.

She smiles at the thought of her father, who she loves very much, but then thinks of her mother and sighs. From the time Sonya left home and married Harry her mother has hardly spoken to her, and has had nothing to do with her grandchildren. For years her mother's attitude upset Sonya, but now she feels nothing but pity for this foolish old woman who has missed out on so much by her hidebound attitude.

As she drives up to the house she notices that it is in darkness except for a light in Deirdre's bedroom. Sonya tiptoes past the lounge room, where she knows her father will be sleeping on the pullout couch, and along the passage to Deirdre's room.

Her daughter sits up as soon as Sonya enters the room and asks anxiously, 'Daddy is going to be all right isn't he Mum?'

Sonya puts her arms around her slim pyjama-clad girl who will soon be a woman. She loves her so much. At times she thinks with horror at the thought that she could have had this precious person destroyed if she had had her selfish, self-centred way.

She smooths back her daughter's hair with a loving hand and says with false cheerfulness, 'It looks as though everything went well. The doctor said he removed all the tumour, and except for looking a bit puffy in the face your Dad looks good.'

'But will he need chemotherapy or radiotherapy? From what I've read that can be pretty bad too you know.'

Sonya smiles. Deirdre may be closer to her father, but in so many ways she is very like her. Both of them have read everything they could get their hands on about brain tumours and the treatment of them, whereas Harry had simply said, 'I'll find out when it happens.'

Sonya gives her a hug and answers, 'We'll know in a few days if he will need further treatment, but for now all we can do is hope it's not necessary. You'll probably be able to go in and see him tomorrow afternoon. Now get some sleep Sweetie or you won't be fit for anything tomorrow.'

The next morning, after the children have all left for school, Sonya and her father sit at the breakfast bar enjoying a peaceful cup of coffee.

She smiles apologetically at her father; 'This place is a madhouse in the mornings. How did you get on last night? Did the kids behave themselves?'

'They were terrific. We had pizzas and they all had some gooey dessert thing that I didn't try. Naturally they were worried about their father and how the operation had gone, but I could feel how they all relaxed after your phone call.'

'And what time did they go to bed?'

Edward McFee looks a little guilty. 'Well, after the phone call Deirdre and John did their homework. I watched a television program with Lisa and Frank, but it didn't finish late. The younger ones were in bed by eight-thirty and John and Deirdre not much later. They're all good kids and a credit to you and Harry.' He pauses for a while, and then gives a big sigh. 'When I'm with them I can't help but think how stupid your mother has been. All these years she's cut herself off from you and her grandchildren because she disapproves of Harry. She won't even listen when I tell her he's been a good husband and a wonderful father.'

Sonya pats his shoulder, 'Look Dad, it's her loss. For years I hoped she'd come around, but she hasn't. It doesn't bother me anymore. Harry and the kids are my family now, and I'm glad you're part of it.'

While Sonya is waving goodbye to her father the phone rings. As she answers it her heart gives a flip and she finds it difficult to breath. Is it the hospital calling to say Harry's condition has worsened during the night? Should she have stayed there with him?

She breathes a sigh of relief when she hears Emma's voice asking, 'How did the operation go? I was thinking about you and Harry all day yesterday.'

Sonya smiles as she says, 'That's so sweet of you. To answer your question I think the operation went very well. The doctor said he removed the entire tumour, but he won't know whether it was benign or malignant for a few days.'

'Well, I just wanted you to know I'm thinking about you both, and so is Phillip. Give me a ring when Harry gets the all clear, which I'm sure he will, and we'll celebrate. See you soon. Bye for now.'

When Sonya puts down the phone she is still smiling.

Since their meeting in Emma's office they have kept in touch over the phone. She had rung Emma to thank her for her advice, and to tell her Harry had agreed to see the doctor. She'd thought that perhaps Doctor Radcliff might have told his wife this, but wasn't sure how far doctor/patient confidentiality extended.

They talked about other things and after that first phone call, have rung each other on several occasions. It has been strange how they have come to communicate like old friends when, in the past, Emma must have hated her, and with good reason. Perhaps they both felt the need to wipe out that old animosity.

Several days later Harry has been given the all clear. Sonya, her father and all the children have visited him in the hospital, and he is to be allowed out in two days time. Edward is taking the children to MacDonald's to celebrate, and Sonya is meeting Emma for a celebratory dinner.

As she waves goodbye to her family and sets off down the street towards the docks area she is worrying about her clothes. Knowing she would be going to an upmarket restaurant she has worn her good black pants suit with a pale green shirt. She hopes it will be suitable.

She and Harry rarely go out to dinner. When they do it is for some special occasion like their anniversary or to celebrate a birthday. At these times she wears one of her few good dresses, but today she needed something that would be suitable for both day and evening.

Emma has booked a table for them at a French restaurant called La Cuisine. Sonya remembers reading a food critic's review of it round about the time it first opened. It had sounded lovely, but the prices were far too high for Harry and her to even consider going there.

When she arrives at the place she pushes open the heavy wooden doors and gazes earnestly around the dimly lit room. She hopes Emma is here before her, for she isn't used to dining in expensive restaurants anymore and she is feeling a bit self-conscious.

Although it is a dull, misty twilight outside it takes a while for her eyes to become accustomed to the comparative gloom inside. Only concealed wall lighting and candles that glow on the white linen tablecloths light the room. The maître d' approaches her and asks if she has a booking.

'There should be,' she says, feeling quite flustered. 'It would be in the name of Radcliff.'

He gives a smirk that twitches his thin black moustache in a comical way, 'Ah yes, Mrs Radcliff has already arrived. Follow me.'

When they reach her table Emma stands and gives Sonya a kiss on the cheek. Sonya is pleased to see that she too is wearing a pants suit, dark blue with a pink shirt.

Emma says, 'I was so pleased about your news I thought we should really celebrate. Phillip said he'd pick us up, so we don't have to worry about what we drink. Let's start with champagne.'

Sonya notices the table is set for three and Emma, seeing her glance says, 'I hope you don't mind, but when I told my friend Jenny why we were coming here this evening she asked if she could join us. Do you remember, you met her in my office? It seems Byron, her husband, is working in Sydney at present, and she also wanted to meet you again. She feels sure she knows you from somewhere.'

Sonya grins, 'I can't think where we'd have met, but I'll certainly be happy to see her again. She seemed very nice.'

'Oh she's a love and very talented too. She's one of the best interior designers in the state.'

As Emma is saying this she looks towards the door, and sees her friend talking to the maître d'. Jenny waves and crosses the floor, a vivid scarlet and black cape swirling behind her.

When she reaches the table she bends to kiss Emma then moves around the table and kisses Sonya also saying, 'I'm so pleased your man is going to be better. It must have been such a worry. I don't know what I'd do if anything happened to Byron.'

With a swish she removes her cape revealing a long scarlet skirt topped by a black cashmere sweater. A gold pendant hangs between her breasts and matching gold earrings shine in her ears below her short cap of blonde hair.

The waiter brings them each a glass of champagne, and they toast to Harry making a speedy recovery before turning to survey the extensive menu.

Sonya is so shocked by the prices she can't help saying, 'But it's all so expensive.'

'Don't you worry about that. This is an important occasion.'

Jenny interjects, 'And I want to pay for our drinks. I was a bit late because I was finalising a deal to do all the interior design work on a small boutique hotel that's going to be built just along from here. There are only going to be twenty apartments, but each one is to have an individual theme and colour scheme. It's going to be fun to do and very lucrative'.

Sonya says, 'What a lovely job you have. How did you get into that line of work?'

'It is a great job. From the time I was a little girl I thought I wanted to be an artist, but when I found I didn't have enough talent to make it as a painter I studied to be an interior designer. I can't think of anything I'd rather do.'

'You're lucky there,' Emma says thoughtfully, 'When I was going through university I thought of tossing in law and qualifying as a teacher. Once Mum won the lottery she could finance me during my remaining years of study, so I felt locked into becoming a lawyer. It was what Mum expected me to do because I'd said that's what I wanted to be from the time I was a kid. Sometimes I think I'd have been better off teaching. I'd have been just as useful and had more time for Simone.'

'Speaking of Simone, how is she? Last time she was at my place I tried to get her to open up about what's bothering her, but she just clammed up on me. Something's worrying her though. She's not as relaxed and happy as she used to be'

'Tell me about it. She hardly speaks to Phillip and me any more. I asked her the other day what she wanted to do for her twelfth birthday and she said, "Nothing" and left the room. Later I went to her room and she was lying on her bed crying. When I asked her what was wrong she told me I wouldn't want to know. It's as if she's feeling terribly guilty about something, but for the life of me I don't know what it could be. Have any of your kids gone through a bad patch like that Sonya?'

'Basically we haven't had much trouble with our kids, but Deirdre went through a stage a few years back when she began behaving differently. She seemed worried and secretive, and it took us a while to find out what was bothering her. Does Simone spend much time on the Internet or e-mailing?'

Emma looks a bit embarrassed, 'Actually I'm not sure. She has her own computer in her bedroom so we don't really know. Why do you ask?'

'Well we'd let Deirdre have a computer in her bedroom, and she'd gone into a chat room and met this guy. They'd exchanged e-mails and been communicating for some time. She said it started out just talking, but then things became more personal. She had felt really close to him, but after a while he started to say rather suggestive things and asking to meet her. She became uncomfortable about their relationship. Fortunately she told me all about it and we changed her e-mail address. Since then all of the kids are banned from using chat rooms.'

Jenny grins, 'How did they take that?'

'They're good kids, and accepted the reason for our restriction. We didn't show them the messages he'd sent Deirdre but told them about them, and they knew how upset Deirdre had been. Harry even went to the police with printouts of some of the cruder messages, but they said there wasn't anything they could do about it. He was ropeable that some jerk could upset our daughter so much and get away with it.'

Emma, who has been listening closely to Sonya, says sadly, 'Our problem is that if something like that is happening we'd be the last to know. Obviously Deirdre felt she could come to you, but Simone won't talk to us about what's bothering her. If she has a similar problem we'd be the last to know.'

Jenny says hesitantly, 'May I make a suggestion? It seems to me, that if we could get Deirdre and Simone together she might open up to her. Sonya, if you explained the situation to your daughter, do you think she would help?'

'I'm sure she would. She's very good with younger kids, and I know she'd like to help anyone who's going through what she did. But how do we get the girls together? If it looks like a set up Simone might clam up.'

Jenny claps her hands and grins, 'I have the perfect solution. Emma, you know how Byron and I have our Ausmas party every year.' She doesn't wait for an answer from Emma but turns to Sonya. 'You must come and bring all your family. You tell Deirdre what's been happening with Simone, and what we think might be the problem. On the night we'll work out a way of getting the girls together.'

Emma laughs so loudly that people at the nearby table turn to stare, 'Oh Jenny, you are such an organiser. And that's the worst invitation I've ever heard. Asking someone to a party just to make use of them. I wouldn't blame Sonya if she turned you down flat.'

Jenny looks chagrined, but then grins and says very formally, 'Sonya, may I invite you and all of your delightful family to an Ausmas party my husband and I are giving on Saturday the twenty-fifth of July. There will be ham, turkey and plum pudding on the menu. Dress is informal; also bring swimwear, as the pool will be warm even though the air temperature will be freezing.'

Sonya laughs and imitating the royalty reference answers in an affected voice, 'My family and I will be delighted to attend.'

The three women are laughing so happily together they haven't noticed the waiter standing nearby until he clears his throat.

Looking up from her menu Sonya says, 'It all sounds so magnificent. What are you two having?'

'I had the beef bourguignon last time I was here and it was delicious, but I think tonight I'll have the pork and veal terrine.'

'I love beef so I think I'll have the bourguignon,' Sonya says, 'It's something I never make because it needs to be slow-cooked and I don't ever seem to have the time for that sort of cooking.'

'With you two choosing different dishes you know you're making it hard for me. I always want what someone else is having.' Jenny looks at the menu again. 'I think I'll try the beef too, and Emma can give us each a bit of her terrine.'

As the night progresses the women talk about their lives, hopes, dreams and disappointments. Sonya tells of her dreams of becoming a teacher being destroyed by her early pregnancy, and Jenny tells her of how she dearly wanted a child, but was unable to conceive normally.

Jenny orders a bottle of full rich Burgundy and when they finish that she orders another. When Phillip arrives to take them home he finds them chatting away as though they have been friends for a lifetime.

Chapter Thirty-two

Deirdre peers through the steamed-up side window at the brightly lit house as her father manoeuvres his car into a parking space between a Porsche and a BMW. She has been cramped in the back with her sister and two brothers, and will be happy to get out of this crowded space. She'll be even happier when she gets her own car.

Mum and Dad have promised her one for her eighteenth birthday. It is only two months away, and then she will be free.

It's not that she doesn't still enjoy being with her family a lot of the time, but a car will give her independence to do her own thing, to come and go as she pleases without always having to rely on one of her parents.

She's had mixed feelings about coming to this party, but when she told her friends at college about it they were all so envious. Evidently the Solange house is a landmark, and famous for having won some big architectural award.

As she gets out of the car and gazes up at the house from the car park she can see why. It is built on a headland and set in parklike gardens. Its curved roofline mimics the outline of the nearby hills, and the pale blue walls and enormous expanses of glass echo the water that surrounds it on three sides. Below the house is an enormous swimming pool on the same level as the car park, then the land slopes down to the rocky foreshore and a tiny curved beach.

Normally Deirdre would have been thrilled with the prospect of attending a party at this gorgeous house, but her mother has asked her to do something here and she's not sure how to go about it. Her mother told her about Simone Radcliff, and how her parents are worried that she might be having a similar problem to the one that she had when she was fourteen. If she is Deirdre wants to help, but she's not sure how to go about getting the girl's confidence. When she was head prefect at high school she often had to mentor girls who were having problems, but in those cases she knew the girls and they trusted her. This kid is a stranger, and as an only child probably a spoilt brat.

She is thinking these thoughts when Lisa tugs her arm impatiently shouting, 'Come on Dee. Mum and Dad and the boys are nearly at the pool. If we don't hurry the boys will be in the water before us.'

Deirdre grins down at the anxious face of her little sister, 'Okay Lisa, let's go, but don't panic. They'll have to be introduced to our host and hostess first so we've got plenty of time.'

She takes her sister's hand and they walk along a white gravelled path leading to a long paved area that is beneath a deck on the upper floor. Here they catch up to the rest of their family who are talking to a small blonde woman and a tall white-haired man with a very tanned face.

As the girls join them their mother says, 'And these are our girls, Deirdre and Lisa. They've both been looking forward to a swim in your pool even though it's a freezer of a night.'

When Deirdre says, 'I'm pleased to meet you Mr and Mrs Solange,' the woman grins and says, 'You don't have to be formal with us, Byron and Jenny will do. Now let me introduce you to my niece and nephew and Simone, and then I'll show you where the change rooms are.'

After being introduced to Jerome, who is eighteen and rather dishy, his younger sister Louise who is thirteen and to Simone, they have all swum together. Not many adults have been in the pool, and none stayed in for long so they have had it to themselves. Deirdre would have liked to spend all of the time with Jerome, but has made a point of getting to know Simone. She seems a nice little girl, but compared with Lisa and Louise, who have been skylarking happily together, she seems to be kind of subdued.

They have been in the pool for about an hour when Jenny comes and suggests it's time they all have something to eat. After they change back into their warm clothes Simone leads the way to a large room that has a wall of glass overlooking the bay.

Although the room is crowded with people it still looks enormous. On one side of the room is a long table covered with plates of ham, turkey and pork, great bowls of colourful salads and platters of different breads and cheeses. Set at an angle to this table is another on which there are a selection of sweets, meringues, cheesecakes, soufflés and mousses. In the centre of this table is an enormous Christmas pudding surrounded by chocolate truffles.

As Deirdre is looking at the lavish spread the boys join them and Jerome says, 'Let's get something to eat and find somewhere quiet to hang out.'

He is looking really spunky in khaki cut-offs and a creamy coloured top. She would dearly love to go off somewhere with him but feels responsible about finding an opportunity to talk with Simone, so answers rather brusquely, 'I think I'd better keep an eye on the little kids for a while.'

He says, 'Suit yourself,' before wandering away and she wonders if she has put him off altogether.

'Damn' she thinks as she moves along the table with the girls, filling her plate with food she now doesn't even want.

After they have eaten Jenny joins them briefly and says, 'Why don't you girls go to the rumpus room? There's a television and a computer with a game set up that was especially designed for girls.'

As the younger girls head out of the room Jenny pulls Deirdre aside and says quickly, 'If you can get Louise and your sister to play the game it might give you a chance to talk to Simone.'

Feeling manipulated Deirdre follows the younger girls back down the stairs with Simone leading the way. Lisa loves computer games so heads straight for the computer and Louise follows right behind her. Soon they are engrossed in the game.

Simone watches them for a while, but then joins Deirdre on the couch where she has been half-heartedly leafing through some magazines that are on the coffee table. She has been thinking how she would much rather be in some nice secluded spot with Jerome, but still gives Simone a welcoming smile.

When she sits down next to her Deirdre says, 'You seem to know your way around this house. Have you been here before?'

'This is like my second home.' Simone smiles shyly. 'Aunty Jenny and I are really close, and I often come and stay with her, especially when Uncle Byron is away on business and during school holidays.'

Deirdre isn't sure how she can head the conversation in the direction she wants it to go so decides to be blunt. With a nod in the direction of the other girls at the computer she asks, 'Do you spend much time on the computer?'

Simone answers briefly, 'Some, for homework and stuff.'

'What about e-mailing your friends? That's what I mainly use mine for.'

Simone looks flustered and mumbles, 'I use it a bit for e-mailing.'

Sensing that this might be her only chance to get the girl to open up to her Deirdre says, 'A few years back I met a guy in a chat room and we spent months e-mailing each other, but then things went bad.'

Simone asks earnestly, 'What happened?'

'He sounded so nice to begin with, but then he started writing really crude things and pestering me to meet him.'

Deirdre watches as a tear slides down the little girl's face and barely hears her whispered, 'That's what's happening to me and I don't know what to do.'

'Why don't you tell your Mum and Dad? That's what I did.'

The girl sobs, 'But I can't do that. I wrote some things to him that I wish I hadn't, about how I wanted to kiss him and hold him and stuff.'

'But that's not a crime. They'll understand.'

'No they won't. They'd be shocked at some of the things I wrote, but it was only words, just a bit of fun. Now he's saying he's printed out some of my e-mails, and will post them to my parents if I don't agree to meet him.'

'Oh you poor little kid.' Deirdre opens her arms as she says this, and Simone buries her head in the older girl's shoulder sobbing uncontrollably.

On the other side of the room the other girls continue their game, their eyes glued to the moving figures on the screen before them, their fingers working the controls. They are totally unaware of the drama taking place behind them.

Slowly Simone's crying stops. She looks up at Deirdre, a woebegone look on her pretty face, 'He's seventeen and he looks so handsome in his photo. I was going to meet him after I turned twelve because I thought I'd look older by then. But about the time of my birthday he started saying really suggestive things, so I said I didn't want to meet him. That's when he started threatening me.'

'Blackmailing you to be precise. Look, the thing is, that photo's probably not who he is. These creeps pretend to be people they're not. Your e-mail friend is likely to be some wrinkly old pervert.'

'What happened when you told your mother and father about the man e-mailing you?'

Deirdre smiles down at Simone's worried face. 'For starters they moved my computer to the television room, and banned me from e-mailing anyone for three months. After that time they made sure I had a new e-mail address, and that I only gave it to people I know.'

'Did they find the man?'

'Dad went to the police station, but they said they couldn't do anything about that sort of thing. I don't think they can do much unless there's been some form of physical abuse.'

Simone sighs, 'Will you help me tell my Mum and Dad about this?'

Deirdre is a very nice young woman, but she is beginning to feel she has done her duty. This is meant to be a party after all, and she would dearly love to catch up with Jerome again.

She pulls Simone to her feet, 'Tell you what, I'll tell Mum about the pickle you've got yourself into, and she can talk to your mother about it. Now let's go and see what everyone else is doing.' She glances across the room at Lisa and Louise. 'Those two don't look like budging, so let's see what the boys are up to.'

'They'll be in the games room. Jerome loves playing eight ball. Come on, I'll show you the way.'

As she eagerly leads the way it occurs to Deirdre that this is the first time tonight she has seen Simone looking really happy.

Chapter Thirty-three

It is a week later, and Sonya, Phillip and Byron are sitting in the lounge room at the Radcliff house, talking quietly and sipping glasses of white wine while they wait for Emma and Jenny to join them.

Phillip looks at Sonya, 'I can't understand why she doesn't want to talk about this with me? We've always been so close until recently, and now she's shutting me out.'

'Deirdre was the same with Harry. She eventually told me, but hated the thought of him finding out that she'd gotten herself involved with some strange man. I think girls know instinctively their fathers find it harder to accept that they're growing up and will have other males in their lives.'

'But it makes me feel as though she couldn't trust me to understand.'

Sonya smiles, 'If it's any consolation Phil, I can assure you Harry felt exactly the same way, and it's not a matter of trust. I know Deirdre felt as though she'd disappointed her father, and I'm pretty sure Simone is feeling the same way.'

As she is speaking Emma and Jenny come into the room and Phillip instantly asks, 'How is she? Has she told you all about it?'

Emma pours two glasses of wine and hands one to Jenny before sitting on the couch next to Phillip. 'Oh darling, she was so upset. I think she'll go to sleep now. She's glad to have what's been bothering her out in the open, but she's still worried that somehow he'll find out where she lives and will stalk her.'

From where she is perching on the arm of Byron's chair Jenny says, 'I could kill him, the slimy bastard. She had a photo, supposedly of him, and a copy of the one of herself that she'd sent to him. The poor little darling had been sleeping with them under her pillow, but since he started blackmailing her she'd put them in the back of a drawer. In the photo he looks a gorgeous young man, but who's to know what he's really like'

Emma interjects, 'And she only had one of his e-mails still on her computer because he'd told her to delete his messages so that her parents, as he put it, "couldn't spy on her." My dear departed father had a colourful saying to describe someone he didn't like or trust, "as cunning as a shithouse rat." I think that describes this creep to a T.'

She pulls a sheet of paper from her pocket. 'I took a copy of the only message still on her computer. Listen to this. "Hi Little Doll. Haven't heard from you for a while. If you don't get in touch with your Joel pretty soon I'll have to send that mail to your folks. We have to meet. Let me know where and when. I won't wait much longer Baby. Love Joel."

Jenny cheeks take on a fiery glow of fury. 'Oh, it's disgusting the way that creep was threatening her. It's no wonder the poor lamb has been so miserable. We have to do something.' She turns to Sonya. 'What did the police say when Harry told them about what had happened to Deirdre?'

'Absolutely nothing. It's evidently not a crime to write suggestive stuff, or to try to get someone to meet you.'

'Well if it's not it should be,' Jenny says furiously.

Emma agrees. 'He was blackmailing her after all. And what might have happened if she'd gone to meet him? She could have been raped.'

Sonya sighs. 'Look I know how you feel. Harry and I felt the same way. It seems some form of physical abuse has to happen before the police can get involved.'

Jenny jumps up suddenly, nearly spilling her wine. 'That's what we have to do. Get him to show his hand. Set up a meeting and then see what he does.'

Phillip looks horrified, 'Surely you're not suggesting that Simone should actually meet this guy?'

'Oh Phil, of course not. Do you honestly think I'd want to put her at risk?'

'Well what are you suggesting?' Phillip is sounding decidedly testy. He is feeling left out of what has happened to his beloved daughter, and so helpless.

'We e-mail him and set up a time and place to meet him, but I go instead of Simone. He knows from the photo she sent him that she's small and blonde.' Jenny laughs as she formulates her plan. 'I'd fit into some of Simone's clothes, and if I wear a hoody and arrange to meet him in a reasonably dark place he won't suspect until it's too late.'

'And what if he grabs you?' Byron asks. 'I don't want you putting yourself at risk from some possible pervert.'

Jenny reaches down and pats his shoulder. 'That's where you and Phil come in. You will be parked near where we arrange the meeting, and once he makes a wrong move you two come to my aid. That should be enough to get the police involved.'

Sonya who has been listening intently now says, 'It could be risky Jenny, but it also could be a way of getting rid of at least one of these predators. And stop Simone from having to worry about him. What if I get Harry to also be parked near the proposed meeting place on his motorbike? That way if this guy somehow manages to drive away with Jenny in the car Harry will be able to keep up.'

Byron huffs, 'I think it is a totally madcap idea and it could be dangerous. You don't really know what sort of person you're dealing with here.'

'It's not going to be the least bit dangerous.' Jenny grins and pats her husband's knee. 'What with you and Phil and Harry all looking out for me nothing could go wrong. Now let's drink to getting this slime ball behind bars.'

Chapter Thirty-four

Emma and Phillip have talked to Simone about what they plan to do. They had been unsure about how their daughter would react, but she seemed relieved that something was being done to remove this fear from her life. Together they drafted the e-mail in which Simone arranged to meet Joel. They chose a bus shelter on a busy street as the meeting place.

On the evening of the proposed meeting Emma answers the door to see Sonya standing on the step, with Harry looming behind her looking ominously threatening in black leathers.

As she kisses Sonya's cold glowing face and greets Harry, Sonya says gaily, 'That's the first time I've been on the back of a motorbike in years. I'd forgotten how exhilarating it is.'

Harry grins happily, 'Now that the kids are old enough to be left we ought to do it more often.'

Emma laughs at her friend's enthusiasm. 'At least you two seem relaxed. Phillip and Byron are so tense. I was just making coffee to try and calm them down before they leave. Why don't you join them in the lounge room Harry? See if you can convince them everything will be okay. Come and help me make the coffee Sonya.'

As they walk to the kitchen they hear peals of laughter coming from Simone's room.

'And I don't think those two are taking this seriously enough. They've been in there for the past half hour deciding what Jenny should wear. It's so good to hear Simone laughing again.'

Sonya is setting out the coffee mugs and Emma removing the perked coffee from the stove when Jenny enters the room.

'Ta rah. What do you think? Will I pass for a teenager in a dim light?'

She is wearing a pair of Simone's cut-offs, a tee shirt and a hoody. Her face is bare of makeup except for a pale pink lipstick, but her blue eyes are sparkling and her lightly tanned skin looks almost unlined, even in the brightly lit kitchen.

Sonya says admiringly, 'You look amazing.'

'She fits perfectly into my clothes,' Simone enthuses.

Jenny grins. 'I know why you're so pleased about that. It means my clothes will now fit you. I think I'm going to have to put locks on my wardrobe doors when you come to stay.'

'Enough levity,' Emma admonishes, 'Let's take these coffees to the men and then go over the plan.'

As soon as everyone has finished their drinks Jenny leaves to catch a bus. It had been decided that it would be better for her not to go in the car with Phillip and Byron as the predator could be watching for her arrival.

Before she leaves Byron holds her close and says, 'Don't take any risks, and remember we'll be nearby. Just yell if he puts a hand on you.'

She walks down the path to the street and stops to give a jaunty wave before heading off along the street to the nearby bus stop. Watching the small figure disappear down the street in the evening dusk Emma feels such gratitude to her friend for putting herself in possible danger for the sake of Simone's peace of mind. She also feels fearful though, and will be glad when this evening is over.

When Jenny gets off the bus she sees that the men are already in position. Byron's car is parked a block away from the bus stop, and Phillip is in the passenger seat. In the other direction Harry is sitting nonchalantly on his bike smoking a cigarette, his helmet held loosely in his other hand.

She crosses the road and checks her watch before sitting down on the hard grubby seat. It is eight twenty-five and the meeting had been arranged for half past. Her stomach gives a nervous rumble, and she takes a deep breath in an effort to slow her rapidly beating heart. She is nervous, but earlier had pretended a bravado she was not feeling. She'd hoped, by acting this way, to assuage any guilt Simone might feel and to help Byron relax a bit. All week he has tried to talk her out of it, but she wants to do this for Simone, wants to get the creep who has made her precious girl so unhappy.

She is glancing up the street towards where Harry is parked when suddenly a car comes around the corner and pulls to a stop in front of her.

The door opens and a voice says, 'Hi, I'm Joel. Hop in and let's go someplace quiet.'

She takes a look in the direction of Byron's car before dipping her head to enter the stranger's vehicle. As she does so she feels a strong arm pull her in, and a cloth of some sort pushed into her face. She tries to scream but there is something on the cloth, something smelly that is taking her breath away. She slips forward, and hears the door slam and tyres screaming before she loses consciousness.

It has all happened so quickly that Byron takes a while to respond. The car is already a block away before he gets the engine started. He swears loudly and Phillip says in what he hopes is a reassuring voice, 'Harry's not far behind him and I got the registration number.'

He knows Byron is tense and worried and wonders if, perhaps, he should have insisted on driving.

Byron is frantically trying to keep Harry's bike in sight as he yells, 'Call the police. Tell them what's happened and give them the number. See if they can get some patrol cars on the lookout for that car.'

They see Harry's taillight turning left into a steep winding street that leads away from the city, and Byron tries desperately to keep up. Phillip is trying to explain to the person on the other end of the phone what has happened when Byron says impatiently, 'Just tell them a woman's been kidnapped, and give them the direction in which we are heading.'

He hunches forward, changing down gears as the road becomes steeper, and mutters under his breath, 'I knew this was a damn fool idea.'

Phillip gives the direction in which they are travelling, and then listens for a while before turning to Byron, 'They've put out an alert to all their cars, and told me to keep in contact.'

When he turns his eyes back towards the road he can no longer see Harry and the car they are following. A feeling of panic clutches his heart, and his eyes sweep from right to left until he sees a light.

'Stop. They've turned off at a track back there. About three hundred metres down the road.'

Swearing under his breath Byron slows down, and then turns the car on the narrow road, hitting a soft embankment on one side before managing to reverse back to the direction from which they had come. He turns onto the track, which is narrow and deeply rutted. Ahead he can only hear the faint sound of Harry's motorbike.

His mind is whirling with random fears, 'Why can he no longer hear the car's engine? Has the predator managed to give Harry the slip? What's happening to Jenny? Why did he let her put herself in this risky situation?'

The car bucks over the rough ground and, as they round a corner, in the dim light they can just make out the outline of Harry's bike lying on the ground its headlight still shining. As they pull in behind the bike they see the car, and Harry holding a person in a headlock.

He calls, 'Over here. I've got this cretin but see how Jenny is.'

Byron races to the passenger side and opens the door. His wife is slumped forward and appears to be out to it.

As he takes her in his arms she mumbles, 'Drugged. No chance. Glad it not Simone,' before lapsing back into unconsciousness.

Phillip is giving directions on the phone, and in a few minutes they hear the whine of a siren out on the road. A car passes the turnoff but then brakes suddenly, reverses, and soon the waiting men can see two sets of headlights winding their way up the track.

The cars come to an abrupt halt, and as Phillip walks towards them four men jump out and advance as a group. Before he can speak he is grabbed roughly by one of them who has noticed the phone in his hand. 'Looks like you're the contact. What exactly is going on here?'

Phillip points to where Harry is still holding the man in a headlock and says, 'That man kidnapped my friend's wife. He pulled her into his car and we followed him to here.'

The policeman looks bewildered, 'How exactly did this occur sir?'

Phillip begins, "Well it's a long story. My daughter was being harassed by that man and we wanted to get him.'

While they have been talking two of the police officers have separated Harry and the predator and handcuffed them both. The other officer is kneeling beside Byron who is holding a still unconscious Jenny in his arms.

He calls, 'There's a woman here who's been drugged or something.' He shines a strong flashlight into the car. 'I think I see what's been used. Bring me a bag from the car.'

The officer who has been talking to Phillip gets a bag from the glove box, and pulls Phillip roughly with him as he takes it towards the car. He carefully picks up a scrap of cloth and sniffs it before placing it in the bag.

'That's chloroform,' Phillip says decisively.

'Yer, and how would you know?'

'I'm a doctor. I'd know that smell anywhere.'

Meanwhile Harry is protesting loudly, 'For God's sake man, take these things off me. I haven't done anything wrong.'

Byron joins in, 'In fact he possibly saved my wife's life.'

The predator, who has been silent until now screams, 'They set me up. It's not what it seems.'

The officer who had been talking to Phillip says, 'If what you told me is true, it looks as though you tried to take the law into your own hands and things went wrong. We'll have to sort this out at the station.'

He motions to the man holding Harry, 'Put him and the other bloke in your car and I'll take these three.'

Despite protests from Byron that he needs to get his wife home, and from Harry about being forced to leave his motorbike where it lies on the ground, they are all bundled into the police cars and taken to the station. Once there, they are allowed to make a phone call. Phillip explains what has happened to Emma and Sonya, who have been waiting anxiously to hear from the men.

It is after midnight before statements have been taken, they have been reprimanded for trying to deal with the problem themselves, and they have been driven back to retrieve their vehicles. The predator has been gaoled for the night, and a search warrant will be obtained the next day to search his property.

When they arrive back at the house the men all look tense and exhausted, but there is a sense of bravado about them. They are a bit like naughty schoolboys who have been involved in some prank.

Jenny looks pale and fragile and is still feeling slightly woozy, despite being plied with numerous cups of coffee by a kind policewoman. Sonya and Emma make them all coffee laced with whiskey, and they sit around the lounge room talking over the events of the night.

When Jenny tells of how helpless she felt when the chloroformed rag was put over her face Byron says, 'We shouldn't have let you do it.'

She answers tetchily, 'What do you mean, let me do it? It was my idea and I'm glad I did. Once we were at the station, and I was with it enough to get a look at that little worm of a man, I felt so pleased with what we'd done.

Simone can stop worrying now, and we've probably saved lots of other girls going through what she has.'

Byron hugs her. 'I know darling, but I was so frightened for you, especially when we almost lost track of where Harry was.'

Phillip pats Harry on the back, 'Yes mate you were the hero of the night. We'd lost him before we were even off the main road. I was so glad you were there on your motorbike.'

Byron adds, 'I'm also grateful to you for grabbing him before he could do anything more to Jenny.'

Harry grins self-consciously. 'Well I got handcuffed for my troubles. It will be something to tell the kids.'

Sonya stands and pulls Harry to his feet. 'And speaking of the kids it's time we were heading home hero.' She kisses Jenny's pale cheek. 'You take it easy. I think you were incredibly brave. I'll ring tomorrow to see how you are.'

As Emma escorts Harry and Sonya to the door she puts and arm around Sonya's waist and says, 'Thanks for sharing the waiting with me. I couldn't have stood it on my own, but you seemed so confident that everything would be all right.'

Before Sonya dons her helmet she kisses Emma on the cheek and says with a grin, 'How couldn't I be, with Hero Harry on the job?'

He is already seated on the motorbike and calls, 'Come on woman. Let's hit the road.'

She settles herself on the pillion seat and puts her arms around Harry's leather clad body.

As they gain speed she feels the wind whistling past, and thinks of a night long ago and the excitement of that trip up the winding mountain road. She presses her face into his back and puts her hands under his jacket so she can feel his heart beating.

Barbara Knight

One World Revisited

Chapter Thirty-five

Emma sits alone and sips a glass of water. She has so looked forward to tonight.

Now that Jenny is no longer teaching they only manage to catch up over the occasional cup of coffee, and neither of them has seen Sonya since she left so suddenly for France. This will be the first time the three of them have been together in over a year.

It has been a year of change for both of her friends.

Shortly after the previous Christmas Sonya rang them both and they had met for coffee. Excitedly she told them she had resigned from work, and planned to go to France with Pierre where they would be married. She even hinted that she might be pregnant, but said it was too soon to be sure.

They had waved her off at the airport, promising to try and make it to her wedding, but Jenny's life was in turmoil at the time and Emma felt she needed to be there for her.

As it happened Jenny had coped amazingly well when she and Don separated. Evidently she had suspected he was being unfaithful, and when she accused him he admitted he was having an affair with a woman he had met at work.

When she told Emma about it she had seemed relieved to have what she suspected finally out in the open. She showed none of the sadness or anger one would expect, but instead behaved more like someone who had been released from prison. She'd been eager to make changes to a life she felt had become almost unbearable.

Within days of Don moving out of their home she resigned from her teaching position and enrolled to do the Interior Design Course.

She told Emma, 'I'm finally going to put myself, and what I want to do, first. I've always regretted not doing that course when I was young or continuing with it once I became pregnant with Grace. Now that Don's gone and the children are older I feel free to follow my dream.'

Often during the past few years Jenny had seemed stressed and harried, finding the balancing act of working and caring for her children, home and demanding husband overwhelming.

This year Emma had seen an enormous change in her. She seems to have boundless energy, for both her children and her studies, and to enjoy being free of Don's dominating presence. Now, since falling in love, she positively sparkles.

As Emma sips her water she gazes around the room. It is unchanged. The white tablecloths, the single red rose on each table, the warm rosy glow from the concealed lighting, even the prissy little maître d' is the same one who had fussed around them last year. She has been here once since, with Bruce to celebrate their wedding anniversary, but it is too expensive for a normal night out.

Under the table she eases off her shoes, cursing herself for being so stupidly vain and deciding to wear them again.

She checks her watch, and then looks expectantly towards the door. The others should be here soon. As she is thinking this she sees Jenny talking to the maître d' and waves to her. Watching her friend walk across the room she thinks again of how much Jenny has changed this year. For one thing she looks years younger. She's had her previously dull blond hair lightened and cut in a short pixyish style, and now radiates an aura of self-confidence, which was lacking during her years with Don.

When she reaches the table she kisses Emma on the cheek before collapsing into a chair with a sigh, 'I'm not late am I? It took me a while to get away from Mum when I dropped the kids off, plus I was a bit late leaving college.'

'Don't apologise. I was here early and, as you can see, Sonya still hasn't put in an appearance. Oh, I'm so looking forward to seeing her again.'

'Me too. Do you think she'll bring the baby? I'm dying to see her.'

'I reckon she will. The bub's only two months old so she's probably still breast feeding her.'

'You know I can't imagine Sonya with a baby. She never talked about wanting one.'

'I think she had her reasons for not having a baby before this. She might tell us tonight about why she changed her mind.'

'That sounds mysterious Emma. What do you know that I don't?'

Emma looks embarrassed, 'It's just something she told me years ago. As I said she might talk about it tonight.'

The heavy wooden door opens, letting in a gust of wind that causes the candles on nearby tables to flicker in their ruby red shades. They see that Sonya has arrived; a carrycot is in one hand and a large leather bag slung over one shoulder. She is dressed in a camel coloured suit that shows off her tall curvy figure. Her tan shoes, bag and scarf match to perfection. Her auburn hair is pulled back into a large chignon with a few stray tendrils wisping around her face. She looks fabulous, and as she walks across the room both her friends stand to greet her.

She carefully places the carrycot on a chair before turning to greet them. She kisses them on both cheeks in the continental way, and then says in a slightly accented voice, 'Ah my darlings, it is so good to see you again.'

They stand for a moment grinning at each other then Jenny asks, 'Can we see the baby?'

Sonya pulls the baby's covers down gently and whispers. 'She's sound asleep and I'm hoping she stays that way.'

The other two women look down fondly at the tiny face surrounded by a pink bunny rug and say quietly, 'Isn't she beautiful? She's so tiny. She's got your colouring.'

Sonya smiles fondly, and then gently replaces the covers before sitting back down and saying to Jenny, 'Look at you. You're looking marvellous. Obviously your new life's suiting you. Tell me all about it.'

'Well I wrote to you about the divorce. Things should be finalised early in the New Year, and Don's been very generous about alimony and child maintenance; in fact so generous I could give up teaching and enrol in the Interior Design course I always wanted to do.'

'And so he should be generous. He was fooling around with some woman in publicity, wasn't he?'

Jenny grins, 'He was and she probably wasn't the first. We'd really drifted apart and I'm so glad it's over. I feel free to be myself for the first time since I was a little girl. And I'm absolutely loving the course.'

'And a certain lecturer,' Emma interjects, 'Tell her about the fabulous Byron.'

Sonya says delightedly, 'Don't tell me you've found a new love already. How wonderful. So this is what accounts for the glow.'

'Yep I'm in love, completely dotty about the man and he loves me. We didn't get together until the middle of the year, but from the moment I saw him I knew he was meant to be someone special in my life. It just took me a while to convince him.'

'Tell me all about it.'

'Well I felt drawn to him from the start, but he seemed sort of aloof, didn't mix with the students at all outside the lecture room. Although I only remembered him vaguely from when I'd started the design course before he seemed so familiar to me.'

Emma says cynically, 'Don't get her started on this. She's quite convinced they must have known each other in a previous life or a parallel world.'

Sonya pats Jenny's hand, 'If she feels that way they may have. So where do things stand at present. How did you two get together?'

'He came to the midterm party and we talked a bit. Afterwards I couldn't get my car started, and he helped me with some jumper leads. This gave me the perfect opportunity to invite him to dinner, as a thank you for his help. I packed the kids off to Mum's for the night, cooked a sumptuous meal, and then seduced him.'

Emma says teasingly, 'See how our Jen has changed. She's become a new woman.'

Sonya laughs, 'It certainly doesn't sound like something the old Jen would do.'

Jenny flushed a little before saying, 'Probably not, but I knew I had to take the initiative, and it seemed so right at the time. I knew it was exactly what I should do.'

'So now it's really serious?'

'You bet. That night he admitted he'd felt attracted to me from the start. The problem was he had this self-imposed rule about not fraternising with his students, because of something that happened in the past. Anyhow I convinced him to get rid of his silly feelings of guilt, and now it's all terrific. He loves me as much as I love him, and as soon as my divorce is finalised we plan to marry.'

Sonya takes Jenny's hand and says, 'Oh, I'm so pleased for you.' She pauses before asking, 'And how'll he cope with a ready-made family? What's he like with your kids?'

'He's really good with them; in fact he gives Grace more attention than Don ever did. He has two grown up sons but no daughter, so she's a novelty for him. He has this marvellous piece of land, and he's already planning the house he will build there for all of us. He's even including a games room for the kids. He took me out there last Saturday.'

She pauses for a moment and then continues. 'I must tell you about this Sonya. Emma thinks I'm crazy, but the strangest thing happened. I was standing where the house is going to be, but suddenly I was in the finished house. Byron and I were standing on this big deck drinking wine. Below us, in the pool, a group of teenagers were playing around and behind us was a big lounge room full of people.'

Sonya asks, 'Do you mean you imagined this happened?'

'No! I felt it happening; felt as though I was living in that house with Byron and we were giving some sort of party.'

Emma jeers, 'See how weird she's become.'

Sonya says quietly, 'I don't think the feeling she had was all that weird. A long time ago I experienced something similar. For just a brief moment I felt as though I was living another life in which I was married to Harry, my first lover, and had a family with him. Because of that I know what you're talking about Jen.'

Exasperated Emma says, 'Don't encourage her.'

Sonya says earnestly, 'Well I really think that at times you can get a glimpse into another life you might be living because of different choices you made in the past. At some time Jenny, you may have made a different choice that resulted in you and Byron being together at an earlier time. You were getting a glimpse into another possible life as I think I did.'

Emma says impatiently, 'You're as bad as she is talking this delusional rubbish. Let's change the subject.'

Jenny says, 'Well to talk of something different, I want to know what made you finally decide to marry Pierre, and have his baby. Emma has hinted there was a reason why you didn't want a baby earlier and she's piqued my curiosity.'

Sonya puts up her hand to signal the hovering waiter and when he approaches says, 'We'll have a bottle of Bollinger thanks.' She turns back to her friends. 'Let's see what we want to eat and then I'll tell you all about it.'

After the waiter has poured the champagne and taken their orders Sonya says, 'A toast to us.' They clink glasses and she add. 'This one glass is all I'll be having as I'm breastfeeding. Even though my darling mother-in-law insists champagne in any quantity is all right, I'm being careful.'

They sip their champagne then Jenny says, 'Now back to your reason for always saying you wouldn't have a baby, and why you changed your mind.'

Sonya sips her champagne before commencing, 'I told Emma about this years ago but I haven't wanted to talk about it since. I had an abortion, got rid of Harry's baby, when I was seventeen. Mum made me feel terribly guilty about it, so for years I felt I didn't deserve to have a baby. It's ridiculous how I let her influence me.'

'What made you change your mind?'

'Do you remember that article we discussed the last time we had dinner here?'

Both of the other women nod their heads and Jenny says, 'Actually I've thought about it quite often because of the feeling of familiarity I've had with Byron, and then the strange experience I had out on his land reminded me of it again.'

Sonya agrees, 'Yes, I can see how those things would make you wonder about the idea of parallel worlds. When I reread the article I remembered that time I told you about, when I felt I was living a life with Harry and our children. It got me wondering how my life would have been if I'd made a different choice back then. But it also got me wondering about the part chance plays in everyone's life. Pierre was being very persistent that we marry, but I knew his family expected him to produce an heir, so I had kept on refusing him. After thinking about the decisions I'd made in my life, some of which hadn't turned out very well, I decided to leave things to chance. I stopped taking the pill and the next month I was pregnant.'

Jenny asks earnestly, 'Do you think a parallel world was created when you left things to chance?'

'I've no idea, but I do know I couldn't stand the thought of there being a world where Pierre went off and married some little French woman who would have his babies, and I spent the rest of my life without him. Actually I so badly wanted to marry Pierre I think I willed myself pregnant.'

Emma laughs, 'So perhaps it was your decision after all. Anyhow, enough of this mystical stuff. Tell us about your life in France. What's it like living in a chateau? Do you have servants?'

Jenny joins in the interrogation, 'And what are Pierre's family like? Are they okay with you, or would they have preferred him to marry a French woman?'

'Hang on there. One question at a time. Firstly, I love living in France and we don't have servants, although we do have a couple of girls from the village who come in each day. They do the bulk of the housework but Mamma cooks the meals. She is a fabulous cook, and is sharing all her favourite recipes with me.'

The three women have all ordered coq au vin, and after taking a mouthful and considering the flavours Sonya comments, 'Incidentally, even though this is very good, Mamma's would leave it for dead.'

'So it sounds as if you get on well with your mother-in-law. That's so good,' says Emma who has loved Bruce's mother from the day when he first took her home to meet his family.

'To use a good old Australian term it wasn't all "beer and skittles," at the beginning. I don't think any of them knew what to expect. Some Aussie, blonde surfy chic I suspect. The whole family was completely amazed that I spoke fluent French and knew quite a lot about their country.'

'So was that the reason they changed their minds about you?' Jenny has asked the question, but both women lean forward, eager to hear Sonya's answer.

'I like to think it was my charming personality and my obvious love of both Pierre and their country, but a big thing was that I was pregnant. It's so important in those old French families to have an heir to carry on the family name. I've blotted my copybook a bit by giving birth to a daughter, but we're already working on producing a son and heir.'

She gives lascivious grin that reminds both her friends of how, in the past, she would occasionally speak of a lover.

Jenny had spent all of her life, until the last year, feeling dominated by first a father and then a husband. She is so enjoying the freedom of being in charge of her home and her life she can't imagine how Sonya could be happy living under the same roof as Pierre's extended family.

She asks anxiously, 'Will you and Pierre move into your own home eventually?'

Sonya laughs, 'No way, but don't look so worried darling. The chateau is enormous, and Pierre and I have our own wing. We can be as private or as communal as we choose to be. The big thing is we have built-in babysitters, Pierre has no distance to go to work, and I really do like his Mamma and Papa and his two sisters who also live in the chateau with their husbands and kids. Having been an only child I'm enjoying being part of an extended family.' She sips the last of her champagne and says, 'Anyhow that's enough about me. What's happening in your life Emma? You haven't taken a lover or tossed in your job too by any chance.'

'Not on your life,' Emma laughs, 'I'm still with my Bruce, and I always will be. The boys are doing well at school and growing at a rate of knots, and I enjoy my job. I really can't imagine any other way I would want my life to be.'

The women have been so engrossed in their conversation they don't notice Pierre's arrival until he bends down and kisses the top of his wife's head.

She is startled but turns immediately and says, 'Hello my darling. Are you here so soon to take me away?'

He smiles at the other women, 'Is it too soon Emma, Jenny? I will wait at the bar if you have not had enough time together.'

Jenny gives him a welcoming smile, 'Why don't you join us and have a glass of champagne? Our old drinking partner hasn't been keeping up with us.'

He gives a charming smile and answers, 'I had better not. I have my two princesses to drive home tonight.' He gazes down fondly at his sleeping daughter. 'How has she been?'

Sonya smiles, 'Totally civilized. There hasn't been a peep out of her all evening. I reckon she'll want a feed when we get home though, so we'd better be heading off.'

Pierre offers the women a lift home, but when they refuse he says, 'Well at least let me settle the bill.'

Sonya bends to kiss them each goodnight before gently picking up the carrycot. 'It's been lovely. I'll be here for a week, so give me a ring and we'll get together again. I'd like to catch up with your kids too.'

As she starts to move away Emma asks, 'Are you staying at your parents' place?'

Sonya grimaces, 'Pierre thought we should, though I still have problems with Mum. He had to come back here on business, and I really only came with him to see Dad and to catch up with you two. I spent so much of my life trying to be what Mum wanted and now, when I couldn't care less what she thinks, she's over the moon because I've married into French aristocracy and had a child. I just find her so artificial she annoys me.' She shrugs. 'Ah well, c'est la vie.'

As Emma and Jenny share the last of the champagne a man advances across the room, his silvery white hair shining in the dim room.

Jenny stands and waves him over then says happily, 'Emma meet Byron.' She curls her hand around his arm. 'Emma is one of my oldest and dearest friends.'

Emma looks up at the man standing above her, and can see why her friend finds him so fascinating. He is extremely handsome with strong masculine features, a tanned skin that contrasts dramatically with his thick mane of white hair and gentle dark hazel eyes. He looks rather like George Clooney, but older and more intelligent.

He asks quietly, 'Are you ladies ready to go?'

They agree that they are and as he wraps the colourful shawl around Jenny's shoulders Emma senses the bond between these two people. She feels so glad her friend has found someone to love who obviously adores her.

Byron's car is parked right outside the restaurant. It is an older model Jaguar in pristine condition. As Emma sinks into the lush leather seats she can't help but think they don't make cars like this anymore. It is probably a collector's item, but from what Jenny has told her Byron uses it as his every day vehicle. Emma compares it to her practical Toyota and Bruce's four-wheel drive station wagon that they use for camping trips with the boys. She thinks it might be nice to have a bit of luxury in her life, but she really doesn't care.

When they arrive at her house Byron escorts her to the front door, and waits while she fiddles with the key before saying a cheery goodnight and loping off down the path. The light is on in the hallway, but all is quiet except for a soft murmur coming from the lounge room. She opens the door to see Bruce, sound asleep as usual, in front of the television set. His hair is awry and his glasses have slipped to come to rest on the end of his nose. She tiptoes across the room and gently strokes his hair into place.

He wakes abruptly, pushes back his glasses and says sleepily, 'Hello darling. I must have dozed off. Did you have a nice evening?'

She sits next to Bruce on the couch and answers happily, 'I've had a lovely time. It was great to catch up with Sonya again, and to see Jenny without our kids around.'

Bruce yawns sleepily, 'Where did you go for dinner?'

'We went back to La Cuisine as a memorial to when we three last had a meal together. How did you and the boys get on?'

'We actually cooked a very good chicken stir-fry. Xavier helped me do the vegetables and John cooked the rice. They're getting to be pretty handy in the kitchen now.'

'Yes, and they don't think it's women's work because they've seen you doing your share of the cooking. You're such a good Dad.' She gives him a hug. 'I do still love you very much.'

Bruce grins up at her, 'What's with the still? Will you stop loving me someday soon?'

'No silly, it's just that tonight I've been with my two best friends, one with her third husband and the other getting ready to marry her second.'

She wonders if she should tell Bruce about her two friends' beliefs that they may have led other lives, but decides against it. He wouldn't understand it any better than she does.

She moves closer to him on the couch and rests her head on his shoulder. 'Hearing those two talk about their lives has made me think how lucky we were to find each other the first time around. Both Sonya and Jenny are very happy, but they've gone through a lot of heartache to get to the place in their lives where they are now.'

'What's Jenny's new bloke like? Did you meet him?'

'Yes, actually he drove me home. He has a beautiful vintage Jaguar that he drives all the time. It's very comfortable and luxurious.'

'Didn't you tell me she was going with a fellow from the college? I wouldn't have thought you could afford to do that on a lecturer's wage.'

'Oh, he only lectures part-time. He's also a very successful architect and evidently quite famous. He's going to design a beautiful home for them to live in when they marry.'

Emma gets up and pours two Glayvas. She hands one to Bruce before settling herself back down beside him on the couch. 'Sonya looks fabulous and she already has this slight French accent.'

'And the baby? I thought you'd be all talk about her.'

'Well actually, she was so good we hardly noticed her. She's very tiny and beautiful and looks as if she has her mother's auburn hair. We mainly talked about Sonya's life in France. She seems to have fitted in amazingly well and even likes her mother-in-law.'

'Why do you find that so amazing? I always thought you liked your mother-in-law.'

'You know I do, you dope. I loved your mother from the first moment I met her. It's just that Sonya's in-laws are members of one of those old French aristocratic families. I understand they can be very insular, but Sonya appears to have settled in very happily with them.'

'So both your friends are with wealthy, successful men. Do you ever wonder what it would be like to be married to someone more exciting than a boring accountant?'

Emma finishes her drink, and then puts out her hand to her husband. 'I think you're fishing for reassurance and you ain't going to get it. Let's go to bed, and you can show me just how exciting you can be.'

Bruce puts his arms around her and says huskily in a mock French accent, 'That eez a challenge zat I will enjoy, ma cheri,' and they laugh together as they head towards the bedroom.

Biography – Barbara Knight

After many years as a teacher, housewife and mother I completed a Bachelor of Arts at UTAS, majoring in English Literature and History in the 1970s. I followed this with a graduate Diploma in Librarianship and worked in public libraries for sixteen years before my retirement.

During retirement I spent several years attempting to become partially self-sufficient by fishing and growing a huge variety of vegetables and fruits before turning to the more cerebral pursuits of writing and painting.

I am an avid reader, a long term member of book discussion groups and have been writing seriously for many years. I have had six short stories published in anthologies or magazines. I have also written a number of novels and a memoir.